Old Habits Die Hard

by

Chris Sheerin

A book by

darkWolf press

darkWolf press, 5 Orlan House,
20 Strand Road, Derry BT48 7AB
Tel: 07597691377
Email: darkwolf62@rocketmail.com

PRELUDE

'Y'know the difference between a professional poker player and a dog, Mr Shale?'

It's close on 3-00am, a pungent breeze drifting across the construction site on Luciano Heights smells like wet Chihuahua, and dawn's first bloody tendrils have skewered the dark wings of night, leaving the sky looking like a badly-mauled raven. Below, the city slumbers, yet gangs of lowlife are still living the highlife in the dank gin-mills and fleabag motels. In the backdrop, the sluggardly drone of traffic soothes the hive, but suddenly that tranquillity is shattered by firstly a gunshot, and then someone, somewhere, screaming louder than a banshee working two wakes. Within moments, the weeping mewl of a police cruiser's siren resounds loudly up amidst the tenements and alleyways, before losing itself as quickly in the night.

Up here on the Heights, however, an even greater drama has begun to unfold. In this one, Yours Morosely is tied upside-down from a crane-jib and swaying precariously about six-feet above a batch of wet cement that four thugs – labouring under the command of mob captain, Vinny 'Happy' Valentine – have just poured into the founds of the new Dillinger Freeway. Other than that, it's a standard enough night in the city in many respects, and later on today it'll probably be hotter than Satan's home sauna, though just now I'm not sure I'll live to see it.

I shake my head anyhow, uncertain of the answer to Happy's rather flippant question.

'Y'don't know? Well, the dog stops whinin' after about ten years!'

As his four henchmen chuckle menacingly, Happy smiles a 24 carat toothy and stares at me expectantly. I grin thinly,

3

feigning an appreciation for this stand-up guy's stand-up, but Happy is far from happy, that much is evident from the way his smile slowly downturns into a sneer.

'But that's enough shit-chat, Mr Shale. You owe Gus Diamond two large, and even a Mickey Mouse shamus like you must've figured by now that you can't just run up debts and then run off. It's not polite!'

'Listen, uhm, Happy,' I splutter, 'I was goin' to get the money back to Gus today, honest. But my, uhm, stocks and shares are up in the air at the moment, and I need a bit more time to sort them out. I'll make good with the moolah then, honest!'

'Up in the air, eh?' Happy shakes his head sadly. 'A bit like you now, Mr Shale.' He mentally weighs up my less-than-lithe 300lb frame, then shivers briskly. 'Or do I call you Whale, the way your so-called *friends* do? Speakin' of which, one of them told us you were down the track this evenin', and that's where we found you – coincidentally – stickin' 500 dollars on Stocks-and-Shares, a pooch so old it couldn't have won had it been blessed with two extra legs. Thusly, your own little Wall Street Crash. Thusly, your current predicament.'

I curse inwardly. In the few minutes I've been here, my eyes have popped so many blood vessels you'd swear they'd just finished celebrating Chinese New Year. Add this to the fact that I've been weeping like a professional mourner since I was bundled into the trunk of Happy's Chevrolet by his henchmen, and maybe you can see why I'm starting to believe that the last few minutes of my life have been somewhat heavenly compared to the hell to come.

'Guys, be reasonable,' I sigh. 'Look, I'll tell you what: Cut me down, I'll go find a case, solve it, and Gus'll get his money. As for this, we'll just chalk it up to experience.'

Happy nods philosophically. 'Experience, Whale, is findin' a fresh toilet-roll outside the john door seconds after you've flushed your best shirt down the crapper. That's to say, you usually get it when you don't need it, and it comes at great expense.' He raises a thumb to the crane's operator and holds it aloft, Caesar-like. 'Still, back to our conundrum: Do you now wish to become pavement pizza, or…'

'Or..?' I grab instinctively onto what I feel to be a very slim handle. 'Or, uhm, what?'

'Or, do I give you a further two weeks to raise the money?' As I'm about to nod my swift compliance to the latter offer, he adds: 'Only thing is, you'll need to pay me another grand to do that. If you agree to do so, I'll simply tell Gus I can't find you – yet! Then you can keep your head down, gather up the money, and we'll meet again in fourteen days time. What d'ya'say?'

'Are you fuckin' crazy?' I begin squirming like a Bishop in a brothel, until I realise from the noise of the straining duct-tape that such unbridled enthusiasm might just be enough to initiate my own downfall, both literally and figuratively. 'How the fuck am I supposed to earn three-grand in two weeks?'

'There's probably more chance of you earnin' it alive than dead,' Happy says with a shrug. His grin brightens by about 80 watts and he tilts his thumb slightly, all too ready to send me south to my maker. 'You don't *really* want to go Hoffa, do you?'

I squirm again, but this time it's because I know I'm lodged between a cock and a hard place and have no other options. 'Alright, alright, but I'll need at least three weeks.'

'Two weeks, that's it! And here's somethin' to remind you I don't kid around.'

Happy points to someplace a little north of the freeway, and the crane-driver spins the jib around 180°. Despite this sudden disorientation, I'm all-too aware that, if it weren't for the benefits of gravity, my slacks would now be brown from the thigh down. Gravity, however, doesn't prove to be the true and loyal friend I'd like it to be, as only moments later I'm in free-fall and the earth is rising quickly to meet me.

Shamelessly, I close my eyes and scream like a supermodel at her hourly weigh-in. Nanoseconds later I'm nut-deep in an untreated sewerage vat, much to the joy of Happy and his ugly crew.

'You keep your head down for two weeks, Whale,' Happy tells me coldly. 'Then I want three-grand in my hand, no excuses. Or, believe me, you'll be in much deeper shit than you're in now!'

ONE

Ask even the most laidback food critic here in the city how they rate Ramon's diner and they'll tell you he's the guy who put the teak in steak and the rat in ratatouille. Such pale references aside, this particular in-delicatessen is now my favourite eatery, partly because its dim nooks suit my currently furtive lifestyle, partly because it's less than two blocks from my latest Chez Shale in suburban Vesperville, but mainly because it's a convenient place to hang out while that same brownstone undergoes major refurbishment.

Now, when I'm talking about fixing up my latest abode, I'm not talking about an architectural labour of love: Fact is, when needs dictated that I purchase that abandoned crack-house for 500 dollars less than the reserve price of 600, I sort of guessed straight off that it might need a little work, but what I didn't realise back then was that it would need renovating from the water-table up. Still, to cut a long story short, after being threatened by the Sanitary Commission with everything from eviction and conviction to fumigation and quarantine, I had little choice but to turn that decrepit mausoleum into something resembling your average home. And, in a bid to keep labour costs down – and despite my every nagging instinct – I was also forced to retain the services of my equally decrepit and nagging 'maid', Greta, for the foreseeable future.

Exactly how I come to have a 'maid' when I'm up my neck in debt is, like most things in my life, a rather convoluted tale. As is the fact that karma has inexplicably decreed that I'm never going to fully rid myself of a certain ex-neighbour of mine named Joe Sinto, who is the millstone that weighs heavily around the neck of the albatross which perches forlornly astride the white elephant that is my life.

However, I'm going too fast, so let's just back up a little here.

As you may recall – just before I started going off at a tangent about Ramon's, Greta and Joe – I was nut-deep in an open sewer. But, minutes later, after Happy Valentine and his cronies drove off chuckling like loons, I somehow managed to wriggle free from that mire, after which I slogged back to the brownstone on foot as every cab in the city refused to drive me.

At home, I showered, slugged deeply at a bottle of gin to calm my nerves, then drove over to Ramon's, where I sat in a dark niche midway between the front and back doors and furtively scanned the menu. Java with a side of pre-breakfast pancakes was the first thing I ordered, much to the dismay of Mrs Ramon – or whatever her name was – whose loud and wearisome sighs always subtly imply that she has more than enough on her own plate without the added burden of ensuring that I forever have enough on mine.

But let's be honest: I didn't care less what Mrs Ramon thought of me just then, and the only thing on my mind was me. Besides, I wasn't getting my eats *gratis* for nothing, if that makes sense. No, I'd promised Ramon that someday soon I was going to help him fend off a few of the local crime-lords and their evil spawn, all of whom were constantly hitting him up for protection money. And the way in which I was going to perform this selfless act was by leaning on one or two of my high-level contacts in either City Hall or Police Administration.

I genuinely hadn't intended to lie to Ramon.

I was just hungry and broke at the time because I'd been on the sauce for a few days straight, and I'd been walking past Ramon's when I spied the upset restaurateur on the stoop. I'd stopped, naturally, because the place looked so warm and inviting, and there was this delicious smell of food emanating out into the street. Then Ramon had suddenly clutched at my leg, begging for help, and I'd instantly sensed an opportunity to help a man out of a desperate situation.

That man, of course, being me.

Of course, I'm now pretty certain that Ramon would be rather dismayed to learn that one local wiseguy currently had plans to use me as freeway-underlay if I didn't meet with a small debt I'd incurred during a five-day poker spree in one of his underground gambling dens. And I'm near certain that the naïve restaurateur would hardly feel much better if he found out that I fled here to Vesperville because a number of beefy bailiffs were intent upon destroying my last bolt-hole because I'd somehow mixed up the words lease and fleece.

Oh, and now that I think of it, I should have mentioned that I'm as popular down in Police Administration as rabies in a pound.

Still, I'd fill him in on some of that eventually. For now, all Ramon and Mrs Ramon had to know was that I'd definitely be there for them at some time in the future, albeit at a time when they didn't truly need me, and perhaps when I had something more pressing to attend to.

Anyhow, back to the story.

There I was, tucking into my food and scanning the daily broadsheets for work, when my pager beeped. Straight off, I knew it was Marcie, my loyal, if inept secretary, who was currently uptown in my office on Dahmler Row. In one way, I wanted to go find a phone and call her right back in case she'd found someone to hire me, yet the downside to Marcie is that she tends to interrupt every serious conversation with inconsequential chatter about back-pay and long-held IOUs and stuff.

Sadly, this holds especially true near the end of each month – and it was now March 28th.

Still, what choice did I have? I needed work, and someone may have been looking to hire me. So, I went out to a phone on the corner and rang the office.

'You got a call, Marty. Someone actually lookin' to hire you.'

'Hey,' I grinned. 'Y'see, that judge was wrong – people *aren't* always put off by corruption and blackmail scandals. So, what sort of work are we talkin' about here?'

'You, uhm, actually know the client,' Marcie replied somewhat hesitantly. 'It's young Tommy Ellis. Y'know, that kid who hangs around the end of the block.'

'So, you're interruptin' me in the middle of a meetin' to tell me one of those society-urchins is stringin' you along with talk of a case?' I paused, took a deep breath and tried counting to 400 in sets of eight as Doc Edgars had advised me to do in times of stress, but I couldn't get higher than thirty-seven. Seconds later, my blood pressure went on the hike and the pulse in my left wrist started doing the cha-cha.

'Tommy was cryin',' Marcie replied sourly. 'He wouldn't go into any great detail, but he said it had somethin' to do with his father and a murder, or somethin'...'

I knew Tommy Ellis well. He was a kid aged about sixteen or so, and he and his gang had been hanging around my office ever since I could recall, perhaps even before my Uncle Don – the original owner of Shale Private Eye Inc., and the guy who taught me all I knew about the business – mysteriously skipped town some five years back and left the place in my 'capable' hands.

But back to Tommy: The first time I'd met the kid, he'd asked if I wanted somebody to look out for my Buick when I was in the office. I told him I'd a dog that'd look after it for me. He asked if it could put out fires. Thereafter, I gave him a small fee each week, figuring ever-increasing insurance would cost more in the long-term.

'Jeez, Marcie, don't you know a wind-up when you hear one? The punk's yankin' your chain because he knows you're...' Again, I paused, aware that tact was often better than fact. 'Well, let's say you're not the brightest bulb in the candelabra.'

Marcie sighed like a locomotive on a down-grade. 'Why are you takin' this out on me, Marty? I take it you're still strugglin' to stay off the cigarettes?'

'Marcie, do you know how many treadmill-lovin' beagles selflessly gave up their time to perfect cigarettes for our enjoyment? I only ever smoked to keep those poor mutts in work. And now, unless they're lucky enough to get into testin' cosmetics, they're all gonna end up on welfare.'

Marcie, despite my scathing wit, had locked onto the source of my anxiety. The fact I was three-grand in the hole aside, this was yet another reason I was going at her like a rabid badger. Doc Edgars – the only doctor in the city who could tell you that you'd six months to live, then offer you twelve if you went private – had warned me to give up my life's every pleasure or, come the end of summer, I'd be suitable only as a mulch. I like life, despite the cards I've been forced, so less than two weeks back, I'd cut back on the drink and cigarettes, and I'd even cut the eating down – a little. Of course, since last night's chance encounter with Happy Valentine my willpower had taken a knock. One minute I'd been idly laying bets on walking corpses at the track, the next I'd been starring in my own version of the Pit and the Pendulum. Was it any real wonder that I was now comfort eating until it was way too uncomfortable? And how long before all my other little vices reappeared?

'So you aren't takin' his case?' Marcie gasped. 'But we *need* the money. And I'd like a few luxuries in my life, like electricity, clothes and food and stuff.'

There it was, regular as clockwork, airy-fairy talk about the redistribution of wealth from the dear-and-greedy to the poor-and-needy. Jeez, in three days time she and I would be going at it like two starving dogs on a glazed ham!

'Of course I'm not takin' the case, woman – *it's not real*! Tommy's probably in the phone booth across the road as we speak, laughin' so hard he's probably shit his pants a dozen shades of brown. You get the picture here?'

'That's a very graphic picture you're paintin', Marty.'

'You only seem to understand graphic, Marcie. Now, if Tommy phones again, tell him that he's been sittin' in the lap of luxury so long its got a fuckin' hernia, but now the gravy boat has just sprung a leak, and if he keeps this up, come mornin' he'll be lyin' in a lily surround. Y'hear me?'

'Yeah, I hear you, Marty,' Marcie sighed, seemingly unfazed by my mixed clichés. 'Sadly, the ears came along with the deal when you hired me.'

'Good, and don't worry about your money. In a few weeks time our recession will be over, and we'll have more cases than you can cock your hat at.'

'Yeah, Marty – cock! It couldn't be any clearer.'

The phone went dead and I rubbed hard at my forehead for a time, before returning to Ramon's to find that my food was as cold and icky as my mood. I thanked Mrs Ramon, but didn't bother leaving a gratuity, as fifteen percent of nothing isn't all that much. Then I strolled out into the rising heat of the day, climbed into my Buick and drove that long fifty-yards home.

***

They say home's a sanctuary for the weary man, but I often return there only if I've no place else to go. There are many reasons for this, some of which I've explained, yet the reason I felt like this today was because Joe Sinto was standing outside my front door as I pulled into the drive, and straight off I knew I was in for a rotten afternoon.

Joe smiled a pearly–white upon seeing me, and I traded him a knife–slash grin in return as I exited the car. I didn't quite catch his first comment, as Greta was going at one of the inside walls of Chez Shale with a jackhammer. And the schmuck didn't hear mine, which was probably just as well as our resultant fight to the death out there in the middle of the street would've made the clamour generated by that moronic Teutonic seem dull in comparison.

Joe's that ex-neighbour of mine I was telling you about, and, to anyone who's ever had the displeasure of having the pleasure, he's known by many monikers, one such being the Ham from Nam.

Two tours of Vietnam had done that to Joe. Two tours in which he'd ended up convinced that wars were never over, there just weren't as many people fighting them in times of peace. Not that he looked your typical Corp type, to be honest. No, Joe always reminds me of a porn-extra. He's a swarthy guy of Italian extract, about 50 years old, with an almost pubic perm and a moustache so thick it would've been difficult for skin-flick connoisseurs to figure exactly when he'd partaken of a chomp-shot. His attire, however, was more telling. Right now, he was dressed in olive-green fatigues which, because he was as thin as a malnourished flute, made him appear a little heavier than his normal 150 pounds.

Needless to say, I never feel too comfortable with him around. So, before I'd undertaken a midnight flit from my last Chez Shale, I'd slyly given him a non-existent address in Vesperville's crime-ridden and dimly-lit Waterfront area, telling him to call around any night just shortly after dark should he need to get in touch. I'd forgotten, however, that he'd once claimed to have served in Special Forces and could probably track a trout through rapids. Now, he came at me quickly down the drive, took my hand in a warrior's grasp and shook me bodily, wearing a demented grin that told me he missed me dearly.

I'd missed him once too – my rifle sight had been off – but I'd made a pact there and then to never make the same mistake again.

'Hey, Whale, you douche-bag!' he cried above the din. 'Just came over to check out your new hooch. But you must've given me the wrong directions, man. So I phoned your office and Marcie told me where you were.' Joe frowned a corrugated. 'That girl shouldn't be handin' out info like that – I could've been anybody at all. Anyhow, I took a slick down here to the A.O., and here I am.'

I fumed inwardly. For a personal secretary, Marcie was way too personal with my details, and I wondered then if she was also the so-called 'friend' Happy Valentine had mentioned last night. If I found out she was, I'd pay her back by not paying her in a few days time. For now, however, I had to deal coldly and clinically with Joe.

'You're, uhm, welcome anytime, buddy, you know that.'

Joe slapped me on the shoulder, hard. 'Ah, you're just sayin' that!'

'Sure I am, Joe. Spooky the way you pick up on things like that. Real spooky!'

Joe Sinto, to be honest, was way more than spooky. He was two bullets short of a clip and spoke mostly in staccato Marine, never having been able to fully readapt to life in the city since our nation quit Vietnam just over two decades back. There are a lot of people like him about, I know, but I honestly can't think of anyone more off the plumb who isn't still in maximum security. Anyhow, figuring I could hardly send him away for at least an hour as he'd travelled all the way across town, I reluctantly asked him inside.

As we entered, I noticed that Greta was in the process of ripping my hall closet into an even bigger closet. Still, as she's of Aryan extraction – and so perhaps of the belief that the only way to build a better world is to thoroughly destroy it first – I wasn't too concerned with her tactics, yet it did occur to me just then that she'd either located Narnia, or that my latest neighbours and I were now sharing communal wardrobe space. But before I could raise this with her, Greta dropped the Kango and took Joe's forearm in the way those fighting types do. I shrugged, realising it would keep, then stumbled into the kitchen across the rubble. Moments later, Joe and Greta followed along behind.

Grimacing sourly, Joe took a look around the kitchen, wiped a coat of thick dust off the table with his finger. 'Hey, I got caught up in a fire-fight in a hooch like this once,' he frowned, his darkly-lit eyes going at the Thousand Yard Stare. 'Only thing missin' here is a gang of pyjama–wearin' Dinks with AK47s.'

'Wouldn't surprise me if they're in here somewhere, Joe.' As I spoke, I saw him tensing and slipping a hand inside his camouflaged jacket. I felt my parts puckering up and raised a quick palm-heel. 'Time-out there, small guy, I'm just jokin'.' Joe beamed a freaky, and I looked at my watch. 'Say, pity you didn't phone before you came over, but I have to go out in about five minutes, and, uhm...'

'Yeah, Whale, sorry about that. But I was goin' fugazi in my place, y'know!' Joe spiralled a finger into his temple to let me know something I knew too well. 'Don't like my new neighbours, either. One of them's been bangin' on my wall day and night, and it's throwin' me off my trombone playin' somethin' awful. So I just came over to shoot the breeze with you and Greta. Hope you don't mind.'

'Hey, I don't mind at all. It's just that I'm in the middle of a murder case. Young Tommy Ellis, his father, a body, blood...' I feigned a sorrowful, aware you had to go easy when disturbing the easily-disturbed. 'So, uhm, as much as I'd really like you to stay...'

Joe raised a palm-heel. 'No problem, Whale. You just go about your business and I'll catch up with Greta. I'll be outta here in five, six hours at most.'

I cursed under my breath, wondering if it was technically possible to investigate one murder whilst being cited as a prime-suspect in another. 'Sure, that's reasonable.'

'But if you have a few minutes now, maybe I'll tell you all about that hooch,' Joe interrupted congenially. He fixed me with a big-eye, more or less to let me know it would not only be rude, but perhaps quite dangerous, to refuse. 'Oh, and some tea would be good. Thanks.'

'Sounds like a barrel of laughs, Joe. And tea you say?'

I regarded my watch again, anxious to be out of there, but unwilling to leave Joe and Greta together. Germans and Italians are dodgy enough characters on their own, but the whole world now knows to their detriment what happens if you leave a couple of them in the same room long enough. So, as Joe sat at the kitchen table alongside Greta, I searched the cupboard for some tea I'd bought years back, hoping he'd swallow it in one gulp, take a whitey and die.

'No green tea, Joe. Black alright?'

Joe pouted, gave me the thumb. As I fixed his drink, I mused that tea was also the only substance Joe hadn't gotten addicted to on his assorted foreign tours. Of course, the Ham would never admit to any dependency habits, but I'd heard him mention Cambodian Red and Laotian Green enough to know he wasn't talking traffic signals. Still, according to him, nothing was addictive so long as you indulged in it every day.

I boiled a kettle as Joe started into his tale without a prompt. Across the table, Greta sat and stared at him in expectant awe, seemingly undaunted by the fact this guy was a regular Hans Christian.

'At the start of the war, I was in the 1st USMC in Vietnam, as you know,' Joe began, as I placed his and

Greta's drinks upon the table before shifting slowly into my seat. 'An E1, Grade-A Private, as low as an enlisted man can get...'

'Never thought you made it that high up the ranks, Joe, to be honest.'

'Yeah, Marty, surprised myself with that one too,' Joe replied seriously. 'But anyhow, where was I? Oh, yeah. I was sayin' that...'

It was then, as a couple of Whizz-Bangs went off in Joe's eyes and his mind boarded a Huey for a different continent, that the phone rang. I waited a second, then asked Joe's permission to answer it. The way you did when Joe was around.

'Your hooch, Whale. Wouldn't dream of gettin' in the way.'

I suppressed something venomous and moved quickly into the sitting room.

'Shale?' a voice started. 'Is that Shale, the P.I.?'

'Maybe,' I hedged. 'You givin' or takin'?'

'Uhm, neither. I got your...home number off your secretary, Marcie,' the voice replied haltingly. 'I need your help. My father's in trouble and he's gonna do a big stretch if someone doesn't help him out.'

'Who is this?' I asked. An annoying memory suddenly resurfaced. 'Tommy, if that's you, kid, I'm goin' to be awful mad. You're drainin' me dry, and...'

'Please, Mr Shale. I know you're a busy man but I'm deadly serious. Didn't you hear about the murder over in Skytowers last night?'

'Can't say I did, Tommy. Bad was it? Anyone dead?'

As Tommy was about to reply, Joe passed the open doorway to the sitting room, his face strained, his pace crablike. 'Need to use your latrine,' he grimaced. 'Got the turtle's head goin' on here.'

'No problem, Joe. Have a good shit, it'll help clear your mind.'

I settled into a reinforced niche in the sofa, lifted the phone again, and heard Tommy midway through a rambling tale that involved murder and death in slightly lesser amounts than the one being recounted only moments before in the next room.

'Give me that again, kid,' I told him sourly. 'From the start. And please, take your time.'

TWO

Sadly I didn't hear as much of Tommy's story as was perhaps necessary, put off as I was by the sound of Hambo in the kitchen fondly recalling the time he'd charged up some hill outside of Khe San and planted the Stars and Stripes in the face of a few foreign nationals who'd been under the wrongful impression they owned it. So, as the kid concluded his strange tale, I told him I'd get back to him, but only if or when the local tabloids confirmed what he was saying. Then I returned to the kitchen, took a beer from the cooler and sat down. Time moved slower than molasses in December after that, and I was forced to listen to several more tales of derring-doo-doo before Greta slowed Joe's tongue by offering him something akin to primordial soup, with a side-order of salmonella and botulism pie with listeria sauce.

Needless to say, when Joe left at 11-00pm – or when he 'executed a withdrawal', as he put it – I was instantly filled with the same sort of warm feeling you get when an old friend drops in. I watched neutrally as he bade Greta a warrior's farewell, listened dispassionately as he hinted about calling around for the housewarming, and smiled wanly as he told me he was thinking of vacationing on the coast. As he climbed into his Humvee and took to the main road as if it had done him a personal wrong, I stood at the door and shivered briskly, my mind filled with bleak visions of him sitting at the shore, gun in hand, ordering the tide to go back.

Back inside, I warned Greta in no uncertain terms that she was never again to admit Joe into Chez Shale while I was alive. Maybe it was a trick of the light, but she stared between me and a kitchen knife for several moments as if weighing that as a proposition. But, several heart-stopping moments later, she picked up the jackhammer and vented her angst on the hall closet until around midnight. Which may've bothered my latest neighbours, now that I think of it, but didn't bother me in the least, as I just stuck on some really loud music to drown out the noise, even as I numbed myself into a deepy with several more beers.

Dawn arrived about noon the next day – pretty much the way it always does in my place – and I ambled into the kitchen. There, I de-tabbed a bottle of breakfast and turned the radio on, hoping to catch the local news. Seconds later, I discovered that Tommy Ellis had been telling the truth after all. His father, Frank, was currently being held in Police Administration and had been charged with killing a former business partner. I phoned Marcie and told her to have Tommy meet me at 2-30pm in a downtown bar called the Gutted Moose. If the kid turned up, so well and so good. If not, I'd down half a dozen beers and try to figure out why my life was slowly going down the tubes.

The Gutted Moose is frequented mostly by the city's hunting fraternity. The most revered customers are those with the biggest guns and the most outlandish opinions. Strangely, even though I'm not really into hunting, I get on quite well with everyone in there. Bernard is the proprietor of this latter day Last Chance Saloon, a boring character who knows everything about talking and nothing about dialogue, and he's never too busy to tell you how busy he is. He greeted me as I came in and tried to engage me in a monologue. But I pointed quickly to young Tommy sitting in a booth to my left.

'Bit of business to get stuck into, Bernard,' I told him from under a worn smile. 'You could bring me a pitcher of beer if you want, maybe talk at me later.'

Tommy was dragging nervously on a cigarette as I edged in alongside him. The fragrant whiff of nicotine tugged on my olfactory nerves, and for a moment it was like a breath of fresh air. But, after mustering up some resolve, I ignored its lure and raised a stalling palm as Tommy was about to speak.

'Before you say a word, kid, let's get somethin' straight. Things are gonna be different this time out, in that if I agree to work for you, *you'll* be payin' *me*.'

As if deeply disturbed by the terms of this unexpected proposition, Tommy's gaze went puppy-dog. 'My mother'll pay you well, Mr Shale, I swear. But she's down in Police Administration now with my father, so I guess she'll be kinda busy for a while. You'll just have to trust me.'

I shook him a no-no. 'Trust's a four-letter word in my book, kid. I'll need moolah up front before I start pickin' at the finer threads in that yarn of yours.'

'It isn't a yarn,' Tommy retorted indignantly.

'Well, I hope not, because I cotton on quick, and it'd take a damn good yarn to pull the wool over my eyes.'

Somewhat inexplicably, Tommy's mood darkened. 'I thought you'd be glad of the work, Mr Shale, seein' as how you aren't exactly run off your feet these days. But, if that's your attitude, I'll go find someone else.'

As Tommy made to rise, I bit hard at my lip. I could let him go now, sure, but he was actually the first person to at least promise me money in the last two months, and I'd probably be taking a step up the social ladder if I started mooning for quarters. 'Alright, kid,' I sighed, 'I'll allow you a few hours grace. We'll have another drink and you can tell me that, uhm, *story* of yours again.'

Nodding dismally, Tommy took a slow sip of his beer. Then, after wiping the back of his hand across his mouth, he began: 'My father was over in Skytowers last night, Mr Shale. He'd arranged to meet a former business partner of his, Abel Shirinski, in a conference room on the 18th floor. But, somewhere in-between times, there was a shootin' and

Abel was killed.' Tommy paused for a second and took a deep breath. 'And now my father's bein' charged with his murder.'

As our drink arrived, I asked Bernard to stick it on my tab, waited until he'd left, then said: 'They sure this Shirinski guy wasn't just fakin' a stone-cold bluey, kid? Maybe just playin' possum until compensation set in?' Before Tommy could reply, I fixed him with a judgemental. 'You'd be surprised the lengths some people will go to where money's involved.'

Tommy shook his head and stared at me sadly. 'No, I don't think so. And I know it doesn't look good, but I know my father and he's no murderer.'

'Correct! He's not a murderer until it's proven in court. Until then, he's just a suspected killer with possible serial-killing tendencies, right?' Tommy nodded uneasily. 'That aside, who was the arrestin' officer?' I knew a few people down in Police Administration and liked less than the smallest amount of them. That feeling was, however, reciprocated by more than the largest percentage.

'Ed Malone.' As I shuddered deeply, Tommy added, 'You know him?'

'Yeah, he's, uhm, a friend of mine.' I suddenly felt sorry for Tommy. Ed 'Tork' Malone was the sort of cop who believed everyone guilty until proven guilty, and he'd have thought nothing about charging the entire city with Original Sin.

'Tell you what I'll do, kid,' I said. 'You go on home, and I'll make a few calls, see what I can dig up. Give me a ring about seven or so, and I'll tell you where we stand. But remember, if this is another scam...'

'This isn't a scam, Mr Shale. I only wish it was.'

With that, we finished our beer and moved outside into the crowded afternoon street. As I stood upon the baking asphalt, the sun splitting the sky overhead, I wiped my brow with a handkerchief and watched as Tommy ran off towards centre city. As he did so, I wondered if I'd been a little harsh. In days gone by, I'd vented my wrath upon the older generation, yet these days I seemed to spend more time criticising young people. Still, that was back in the days when I had a narrow waist and a broad mind, and near everything in my life had wheeled 180° since then.

I shrugged undecidedly, climbed into my Buick and drove off, careful to keep the needle under 80mph as I was in a built-up area and a little drunk. Minutes later, I pulled in at one of the few un-vandalised phone-booths in the city and called Police Administration. I've a half-friend down there who occasionally gives me the upshot on current events, depending upon his mood.

'Mo?' I said. 'That you?'

I heard a click, then re-dialled. Mo always hangs up the first few times I call. It's a ritual he has going on, so I play along. I got him the seventh time, and he answered with a short bark. 'What the fuck do you want, Whale?'

I skipped the unpleasantries. 'Just thought I'd call you up and see which way the wind is blowin' on that Skytowers thing. Apparently some guy Shirinski croaked the Big Croak there two nights back. So, what's the verdict?'

Mo sighed deeply. 'I don't want to talk to you, Marty,' he snapped. 'You're nothin' but trouble with a capital F. We've got everythin' we need to fulfil our needs on the murder, thank you very much. We got a victim, a murderer, a weapon and a motive. What we *don't* need is a red herrin' and a stumblin' block.'

'One more thing, Mo, before you slam down the gavel and start shoutin' that Ellis deserves a thirty-second ride on Old Smoky. What was the *exact* motive?'

'Look, Marty, y'know I can't hand out that kind of info over the line.'

'One word, Mo. One word to point me in the right direction on this thing.'

'This isn't a *thing*, Marty. It's an open and shut case, and if Malone finds me talkin' to you, I'll be out on patrol faster than you can say "pass the pies". And that's fast!'

'A word, Mo. One word, that's all I'm askin'.'

'Jesus – blackmail!' Mo seethed, clearly unimpressed with my fortitude. 'Now, if you're collectin' words, here's another three for you...'

I hung up before Mo could pollute the line with his unsavoury request, got back into my car and took the freeway out of the city towards Torrio Hill, another of the city's suburbs that's so small the speed-limit signs are hung back to back. There, I planned to meet up with an old friend of mine, Clay Rivers.

Clay is African-American, tall, built like a jockey's whip and perhaps my only real friend. For that reason, I even visit him when I don't need anything. What I do like about him, though, is he's easygoing, intelligent and possessed of so much optimism that he'd go out and build a stable if he happened upon a horseshoe. The downside to such an outlook, of course, is he's far too upbeat where love is concerned, and Cupid's arrow has been barbed on every occasion the man has fallen under the Big Delusion. For ten years, Clay was happily married to a girl who wasn't, before falling for another young lady who had promised herself to another...dozen teamsters. Consequently, like many men, Clay had started a family but hadn't hung around to finish it. Still, who am I to judge anyone? I've also had a few near-Mrs myself, yet I've always managed to avoid that knotted complication by remembering two very important rules: One, you aren't complete until you're married, and then you're finished; and two, you should always get married at least three times before you settle down.

Clay greeted me at his front door with a wide, amiable grin. I strolled into his quaint abode, took off my jacket, and sat down on the strongest chair in the room, as is my way. Clay shook his head in mock despair. 'Make yourself at home, Whale. But weren't we supposed to meet up last night?'

'Yeah, well the Danger Ranger stopped by, and he wouldn't shut up, so I couldn't get shot of him without doin' somethin' short of actually shootin' him...'

I paused for a moment, hoping some grammar would kick in.

'Anyhow, I ended up havin' to shoot the shit with him, until he shut up and shot off, the little fuckin' shit! But I'm not stayin' too long because I've got a case on. I just called in to say I'll meet you later tonight for a beer if you want.'

'No problem. But, you didn't tell *him* you were comin' here, did you?'

I smiled wanly. Like me, Clay knew that Joe Sinto was a primitive if ever there was one; and to the guy with the bow and arrow, everyone's a target. 'Sure I did. He's comin' over here shortly. Why should I have all the fun?'

Clay grinned uncertainly as he moved into the kitchen and returned with a couple of beers. He offered me one and seemed about to question me further when the front door was keyed open. We both turned as a tall, dark-skinned youth entered the room. 'Oh, Whale, this is my son,' Clay beamed, making his way back out to the kitchen. 'You've met him several times before, I believe.'

Which was Clay's idea of a joke. Nineteen year old Jason – or Muddy as I call him in jest – was actually my godson, and the eldest of Clay's two children, the other being a pretty teenage girl called Martella. In his own inimitable fashion, Clay was trying to tell me I wasn't much of a godparent, and maybe not much of a friend. Still, we had a history, Clay and I, stretching back to the early '70s when

Clay worked as a Salvation Army chef in one of the city's poorest ghettos after his dishonourable discharge from the forces – the same poorhouse I'd visited regularly during stakeouts when trying to save my hard-earned for necessities like drink, gambling and broads. Whatever the reason, Clay and I had bonded, and our common interests at that time were living it up at night, living it down in the morning, and generally hanging out in the sort of place where girls went to look for husbands and husbands went to look for girls. Then, about two years later, Clay got hitched. Naturally, I'd been at his bachelor party, his wedding, both christenings and his divorce party, though I can honestly say I now recall very little about each of those events, except maybe for the faces of the bastards I was fighting.

'How's it goin', kid?' I grinned as Muddy sat down beside me and flicked the television to life. 'Still shacked up with that lap-dancer across town?'

Muddy's gaze went hound-dog. Suddenly he was possessed by teenage angst – a forehead full of frowns, and a look that said he was going to spend his next few years beset by thoughts of troubles which would never befall him. 'Alice? Well, uhm, no. She threw me out,' he said sadly. 'She said I should find myself a decent job, because she wants a white weddin' with all the trimmin's.'

'She wants what?' I barked. I knew that girl would only have a white wedding if it snowed hard for a week. She wasn't good enough for my godson, and she turned his every living day into a soap-opera climax. Still, Muddy was also a Walter Mitty type character who wandered in and out of his own life at regular intervals, so that didn't help. Of course, I'd done my bit for the kid: Many a time I'd told his girl what I thought of her as I'd leered at her on stage. 'Why that little fuckin' harlot! She's havin' carnival knowledge with everyone. You want me to go beat some sense into the little mattress-back, kid?' I saw Clay hiding his face in his hands and wincing. 'I'm serious, Clay. She's an adventure playground, and you have to take penicillin every time you look at her!'

'Thanks for the offer, uncle Marty, but no,' Muddy said, forcing a smile. 'I'll just have to work this thing out for myself, y'know.'

'Yeah, well don't you go gettin' all emotional over her, she aint worth it. Remember, emotions are only for women and the weak and feeble.'

'I know. You told me that last time you were here.'

'Yeah, well there's a lot of things you *don't* know where women are concerned, Muds. And, as you're my godson, I feel it's up to me to keep you straight. Just remember the old proverb: If you love someone set them free; if they return, they were always yours; if they don't, then hunt them down and kill them!'

'Sure, uncle Marty. I'll keep that in mind.'

I patted his shoulder affectionately. 'You're a good kid, Muds. But you've no idea how to treat women. Still, that'll all come to you in time. Hey, tell you what – I've got to run an errand for a new client of mine now, but your father and I are meetin' in the Moose about ten this evenin'. Why don't you join us, and we'll talk this thing through?'

Muddy nodded glumly, and Clay shrugged as if he didn't mind one way or the other. 'I'll take that as an affirmative then,' I grinned, finishing my beer and putting my coat on. 'You just hang in there, Muds. If this thing doesn't work out for you, I'll find you another nice young lady to ease your pain.'

At the front door Clay whispered, 'You don't know any nice young ladies, Whale. And even if you do, they cost more than he can afford.'

'Oh no? Just be there at ten.' I waved to Muddy. 'Remember, kid, the night belongs to livers, not lovers. And one thing I know about the demon drink is it can get you an old demon any time you want.' I winked playfully at Clay. 'See, I'm a regular Doctor Ruth. I'll have that kid sorted before the clock strikes midnight.'

Clay didn't reply. He merely shook his head and laughed sourly as I climbed into the Buick and drove off into the night.

***

Skytowers is a multi-storey conference centre which stands midway between Masseria Park and the Siegel River. Being equidistant between those two scenic landmarks, it also has a reputation as one of the city's most luxurious skyscrapers. Still, despite the glorious references given to it by our town-planners, I personally think it breaches the skyline of our city on a par tantamount to rape, and, unlike Abel Shirinski, I wouldn't have been caught dead in it if I hadn't needed the money.

I arrived there about 8-30pm but parked a little down the block, as the dark-skinned Ed Malone – who's secretly called Tork by his subordinates, because of his spiritual affinity with the Spanish Inquisitor, Torquemada – was way too familiar with both me and my car. To put it more succinctly, this senior detective believes you don't have to be a knight of the road if you own a ten-tonne truck, and his truck happens to be the city's police force. Sadly, according to Tork, Yours Gratingly is forever driving his own un-roadworthy ramrod through every red-light in his precinct, which means I'm always on his to-do list.

As it was, I didn't see his car out in the street, and there was only one patrol car parked in the lot across the way. I knew there'd be at least two officers outside the room of the murder until forensics had taken samples of everything they needed, which meant I just might have some trouble getting in to poke around.

The security guard at the front desk halted me with a whistle as I tried to pass him by. He had the look of something from way down the food-chain, as well as the vacant glare of a night-club doorman. This was another guy who looked as if he'd trade off everything he owned in the world for some magic beans, so when I flashed a false badge at him, he didn't consider things too deeply. He straightened in his seat and directed me to the crime-scene on the 18th floor.

Once inside, I called Marcie from a payphone in the lobby, told her where I was, and asked her to arrange a meeting for me with young Tommy's mother the first chance she got. Of course, as soon as I stopped talking business, Marcie predictably started talking wages. Needless to say, I told her the connection was fading midway through that pathetic monologue and moved towards the elevators. Just then, I'd more pressing concerns, and the first was how I was going to get into the scene of the crime.

THREE

As I rode the escalator to the 17th floor – one floor beneath the crime-scene – I smiled thinly, hoping this was the start of a financial upturn. All I had to do was drag this case out for at least two weeks, charge Mrs Ellis 200 dollars a day, and hike up my expenses. Then, after paying off Gus Diamond and his lackey, Happy Valentine, I'd be in the clear. That latter payment, of course, was non-negotiable, because Happy had one hell of a bad rep, and even now was probably considering way to sex-up my demise. Despite his pleasant demeanour, urban myths abounded as to how many of his victims were cudgelled into a Merrick, how others were forced down to the banks of the Siegel River to drink the Big Drink until they could drink no more, and how still others were shot so many times the city pathologist had difficulty picking out their nether-eye in the autopsy.

I shivered coldly, returning my thoughts to what I'd do with any money I had left over. I'd have to give Greta twenty bucks, of course, as I hadn't paid her in months. And I could probably stop Marcie from playing 'Back-Pay or Payback' by giving her a few hundred, whilst simultaneously explaining that it was just a pre-instalment on the instalment I'd eventually give her as a small down-payment on a large down-payment of what I owed her overall. Anything after that would, needless to say, help Yours Deservedly pay off a few bills, have a few tipples and maybe even a little flutter or two down the track – normal stuff like that.

All this, of course, depended upon whether Lady Luck was standing at my side or, as was more usual, going at me from behind with a strap-on. The only other way I could think of making three-grand in a hurry was one I'd been considering for some time, though was as yet understandably reluctant to commit to until I was faced with a real and genuine emergency. In short, it involved me going down to the local hospital and selling off one of my spare livers.

Anyhow, as the elevator reached the seventeenth floor, I got out and found the nearest stairwell. Then I moved silently onto the next floor, knowing it was essential to maintain the element of surprise. A furtive glance through the stairwell door into the corridor soon told me I'd found the room I was looking for, though, as I suspected, it was currently being guarded by two of the city's finest.

I hung out of sight, wondering how to proceed. Fake ID was out as I'd been on a first-name-and-blame basis with every cop in this city for years. Moreover, it was rumoured that Tork had recently given his men the go-ahead to shoot me for anything from whistling-in-a-built-up-area, to looking-large-in-a-40-mph-zone; and, as grim as my personal outlook was just then, I'd no desire to end up a modern-day Clive Barrow. Within moments, however, someone exited a room to my left. He was middle-aged and of Asian origin by my guess, so I quickly sidled in close to the wall, took a good hold of myself, then dived around the corner and took a better hold of him.

There was a bit of a struggle at first in which he thrashed about like a fish on a trawler, and for a moment he had me worried – I thought I'd killed him. But shortly before he turned Smurf, I took out my fake badge and quietly informed him that I was there to check that my men weren't asleep on the job.

He nodded his understanding and I let him go. Seconds later, when he'd calmed down, he told his name was Rick and that he worked the graveyard shift there in Skytowers several nights a week. As he spoke, I noticed he had a furtive look in his eye, and I got the impression that this was a man who'd skipped immigration only weeks before and perhaps worked a second job teaching basket-weaving in dark basements. Still, after he'd showed me some ID, I asked him what he'd heard about the latest developments in the case.

'I know little other than what I already told your men,' he shrugged. 'This floor has been closed for a week now, for painting and a general overhaul. And no one has been in that room since the murder took place. Except for the Forensics team, of course. Oh, and me – to make the place nice and tidy before they arrived.'

I regarded him incredulously, looking both through him and down at him at the same time. 'Did you just say you cleaned up a crime-scene *before* the Forensics team went in?' As he nodded, I regarded him as I would a corpse, because if Tork Malone ever found out that this guy had messed up his crime scene, he'd do things to him that weren't even described in the Blue Section of the Policeman's Manual. 'And those guys on the door just let you go in?'

Rick frowned uncertainly, as if caught up in an inner debate with a wiser man. 'No one said I couldn't. I just went in through the other door and scrubbed the blood out of the carpet, stuff like that. I wanted to leave the place tidy.'

I shook my head in disbelief, intuitively guessing just then that Rick probably spelt his name with a silent P. 'The, uhm, *other* door?'

He bowed low and smiled inscrutably. 'Come with me and I'll show you.'

As I was deliberating whether I should blow in Rick's ear and give him a refill, he led me down the corridor past plush, glass-walled offices and spacious waiting areas, each accessorised with a variety of tall palms and fronds. Even the 'music' had a relaxed feel and was a composite of bird calls, the sound of running water and the reassuring clack of bamboo chimes. When we arrived at room 18c, Rick produced a set of keys, inserted one in the lock and led me into an expansive conference room which was devoid of furniture, though there was a podium at one end and a movie-screen covering the wall behind it.

Moving towards the furthest end of the room, we arrived at yet another locked door, which Rick again keyed open. 'We keep all our chairs and tables in this storage room,' he whispered. 'We shift them between the two rooms if and when needed.' As we moved into that large communal closet, the light was flicked on by a motion-sensor, nearly sending me under. Rick urged me towards the last door, pulling a flashlight from his pocket as he did so. 'And beyond this door is room 18a. I'll wait here. You just go in quickly, close this door fast so the cops outside don't see a light, then use the torch. It's pretty dim.'

I nodded, realising Rick's cool head had more to do with him having cold feet than anything else. So I waited until he'd moved back into 18c before quickly entering room 18a and shutting the closet door fast behind me. As Rick had said, the torch he'd given me was about as dim as its owner, though it allowed me to determine that I was in a room of a similar size and shape to18c. The next thing that became apparent was the chalk outline in the centre of the floor which marked the spot where Abel Shirinski had fallen and died in a pool of his own juice.

It may've seemed like I was on a wild-goose chase, but I knew that, despite his reputation, the city's finest forensic scientist, Mal Brennan, was getting old and often left more clues lying about than the organisers of a Murder Mystery weekend. I hoped Rick had been equally flippant. As I turned the torch on and shone it around the room, I quickly located a small bullet hole beside the door to room 18a – the door now being guarded by the police. It was only when I pointed the torch at the floor, however, that I noticed a long, winding trail of vaguely luminescent particles which ran from the central closet door to a place about three feet from the innermost supporting wall.

I knelt, examining the particles for a second, then quietly retraced my steps. As I neared the closet door, however, I caught a glint of something metallic lodged beneath the doorframe. I bent over, scooped a small pea-sized metallic object up into my hand and pocketed it. Good old Mal Brennan, I mused: There were times when he couldn't have found a mammoth in a wool shop!

Rick was waiting outside in the corridor, his mop raised defensively. 'Ah, it is you,' he observed, astutely. 'Thought it was someone else.'

I nodded wanly. Lyndon Johnson had once said that Gerald Ford played too much football with his helmet off, and I suddenly found myself wanting to ask Rick if he'd done the same. 'Listen,' I said instead, 'thanks for your help, but if you don't mind, I've a few more questions.' I took out my notebook and pen.

'But I already gave a statement to your officers.'

'Yeah, well, sometimes they don't hear all they hear. Now, you were here on the night of the murder, right?' Rick nodded slowly. 'Right, so what did you see?'

'I was outside cleaning the corridor, the way I always am between 7-30pm and 8-00pm, and I saw the dead guy enter the room at 7-30pm. Only he wasn't dead yet…'

'Really?' I pouted a DeNiro, pretended to write that down. 'Wasn't… dead…yet.' I raised an expectant eyebrow. 'Then what?'

'So I was mopping the floor, as I said, but I knew the guy shouldn't have been there as this floor is closed. Then the other guy entered 18a around 7-45pm. The two of them started to argue for a few minutes, then it went sort of quiet for a while, after which there was a gunshot. So, at that, I stopped mopping, knocked on the door and entered the room. I saw the first guy lying dead in the centre of the room, and the other guy standing directly over him with a gun in his hand. I started shouting for Security, and the second guy, to be fair, just dropped the gun and stared blankly at me. He didn't try to run. He just kept pointing at the closet door, saying someone else had killed the guy on the floor, though I guessed he was just getting his alibi in quick. Moments later, the security men showed up and held the killer until the police arrived.' Rick frowned to a halt. 'Guess that's all I saw really.'

'So, this second guy – the one you think is the killer – he's pointin' to the closet door between the two rooms?'

Rick nodded vacantly, and I had to restrain myself from slapping him. Christ, this guy's brain was as ripe as Swiss cheese, and he probably got woodlice in his hair.

'Yes, Detective Lieutenant.'

'Anyone else got a key to that room?'

'My relief. Victor Fellows. He's the night porter.'

'And where would I find him?'

'Here mainly,' Rick replied. 'At night. But sometimes I cover for him as he tends to drink a bit too much, y'know.'

I nodded judgmentally.

'But he's home during the day.' Rick produced a notebook and pencil from his pocket and scrawled down the address. 'Here,' he said. 'If you want him, that's where he lives. Don't know if you'll get much sense out of him though.'

That was obviously a prerequisite for this particular job, I thought sourly. 'Yeah, well that's enough for now, Rick. I'm goin' down the precinct to drop a dime on those two assholes who are sleepin' on the job back there. But you've been a great help.' He smiled, and I made my way down into the lobby.

There was a tall, well dressed lady standing in the foyer when I exited the elevator, and she seemed uneasy with her surround. She was about 40 years old, pretty, and wearing a blue dress and pink hat. I sat on a nearby bench and whistled her over, figuring she was Tommy's mother. She glared at me incredulously and, despite her all-too obvious instinct to run off, approached me warily. As she neared, I noticed her legs were long and shapely – I'm not really into long or short legs, preferring something in-between – though her breasts were so low-set it was obvious gravity had been tugging on them for a while. Her nose was also so upturned that if she'd sneezed she'd probably have blown her hat off.

'You'd be Mrs. Ellis, if I haven't missed my guess,' I grinned. She nodded warily and I shook her hand, even though she hadn't offered it. 'I'm Marty Shale, Private Investigator.'

She scrutinised me evenly across the tip off her upturned snoot. 'I was talking to a policeman this morning,' she said loftily. 'And I told him I'd considered hiring a Private Investigator. He told me that of all those available, *you* were the one to avoid, and that if you approached me I was to scream loudly until someone came over and clubbed you to death with something pointed.'

'That'd be Ed Malone,' I grimaced. 'Friend of mine. Bit of a joker is Ed.'

'I don't think he was joking. He was foaming at the mouth when he said it.'

'I'm underwhelmed by the reference, lady, really I am,' I replied seriously. 'But then, he's always casting nasturtiums about me. Truth is, I wouldn't look good to that *defective* if I was rolled in gold, know what I'm sayin'?'

'He said pretty much the same kind of thing about you,' she sneered. 'Only he seems to know exactly what he's talking about. No offence, of course.'

'None taken – I'm only offended by things that make sense.' I took a deep breath. This lady obviously wanted to gnaw wildly on the bone of contention with Yours

Insatiably, but she was also my meal-ticket, so I had to keep my temper in check. All I had to do was remind myself that time was money, and if she didn't want Frank doing the time, she'd eventually have to come across with the money. 'Anyhow,' I grinned. 'As for Malone, he's blowin' mud because *he* doesn't do *his* job correctly. And just because he's got a serious face, it doesn't mean you have to take him seriously.'

'Let's stop jousting, Mr Shale. What I want to know is, why should I hire *you* instead of leaving this case to the police?'

'I'll tell you why, lady. Because Malone deals with about eight murders a month on average, and dozens of rapes, muggin's and drug-related crimes. This murder is only *part* of his daily routine, and evidence doesn't really concern him all that much. He's usually happy enough he doesn't leave any.' I tapped my chest with a forefinger. 'I, on the other hand, am a 200 dollar a day–*minus expenses*–one case P.I. who never leaves a case alone until I've solved it. I sleep, eat and shit it, lady, until I can eat, sleep and shit no more! Evidence, you want evidence? There's your evidence lady. Case dismissed!'

'That's an interesting picture you're painting, Mr Shale,' she replied sourly. 'And I've a feeling it's probably *very* you.'

'It's me, lady. All me. I shit you not!'

'Mmm, right, I'll hire you,' she sighed. 'I suppose Frank needs every bit of help I can muster, and it can hardly hurt to have another pair of eyes around...'

She continued talking, but I stopped listening as I'd seen a familiar face entering the lobby. And I didn't like the look of it, as it belonged to none other than Tork Malone, the demon we'd just been discussing. I took Mrs. Ellis by the arm and led her behind some nearby pillars. 'We should go somewhere a little more private,' I urged her quietly. 'I know the perfect place uptown.'

'Why are we hiding?' she asked, craning her head around to see who or what I was trying to avoid.

I kept the pillar between myself and Malone. 'Thought I saw an ex-girlfriend,' I replied softly. 'Bitch smacks me every time she gets the chance.'

She pulled free from my grasp. 'Seems perfectly reasonable to me,' she replied acidly. 'Why don't you introduce us – I like her already.' She made to escape, but I pulled her in close and fastened my hand tightly around her big mouth.

Tork and his ever-faithful echo-man, Mo Breasley, made their way across the lobby to the elevators, no doubt off to look for another clue that would help convict Frank Ellis. When they were out of sight, I released Tommy's mother, waited until she'd calmed down, then asked her for her first name and she told me it was Maria. 'Well, we'll take my car, Maria,' I said, as soon as Tork had vanished. 'You can spare an hour for your husband, I take it?' I helped her towards the front door.

She regarded her watch. 'Well, about an hour is all I *can* manage,' she replied, pulling away from me and fixing herself up. 'Frank's attorney thinks he can get me in to see him tonight, so we'd need to hurry.' She pulled me back by the arm and said, 'But I want this to go no further than you and I, Mr Shale.'

'Murder's a big deal, lady. It'll probably be in all the papers...'

'Not that,' she said acidly. 'I can handle that kind of publicity. I'm talking about the fact I've employed *you*. I don't want anyone to know about it. It'll ruin what's left of my standing in this city. I want our working relationship to remain a secret.'

'We can all keep secrets, lady,' I seethed, fixing her with Japanese eyes. 'It's usually the people we tell them to who can't. But sure, you want to be Ann o'Nimity, we'll do it your way. You're payin' for this, after all.'

'Good. Frank's in enough trouble. And I get the distinct feeling you could swing it for him to be hung, drawn and quartered if you really put your mind to it!'

I so wanted to share my ever-expanding knowledge of invective with her just then, but held off, realising my life was perhaps now literally in her hands. Instead, I chewed on my tongue, exited Skytowers and meekly made my way down the street through a congestion of hard-hats and office workers towards the parking lot.

Maria Ellis trailed a little way behind, and, as we walked, I was near certain I heard my intuition – long since coshed, bound and dumped into the boot of my brain – feebly calling out that I was way out of my depth with this particular case and would probably have more luck trying to whittle a hippopotamus down into a mouse.

FOUR

I took Maria to the Gutted Moose, my reasons for doing
so threefold. Firstly, I'd promised to meet Clay and
Muddy there at 10-00pm, which meant I'd roughly an
hour to interview Maria without interruption. Secondly,
the longer I kept that little snoot in my company, the more
I could eventually charge her. And lastly, and most
importantly, I'd a thirst on me that would've made a
cactus delusional.

'You'll like it in here,' I told Maria as we walked in the
door of the noisy bar. 'Maybe not the people, but the place
is nice enough.'

She nodded wearily, the events of the past few days
obviously having caught up with her. 'Actually, I often
think I like humanity more than I like people.'

Right then, I felt Maria Ellis had slipped momentarily
from her mountain retreat into my underground lair, and
that it was even worth keeping on her right side. After all,
if Frank ended up doing bars-a-la-carte in the Big House,
who was to say she wouldn't become so vulnerable she'd
fall for the charms of Yours Seductively?

Even though the Gutted Moose was brimming with
patrons, Bernard still managed to espy us coming in. I
didn't engage him in conversation because I didn't feel
like slashing my wrists. Instead, I pointed to my favourite
booth to signify I was in the middle of a meeting, then
froze in horror. Joe Sinto was there, sprawled lazily across
two seats, talking to himself in staccato-marine and
sipping greedily at a beer. I tried a timely withdrawal, but
he was obviously in reconnaissance mode. He fixed me in
his sights, gave me his standard A-OK thumb, then
whistled me over.

'Thought you were on your way to the coast,' I said, feeling a rising urge to go at him heavily with a sack of doorknobs.

'Tomorrow mornin' maybe,' Joe grinned. 'Just thought I'd join you for a drink first. Marcie told me this was your favourite slop-chute, so...'

'Yeah, well, I'm workin' at the moment,' I said, pulling Maria towards a booth that was diametrically as far away from Joe as was possible. 'So we'll just leave you alone. You looked like you were havin' a pretty good time by yourself anyhow.'

Joe grinned a cheesy, then pointed a digit in the direction of my designated booth. 'Looks like someone's stolen your office, Whale,' he observed. I bit hard on my lip and watched two young lovers sidling casually into my intended sanctuary. 'You want me to go over and haul them out of there for you?'

His accusing digit was suddenly loaded with 7.62mm and I shivered hard, weighing up that conundrum before shaking him a definite no-no.

'If this man is such a good friend of yours,' Maria cut in tersely, 'then we'll just sit here and talk. I'm sure he won't listen in or interrupt us.' She turned to Joe with a rather gullible look upon her face. 'Will you?'

Joe shook his head. 'Not me, lady. I use my nose for breathin', sniffin' and smellin' with, not for stickin' it in where it doesn't belong.'

Maria nodded evenly, obviously unaware that Joe never interrupts a conversation when he can invade it. Then we both sidled into the booth alongside the Irrational National.

'Can we begin?' Maria asked, biting nervously at her lip. 'As I say, I'm in a hurry.'

'Sure.' I whistled Bernard over, ordered a pitcher of beer for myself, nothing for Joe, and a diet-soda for Maria, simply because it looked like something she'd drink and it was cheap. Joe, unfazed by that subtle hint, ordered himself another beer. Bernard brought the drinks over, said something laced discreetly with subliminal messages of boredom, then tottered off to drain someone else of their life, energy and money.

'Frank, Abel and Jim...' Maria began.

I raised a stalling hand and cursed inwardly. Clay and Muddy had just entered the bar. They invited themselves over and squashed in beside Joe. I raised my eyes to heaven, then introduced Maria to Clay and Muddy. Joe they both knew too well, as the Italian Scallion was something of an urban-legend in and around the city, albeit for all the wrong reasons. I then apologised to my new client for the unforeseen interruption. 'If you wish,' I suggested uneasily, 'we can go somewhere else.'

'They can talk with Joe,' Maria said quickly. 'We'll have to begin now or I'll never make it down to Police Administration to see Frank.'

Clay ordered a couple of beers for him and Muddy. 'You just carry on,' he said, almost nervously. 'I'm sure we'll find somethin' to talk about.'

I nodded, suppressing a grin. Strong experience had taught Clay that Joe had a very limited vocabulary. This being so, my best friend must've known immediately that he was about to hear the Paris Peace Accord denunciated in boonie-ese.

'Frank, Abel and Jim were partners in a computer export business in the late 1970s,' Maria began. 'They were pioneers, if you like, of the computer industry in the city. Jim couldn't hold out to the initial setting up costs, however, and he left after about a year. Frank and Abel persevered. They tightened their belts, kept on ploughing their profits back into the business, and slowly, after about three years, it took hold. I met them both about that time, though I *knew* Abel first...'

Maria paused and shot me a wide-eye that went straight across my bow. I sat there oblivious for a few seconds, thinking her mouth had healed over, but I soon realised she was simply waiting for me to catch onto what she was saying.

'Ah!' I exclaimed brightly. 'You *knew* Abel first.' I made a rather Italian-type gesture with a thrusting, clenched forearm to indicate I knew the bigger picture was probably X-rated and we were now talking biblical. She smiled uneasily. 'I see! I see! Say, now this case is actually gettin' interestin'...'

'Well, it didn't last all that long,' Maria winced. 'A matter of months, not much more. As soon as I met up with Frank, I realised he was the man for me. So, I terminated my relationship with Abel...'

I snorted in disbelief. 'And went out with Frank?' I shook my head in disgust. 'Jeez, lady, you don't believe in lettin' the grass grow under you ass, do you? Talk about bein' an eager beaver – if you'll pardon the expression.'

Maria nodded and blushed simultaneously. 'Yes, but I didn't go out with him in *public* straight away, Mr Shale. We kept our love affair under wraps for a time before we brought it out into the open. I wouldn't have been so tactless.'

'But it didn't bother you that you were doin' the bedroom boogie with your former lover's business partner and closest confidante, someone whom he'd trusted...'

'It wasn't like that,' Maria sobbed. 'I didn't want to hurt Abel. Nor did I want him to hurt me or Frank because, at that time, well, he had a bit of a temper. But, yes, we told him. Eventually. We had to, I suppose, what with me being pregnant, and Frank moving me into the office to work as their personal secretary.'

'Jeez!' I snorted. 'Frank had some nerve! First, he steals his partner's girl. Then, when he's had his fingers in the proverbial pie for a while, he flaunts the growin' fruit of his loins in front of him. Joseph H Crucifix, what a friggin' nerve!'

'But I loved Frank from the moment I saw him. I...'

I interrupted her, and pushed Muddy's hand away from the pitcher. 'That's my beer, kid!' I stormed. 'Go buy your own, you thievin' lump of shit!' Muddy turned away from me, obviously perplexed. Shaking his head, Clay gave Muddy five bucks to get his own beer, then smiled wanly as Joe showed him a stranglehold technique he'd apparently used on at least six Viet Cong. I turned to Maria and said, 'If there's one thing I hate it's untrustworthy, manipulative people out for their own gain. But sorry, I'm gettin' *way, way* off the subject here. What were you sayin'?'

'Anyhow, that was all in our past,' Maria frowned. 'Frank and Abel sold the business soon afterwards. That was in the fall of '82, I think. They were shrewd businessmen and the market was becoming saturated with similar mass-manufactured products from California, which is, as we all know, the Japanese capital of America.' Maria smiled as if she'd made a funny. I didn't bother because, if she did, I didn't get it. 'Anyhow,' she continued, 'both of them made a tidy profit on the sale and they parted on good terms.'

'Did they both stay here in the city?' I asked.

'You're anticipating me, Mr Shale...'

'That's my job, lady,' I told her smugly. 'I'm paid to be one step ahead of the guy in front, maybe two steps in front of the guy who's four or five steps behind. It's all arithmetic. That's why I always get things to add up in the end.'

She shivered like a priest who'd been ordered to confront a powerful wraith with a cheap and heavily-abridged bible. 'Well, Frank and I stayed here in the city,' she continued after a moment. 'We set up a hardware business that's still thriving today. As for Abel, he moved to Canada where he got into electronic surveillance equipment. He'd phone us every now and then, or drop a card. He met a girl in Toronto who became his secretary and, eventually, his wife. He even invited us to the wedding, but we didn't go. Frank didn't want to, you know. He thought it best that we maintain our distance and let time heal that rift.'

I nodded sagely. 'Yeah, well you can nurse a grudge for as long as you want, but it'll never get better, that's what I say. Anyhow, where did it all go wrong? It sounds as if everythin' worked out all right until then.'

'Well, we last heard from Abel about three years ago. But then I...'

I held up my hand once more. I was engrossed in her tale by then, but something had distracted my attention. This was, namely, a silence that shouldn't have been there. Not that it's ever completely silent in the Gutted Moose, you understand, and just then the place was an open air asylum with everybody talking and nobody listening. As usual.

Except for those people who shouldn't have been listening: Those people in *my* company, who should've been talking amongst themselves.

In hindsight, I can understand why that was so. When you stick three normal people into each other's company you can expect them to sustain a conversation of some description for at least ten minutes. And it wasn't as if Joe, Clay and Muddy hadn't enough in common. Clay and Joe had both served in Vietnam; Muddy and Joe liked to spend all their spare time in strip-joints and similarly low-brow establishments; and Muddy and Clay were both spawned from the same strain – apparently. However, the drawbacks here were manifold. Clay and Muddy were at a stage in their lives when they agreed on everything but at different times. As for Clay and Joe, they'd both served in the East, but, while Joe liked to constantly remind himself and everyone within 999 yards of his exploits, Clay was forever trying to forget his own. I mean, if you mention a dishonourable discharge too often, you aren't going to make too many friends. And that held especially true in the patriotic Gutted Moose where, if you shared a slice of pie amongst three you had communist tendencies, and where it was often considered un-American to get into passing conversation with a Canadian.

'Hey!' I snapped. 'This is a private conversation. Can't you talk about the weather or somethin'?'

'We were,' Clay seethed. 'The weather in Saigon durin' the Tet Offensive.'

I looked at Joe and he shrugged so sheepishly that I felt like going at him with a pair of shears. 'Thought it was a mist,' he explained. 'Turned out to be the smoke flyin' from our boy's asses as those fuckin' Dinks decided to fight back.'

'They may as well hear the rest of the story,' Maria sighed. 'God knows how long they've been listening to us anyhow.'

'I think you did the right thing,' Muddy confided in Maria. 'Everyone should screw around a little before they get hitched. It's only natural.'

Bernard approached our booth just as I was about to slap some respect into Muddy, a tray of brewskies to his front. 'Got you all a free beer,' he smiled. 'This looks like an interestin' place to be. You mind if I sit and join you durin' my break?'

'Yeah, we do actually,' Joe said indignantly. 'This is a private conversation!' He gave Bernard his favourite death stare, then laughed satanically as the bar-owner took a whitey. 'Look at that face,' he added bitterly. 'Looks like someone went at it with a Louisville slugger and forgot to stop.'

'Maybe later,' I consoled the bar-owner. 'And don't take any notice of that remark. I personally think you've got a face like a saint, Bernard.'

Bernard sloped away to the bar. 'I'd stay and have a battle of wits with him,' he sneered at Joe, 'but he looks like he wouldn't have enough for a skirmish!'

'*Anyhow*,' Maria cut in shortly, 'that's the history of the situation. Now I'll continue into modern day.' I nodded, warning everyone to silence with a raised finger. 'About six months back we started gettin letters from someone here in the city. The topic of the letters was, let's say, *indelicate*.' Maria frowned uncomfortably and dropped her gaze. 'Frank wouldn't let me look at them. He told me they concerned my past, and that their content indicated they could only have been sent by Abel.'

'Can't you be a little more specific?' Clay asked. 'I mean....'

'I'll ask the questions here,' I snorted. I looked at Maria. 'Well, can you?'

'Let's just say they contained *specific* references to our affair,' Maria replied, delicately. We all nodded, exchanged knowing glances, and I made a few more Italian hand-signals under the table. 'We must have received one every week for an entire six-month period. 'And each was more explicit than the last.'

'So why didn't you go to the police with them?' I asked.

'That's a good point,' Joe mused. 'Better still, you could've printed those letters in the tabloids and embarrassed this guy out into the open.'

Maria glared a frosty at Joe. It hadn't taken her long to get the measure of him – it ran to a glass of beer. Give Joe one glass and he was a happy fool; give him a pair of glasses, however, and he made a spectacle of himself. She upturned her nose ever so slightly, then turned her back on him before continuing. 'Well, Frank destroyed the letters because they contained references to my affair with Abel and were vile. But in the last letter the perpetrator asked Frank to meet him in Skytowers. Naturally, Frank was livid and I asked him not to go, but he said it was a matter of honour. The meeting was arranged for 7-30pm in room 18a. Frank turned up a few minutes late, and, sure enough, Abel was already there. But Abel was in a foul mood, and the first thing he did was accuse Frank of sending *him* abusive letters, letters which alluded to the ease with which I was apparently taken away from Abel. Naturally, Frank denied that, and he quickly suggested they'd both been set up.'

Here, Maria paused and sighed heavily, wringing her hands as she fixed me with a serious. 'But, Mr Shale, this is where the story gets a little crazy. Frank said that, as he was speaking, an armed and masked figure stepped from the central closet and approached both men, warning them to raise their hands and remain quiet. They both did so, of course, thinking it was a robbery, but then the figure moved behind Frank, knocking him unconscious. Frank said he was then awakened by the sound of a gunshot, and when he opened his eyes Abel was lying dead to his front with a gun – which the police say was fully loaded – at his side. And, well, *another* gun – the actual murder weapon – was in Frank's hand. Of course, the masked man was gone by then, so Frank stood up, trying to work out what had happened. Unfortunately, he was still holding onto the murder weapon when the janitor entered the room seconds later.' Maria stopped speaking and gauged the reactions on our faces. Upon noticing her story was having much the same effect as a head rabbi ordering the Pork Surprise at a bar-mitzvah, she dropped her head in dismay. 'Then, Frank just dropped the gun and stood there, figuring...'

'That justice would prevail,' Joe cut in with a dismal shake of his head. 'But it's not like that in the real world, lady. Y'see, the same thing happened to me once. I was standin' outside a village in Da Nang all by myself. Thing was, someone had torched the place and killed two dozen slants minutes beforehand. Sadly, I was the only one around for six-clicks, so I got tagged with the blame.'

'It must have worked out all right?' Maria asked, hopefully. 'You're here now.'

'Sure it did,' Joe grinned. 'I got a fuckin' medal for it! Y'see, it's all geography. Kill someone out there, you're a hero. Kill someone here, you're a cold-hearted, murderin'...'

'And so the police were called,' I cut in. There's a universal law which states that if you get a small mind, you also get a big mouth to make up for it, and Joe was following that particular law to the letter. The guy was an insensitive bastard! 'But Frank didn't try to run, did he?' I soothed. 'Maybe he figured he'd only get ten to fifteen if he acted like a dumb schmutz, eh?'

'He gave himself up willingly to Detective Malone,' Maria sighed, tears forming at the corner of her eyes. 'He's innocent and knows he has nothing to fear.'

Again, Maria looked between Clay, Muddy and me as if seeking reassurance and consolation, only to be met with averted gazes and fake toothies. As I say, Malone has a wide-reaching reputation of thinking the public are there to be offended, not defended. Unsettled by this, Maria's gaze finally rested on Joe.

'What can I say, baby?' Joe shrugged. 'You're in a bit of a Dali Llama, but don't go countin' your Chi-Coms just yet.' He nudged her sharply in the ribs, 'That's an old in-country joke.' Maria tried a grin that looked as if it had already been tried and convicted. 'But seriously, who knows what'll happen? There are no certainties in life except debts and taxes. Marty taught me that. That right, Whale?'

'Sure, Joe. And uncertainty, which is maybe the most certain thing of all.' I smiled at Maria, but she didn't look all that impressed with our uncultured pearls, and she even seemed set to go at the waterworks. 'Look, lady,' I said finally, 'I'll get you a cab. Then I'll get straight to work on this. That alright?'

Maria nodded uncertainly, and about ten minutes later I left her to a cab rank at the furthest end of the darkening road. As she was feeling pretty vulnerable, I told a couple of drunken bums to watch over her, after which I made my way back to the bar. When I got in, Joe was shaking his head.

'Say, Marty, that's an unbelievable tale if ever I heard one.'

Coming from Joe that was verification in spades. I gulped hard at my beer to make up for lost time. 'Well, we'll leave it for now. Let's sink a few more brewskies and talk about something interestin' for a change.' I noticed that Muddy was being eyed up by a pretty young girl at the bar whose skirt doubled as a belt and who was sucking seductively at a bottle of beer. 'I've a theory about women who drink from bottles,' I told him with a grin. 'You want her?' I sank another beer and noticed the room blurring around the edges. 'She's better lookin' than the rest of the bargoyles around here, and she's sportin' a fine set of blouse-puppies.'

As the young lady winked seductively at Muddy, he blushed shyly. 'No, thanks, uncle Marty. She's with that big guy over there.' He pointed to the tall, dark-skinned fellow on her left with the barrel-chest and arms like loins of pork. The guy was a regular Schwarztenegro, and he seemed quite protective of his girlfriend.

None of which made the slightest dent in Yours Leeringly.

Y'see, I've this attitude whereby I always try to enter a bar optimistically, and leave it misty-optically. In-between times, sure, I'll drink like a drain and eat like a carnie at a stranger's wedding, but I try not to get into scrapes unless I feel the world has done me wrong, unless I'm feeling really paranoid, or unless I feel like starting them.

Saying that, I've a few rules there as well. Firstly, I'd rather have a full bottle in front of me than a full frontal lobotomy, so I always try to vent my wrath upon someone who looks as if they'll come in a handsome second to my first. And secondly, I also tend to steer clear of guys who look as if they're carrying a carpet under each arm.

Still, as the late John Lennon once wisely noted, life's what happens when you're busy making other plans!

FIVE

'You let me offer that gorilla one-on-one?' I screamed at Clay. 'What the hell were you thinkin'?'

The fight hadn't gone well. It seems that Schwartzenegro – who, sadly for us, also had several large friends in the bar – could've heard a Ninja sidling headlong up a wind-tunnel, so my remark about his girlfriend's puppies was met with much disdain. In age-old saloon tradition, therefore, insults were deployed soon after by those skilled in the use of piercing invective, threats were dispensed by those limited in imagination and ability, and punches and kicks traded by those devoid of reason and logic.

As luck would have it, I threw in the first punch, while avoiding one in every six thereafter. Near the end of the fight, I also threw in the one that counted – the one with the chair attached to it. Which was just as well, as both Clay and Muddy's attempts at self-preservation were akin to a pork chop defending itself from a glutton. And Joe Sinto? Well, for all of his alleged experience, he was as green as unripe bananas when it came to hand-to-hand combat. Sadly, this meant that, overall, the opposing team batted a higher average in that particular game, whereas me and mine, well, we mainly supplied the balls.

We stood now, all four of us, before my dressing room mirror, like extras in a Zombie flick. I shook my head wearily as Clay, Joe and Muddy sought to catch a glimpse of themselves in a fraction of spare glass through panda-like eyes.

'The guy told you he was a wrestler!' Clay stormed. 'But what did you say?' He screwed his face up and mimicked me rather unflatteringly. '"I'm into Sumo myself, so come ahead if you think you're hard enough!" Christ, Whale, if ever a man was born with a silver foot in his mouth..!'

'I was tryin' to do Muddy a favour,' I feebled. I winced as I sat on the bed, realising that even my very hair hurt. 'Wasn't I, Muds?'

Muddy shrugged lamely. Someone had apparently tried to perform open-heart surgery on him with an ashtray, so now he had a third pectoral muscle growing out of his ribcage. 'I guess so, uncle Marty.'

'That aside,' I grumbled, 'how come we all stayed here last night? I woke this mornin' and there were so many limbs in my bedroom, I thought I was in one of Joe's stories.' Joe stiffened at my remark, and I raised a hand to stall the incoming. 'Just tryin' to lighten the mood, big guy. Come on, let's go eat.'

I led them downstairs through the ruined hallway into the kitchen. There, Greta had heaps of inedibles sizzling away in the frying pan, and she was attending to them with a toasting fork the way a ringmaster attends his lions. She saw me and turned sour-kraut, then noticed her buddy Joe and smiled an upturned gummy that could've put me off my food, but didn't, because her culinary skills are enough to do that on their own. Deep down, I know Greta thinks I'm a pagan-god because of the amount of burnt offerings she lays before me on a daily basis. Actually, as I recall, the first thing she burnt in my kitchen was the cookbook, and everything else fell sharply into line thereafter.

I moved through the kitchen at speed, grabbed my denim jacket and made for the back door.

Joe looked perplexed, but Clay knew the drill: He urged Muddy and Joe after me. 'Goin' to Ramon's,' I explained to Greta. 'Just keep that stuff in the pan a minute longer and we can use it to repair the hallway closet later!'

But I didn't take my companions to Ramon's, because – to put it plainly – I didn't want my meal-ticket cashing in his ticket. I drove, instead, to another diner on Cagney Way. As we drove, the DJ on Clowntown Radio told us it was going to be hotter than a bucket of fresh spit that morning, then spun a couple of jingles that had Joe bouncing around in the back seat of the Buick like the rear-gunner in a Huey. As a result, by the time our food was ready, my intestines were tied up in a Gordian Knot and I could hardly even look at it.

'What you doin' today?' I asked Joe as he polished off my breakfast for desert. 'Any plans for, say, out of town? The Apple, maybe? Or further off even?'

Joe's brow furrowed, and I knew he was thinking as he had to stop eating. 'Y'know Whale,' he said, sucking at a lump of gristle, 'I haven't worked in a while. Those MEDCAP guys reckon I'm unfit to hold a job.' He looked at me through eyes so haunted they'd have given Casper a case of the Heebies. 'And there's not much to do at home, except take your meds and get stuck into your C-rats every few hours. It can make a man think and do funny things at times.'

Joe had obviously been at home far too long – that much I figured instantly – yet whatever else he was trying to say eluded me. 'And you, uhm, think you might be able to find somethin' to do up in old 'so-good- they-named-it-twice'?'

'You're a true friend, Whale,' Joe replied suddenly. Clay and Muddy, who'd hitherto chosen to squabble amongst themselves as the lesser of two evils, ceased speaking, as if they had a premonition of what this cuckoo was about to say. But I had a hangover and a mild concussion which allowed me to remain several inches below the surface of surreality. 'And I was thinkin' that...'

'You're thinkin' now, eh?' I grinned. Joe nodded slowly, and for a moment there was a faraway look in his eyes as if he'd just landed from another planet and yearned to return home. 'Sure you are. And you want to borrow the fare for a one way ticket to Capital City? Sure you do.'

I fumbled for my pocketbook, recalling someone once saying that if you lent a friend twenty dollars and never saw either them or your money again, it was worth it. Just then, I so wanted that to be true.

'No, Whale.' Joe grinned an aw-shucks, shaking the contents of his fork all over the table 'Just the opposite. I want to stay here and help you out of your per-dicament.'

I frowned uncertainly. 'What, uhm, *predicament* is that, Joe?'

'This murder case you're workin' on,' Joe smiled. 'Face it, Marty, if anyone knows about murder, it's me. And I have a few theories about this thing already.'

'This isn't a *thing*, Joe,' I replied, on the verge of taking a whitey. 'This is *my* bag, and I can handle it as well as the next porter, y'know?' Joe shook me a thicky. 'Look, I'm sayin' this is a shitty game and I'm always in the shit, though sometimes the depth varies and I get to stick my head out a little, but *only* because I'm a lone wolf who wouldn't even cry wolf if the Big Bad Wolf wolfed down my grandma, and... Look, I really can't be any clearer here, so is any of this getting' through?'

'You're talkin' shit, wolves and luggage here, Whale. To be honest, it's all a bit vague.'

'Well, what I'm sayin' is, there's no one I'd rather have standin' in front of me when I'm starin' death in the face, Joe. And I *really* wish I could prove that to you now, honest. But wishes don't do dishes, and...'

'You gotta take me, Marty,' Joe pleaded, clutching hard at my shirt. 'I'm goin' stir-crazy in the hooch, and I know I'm gonna do somethin' drastic real soon.'

Joe stared at me through eyes as dead as pork, and I clenched my buttocks hard to prevent a serious breach of professional etiquette. 'It's just you nearly got me killed the last time we worked together, Joe, and...'

'Give me another chance, Marty. I'll come through for you next time, swear!'

As he released his grip upon my shirt, I found myself transfixed by his cobra-like gaze, and somewhere deep in the place my heart used to be I became aware that if I kept on beefing I'd only end up in a stew.

'Well,' I said lamely. 'If that's, uhm, the way it is, then I guess you'd better tag along.'

Joe slapped me on the back and broke the mesmerising trance. 'I'll just go drain the main vein,' he said, beaming another freaky. 'Then we'll formulate a set of plans.' He left to go to the toilets and I returned my gaze towards Clay and Muddy.

Their jaws were nearly touching their knees.

'What are you thinkin'?' Clay gasped. 'Do you realise what you just said?'

I sat there numbly and gulped my beer straight from the pitcher. Suddenly life didn't look so pretty and I had to daydream about spoon-feeding myself from a sewer to prevent myself from retching. I knew, of course, exactly what had transpired, but you have to get into my way of thinking here. In all honesty, I knew Joe Sinto was about as much use as a flare-gun in a munitions store, but then he'd also helped me out with a few cases over the years, at times providing me with alibis and the sort of hardware that wasn't pots and pans.

'Wake up, Shale.' Clay slapped my face, hard, and I realised I was dribbling beer down over my slacks. 'You've just committed professional suicide. Again!'

'Yeah?' I snarled. 'How was I supposed to disagree with him in an enclosed area?' I stared at Clay as if he was a life-belt in troubled waters. 'Look, I'd rather have a burglar riflin' through my office than be seen dead with Noddie the Squaddie out there on the street, you know that. So *you're* gonna have to help me out. You can keep him distracted for a few days, can't you?'

'Oh, no! You'd need to be an idiot to do that job. And I'm not that idiot.'

'You are,' I said quickly. He regarded me darkly and I willed my eyes bloodhound. 'Y'know what I mean.' He half-nodded, then shook me a no-no. 'Look,' I pleaded, 'you remember that time he got the tar kicked out of him in Harlem?'

Clay shivered briskly. 'How could I forget that one?'

'Yeah, those three guys were gettin' stuck into him, giving him an awful beatin'. Then this patrol cop happens along...'

'Did the policeman save him, uncle Marty?' Muddy asked, wide-eyed.

'No, kid, he helped them out, because he knew an asshole when he saw one. But a few days later that same cop walked out his front door, got in his car and turned around to see his house explodin' all over the place. Forensics put it down to gas, but the local postman reckoned it was a package he delivered that mornin'. And those other three guys also got caught up in similar incidents soon after. One got his car torched, another found a herd of pot-bellied pigs trashin' his garden, and the last guy received dog-stogies in his mail every day for months afterwards.' I shook my head firmly. 'Uh, uh, say what you want, but I think the Hand of Fate teamed up with the Hand of Hate and they went at that one together.'

I loosened my tie. It was sure getting hot in there, and I had a real bad urge for a cigarette.

Joe rejoined us less than a minute later. As he did, Muddy and Clay rose nervously from their seats and half-trotted towards the front door.

'Where are you goin'?' I said. 'Don't you want to tag along with us for a while?' I patted my concealed gun-holster to let Clay know what he was getting if he deserted me now, in this my direst hour of need.

'I've a heap of work that needs doin',' Clay winced. He faded Caucasian as he continued sidling towards the door with Muddy in tow.

'And I've got to get back to my future-wife,' Muddy stammered. 'I've decided things aren't nearly as bad as they seem. In comparison.'

They left in a blur of excuses. It was now 1-15pm, and, sighing loudly, I paid for our meal, led Joe out to the car, and drove to the nearest news-vendor. I bought two packs of Lucky Strikes, then made for a payphone. I'd two healthy undercoats of nicotine on my lungs by the time Mo had finished his phone-slamming ritual, after which I asked him for the address of the dear departed Abel Shirinski.

'You aren't gettin' it, Marty! This case is as clean-cut as a neutered tom. Furthermore, Malone's lookin' to *talk* with you, don't ask me why.'

'I'll be honest here, Mo, I'm tapin' this conversation in case I go missin' in the not-so-distant future.' I put the earpiece of the phone next to my chest and clicked back the hammer of my Magnum. As I did so, Joe glared a big-eye, put his hand beneath his jacket and homed in on the noise. 'You hear that, Mo? Tape-recorder.' I eased back the hammer and Joe relaxed somewhat.

'He only wants to talk, Marty. I think he was just jokin' when he said he didn't want to hear your name again unless it was followed by the letters DOA'

'Yeah, well, we'll discuss his professional jealousy some time when I'm feelin' less vulnerable. Now, what about that address?'

Mo gave me an address in Specksville, laughed snidely, then slammed down the phone. I guess he didn't like hearing it straight. About a year ago I'd been working an investigation which involved the local Family and a Triad gang; an investigation, might I add, that had primarily escaped the attention of the city's entire force until I'd single-handedly brought it to light. In all, it had earned me a bullet, a ceremonial dinner in City Hall that would have stunned a glutton into a coma, and a speech from the Mayor that ran like the horns of a steer, in that it had a couple of points and plenty of bull in-between. Of course, as a senior detective, Malone had been there to personally pin the medal onto my chest, but he'd missed my lapel with the pointy bit whilst trying to work the damned thing out through my back. He'd grinned demonically as he did so, before shaking my hand so hard the blood didn't come back into it until later that evening when I was getting into my hobby.

No, Mo didn't have to tell me that Malone was forever on my case. It was as obvious as the nose all over Joe's face. I lit up yet another cigarette, hung up the phone and called Joe over.

'I want to get a few things straight here,' I told him warily. 'Y'know, sort out the peckin' order in this, ehm, let's say, *battalion* of ours.'

'Hit me with it,' Joe said easily.

Christ, I wanted to! Badly. But I resisted.

'Right, big peckers first, little peckers last, that's the first thing, right?' Joe nodded easily. 'Furthermore, I'm a professional who dices with the Grim Reaper on a daily basis. Death and me are old enemies, y'know, and have been since long before I was born. I mock him. I taunt him. I play knick-knock on his door, then run off just as he's about to answer it. Then I come back and stare him in the face before I run off again. But that's just me, and I can't for the life of me tell you why I do that. Y'see where I'm comin' from here?'

Joe grinned broadly. "Course, I do, Marty.' He paused, shrugged an embarrassed shrug. 'Well, maybe not so much.'

'Uhm, well, what I'm actually sayin', Joe, is that, because I'm the guy who sticks his neck out all the time, *I'm* in charge here, and I don't want you stickin' your ladle in my broth. Remember, ability's good, but stability's better.' Joe was staring off down the street after two stick insects with breasts. I pulled his head back, stared him deep in the eyes. 'Now, are we readin' from the same call-up papers here or what?'

'Sure, Marty, virility's good, but mobility's better. And you don't want me gettin' laid in your brothel. Hey, man, I know *exactly* what you're sayin'.'

I nodded uneasily and felt a gang of shivers playing Chopsticks on my spine. Joe put out his hand and I took it in mine. He had a firm handshake and he looked me squarely in the eye – and that can never be good. Still, I ignored my instincts, urged Boonierat Sinto into the Buick and drove out to my first stop of the day, the address across town that Hank had scrawled on a piece of toilet paper.

***

Victor Fellows lived in a run-down tenement on Cahn Street, on the south side of the city, beside the town dump, a scrapyard and a trailer park. The entire block defied gravity and was so damp the gutters were inside. At about 1-30pm, Joe and I ran a gauntlet of roaches, rats and winos on our way to his place on the 7th floor, then had to wait a further few minutes as he shifted a dozen dead-bolts before finally opening the door. The first thing to hit me was that it smelled like the dregs of a wine-vat in the height of summer, and the second was that it looked much the same way.

Now, Victor stood silhouetted against the doorway, but I only got a good look at him when the neon Cola sign beyond his closed sitting room curtains pulsed red for a second or so at a time. During those moments, he resembled a demon from the furthest reaches of Hell. He was about 60 years old, sported a three day beard and looked as if he'd dressed himself with a pitchfork. He reeled slightly, licked dry lips and opened a bleary eye. 'Wassup?' he growled.

This was another guy for whom the bottom of the whiskey bottle was way too near the top, I could tell that at a glance. 'I hope I didn't catch you at a bad time,' I replied evenly. 'I'm Marty Shale, Private Investigator, and I'd like to ask you a few questions about the murder in Skytowers a few nights back.'

'This look like a good time to you?' he asked wearily. He regarded his watch. 'I'm tryin' to sleep off a hangover before my next drinkin' session.'

I turned on my heels, not really in the mood to get myself involved. 'I'll come back when you're sober,' I told him pointedly. 'And remember, it's not always a good thing to be up like a lark and lookin' for a swallow.'

He laughed dryly, slammed his door behind him, and I heard the dead-bolts being unevenly applied once more.

'That's guy's about as coherent as a dyslexic readin' into a tannoy system,' I told Joe, as we walked back to the car. 'We'll get back on that one at a later date. C'mon, let's go see this Shirinski dame.'

'Yeah,' Joe grinned. 'She's probably lookin' for someone like me now that her old man has kicked up his heels.'

As Joe gave me a few of those big hand signals we all tend to get into on occasion, I fixed my shirt, licked my hand and smoothed back my hair.

'Of course she is,' I smiled insincerely. '*You're* exactly her type!'

SIX

Specksville is one of the city's most famous residential districts and it lies east of Baum Creek. The place had changed little since my last visit, and the view from its lofty heights was impressive as ever. If I recall correctly, George Washington once stopped here for a whiz before riding off someplace else for another whiz before fighting the British. As you can tell from that remark, I'm not too good at history, and my own idea of an interesting date is making out with a girl who doesn't keep asking me if I'm a cop. I do know, however, that about two decades back this place hosted the summer residences of the sort of people you didn't ask what they did for a living, but whom.

Mo had given me an address in Marlowe Park, which was a posh suburb where the upper echelons still spent money they didn't have on things they didn't want to impress people they didn't like. Going on 2-20pm, I pulled the Buick in at the bottom of the estate and strolled through its neatly lawned interior, recalling how I'd driven many a young lady up here in my youth and promised them this sort of lifestyle in the future just to get to first-base. At that time, many might have called me a wistful dreamer, yet I can assure you I was drawn here by a pair of tingling love-spuds and not by the Big Delusion.

I never did, nor shall I ever, allow my love-wand to have that much control over my brain.

As I searched out Marlowe Park, Joe trailed furtively behind. Apparently, I was on point. Under the glare of the afternoon sun, I took off my jacket and rolled up my shirt sleeves as the hill rose at a gradual, if more treacherous, incline than I recalled. Joe followed suit, whistling his approval as ever more lavishly designed homes came into view. I had to agree with the Ham there, though I did so in silence.

This was an exclusive area, and the late Abel Shirinski had certainly lived it up in style, yet I doubted his sense of taste would've appealed to anyone dispossessed of the Picasso gene. I suddenly found myself wondering why those with the most money spent it on the most outlandish and garish things. Was common-sense so called because the rich were totally devoid of it? And was it any wonder their offspring became rebels without a clue? Young Tommy Ellis was a prime example. If I guessed right, Frank and Maria also had too much moolah, yet they'd certainly no idea how to keep their kid on the straight and narrow. As a result, Tommy had taken to the streets, where people talked to you and not at you, unaware he'd eventually get talked into stuff he'd never be able to talk himself out of. Yeah, that kid would end up making a porridge of his life because he'd chosen to major in extortion, petty thievery and larceny without firstly getting a degree in law. I knew that as surely as I knew that sometime soon they'd be dragging me bodily out of Joe Sinto.

The Shirinski home was a colonial mansion that had been transformed, through an ingenious series of modernisation tactics, into a mock-colonial residence. It had then been painted in unflattering mauve and stood in grounds dashed with roses, lilac and lavender. I pressed lightly on the doorbell and it announced my presence to the whole neighbourhood. Joe stood behind me in the driveway, no doubt scanning the hedgerows for someone or something that didn't belong. Had he gazed into a mirror at that juncture, he may've found exactly who or what he was looking for.

A youngish, perfectly-formed lady answered the door. She was attired in something bold and red that was only barely legal, and she had eyes as big as lakes. Straight off, I felt hot and wanted to go in for a swim. 'Is your mother in?' I smoothed. I treated her to an ogle and she blushed, obviously flattered.

'I'm Patricia Shirinski,' she smiled. Her accent was Canadian, and therefore naturally flat and devoid of life or tone. 'Would I be the one you're looking for?'

'You're Mrs. Shirinski?' I feigned a startled. 'The widow Shirinski whose husband was smoked up like a kipper in Skytowers two nights back?'

'Yes,' she replied, her lips quivering. Her mood had changed for no apparent reason, and her lakes began to fill and overflow.

'That's good. I thought I'd come to the wrong place. Hope I didn't catch you at a bad time?' I dropped another toothy at her, though this time she hadn't the manners to return it.

'What do you want?' she asked moodily. 'This *is* a bad time for us all actually. My husband is barely cold, and every news-rag in the State seems willing to denounce him without awaiting the outcome of the trial.' She looked at my face as if she'd only just noticed me. 'Who gave you the black eyes?' she asked curiously.

'No one gave them to me, lady – I had to fight for them! And I'm not a reporter. I'm a Private Investigator, and I'm only here to ask you a couple of questions.'

She regarded me warily. 'On whose behalf?'

'I'm defendin' the man who killed your husband, and I was wonderin' if....'

My words were blown away in the gust that escaped the slamming door.

'Probably on the rag,' Joe shrugged. 'PMT goin' on TNT.'

I ignored him, got down close to the keyhole. 'Mrs. Shirinski,' I shouted. 'If you have a minute, there's somethin' you should know.' I waited a second, but there was no reply. 'Mrs. Shirinski, the police think Frank Ellis killed your husband in self-defence, but I think someone else killed him to frame Frank.'

The door opened quickly and a very irate Canadian lady stood there on the doorstep brandishing a carving knife in her right hand. The grin had worn itself down to a snarl, and the lakes had frozen over cold and deep enough to bear anything except me. Joe stepped back onto the lawn, wisely acknowledging that he'd more than enough metal in his skull already. Me, I didn't actually fancy playing an inverse Janet Leigh to this woman's Anthony Perkins, yet something told me that if I made a run for it I'd only be adding to her dark sense of enjoyment by providing her with a moving target.

'What kind of a ridiculous thing is that to say, wide-load? Frank Ellis killed my husband, that's obvious, and I hope he rots in prison forever.'

'That's one possibility, but only one of many.' I upraised my palms to let her know I'd come in peace and had no inclination to go in pieces just because she was going to pieces. 'Lets just say this investigation may not go as smoothly as predicted. I'm on the case, y'see, and I intend to dig deeper than six-foot on this one. I won't let it rest in peace, I wont let it die, and if there are *any* skeletons hangin' around in any closets – or boardrooms for that matter – your financial assets will be bound up in red-tape for months or maybe even years.'

She dropped the knife slowly to her side, her grip now firmly wrapped around my verbal handle. I'd a feeling that last statement of mine would swing this thing 180°. After all, this girl's idea of roughing it was probably three days without a pedicure.

'You'd better come in,' she whispered. I turned and winked at a bemused Joe Sinto as she led us inside. She took us along a marble hallway into a grandly designed drawing room. In the room's centre there sat an ornately carved table, and around it several easy chairs. I made for the one with the strongest legs, then sat gingerly and scrutinised Patricia Shirinski as she paced backwards and forwards across the room like a cage-bound tiger.

Up close, under the bright glare of the drawing room lights, I noticed Mrs Shirinski was older than I'd first imagined. She had a barely noticeable series of scars beneath her chin, and now I knew why her skin was stretched around her face like cling-film and her eyes were longer than they were broader – she'd had so many face-lifts her belly button was most likely at the back of her neck, and one more would probably leave her wearing a beard. Still, she wasn't too bad for all that, and I reflected that any man who didn't want something like that hanging off his left arm socially obviously didn't know what his right hand was for.

'Who are you again?' she asked eventually. 'And what makes your assumption about the murder so different to that of an entire police force?'

'I'm Marty Shale, the city's finest Private Investigator,' I told her proudly. 'And the big difference is that I know *exactly* what I'm doin'. And this is Joe. He's a, uhm…well, he's with me. Now, are you goin' to help me out?'

She moved to a cocktail cabinet and poured herself a drink, but didn't offer one around. 'Let's see what you have to say first. Then I'll decide.'

'All right, I'll tell you my hunch. I went over to Skytowers last night and took a look around. Your husband arrived there just before 7-30 on the night of the murder, fifteen minutes *before* Frank Ellis. Isn't that so?'

She shrugged heavily. 'That's what I've been told, yes.'

'Sure he did, lady. I know because the janitor told me. Then Frank showed up. But, when he entered the room, there was a bit of an argument and, shortly afterwards, Abel was shot. Now, there are those in Police Administration who consider this plain murder, and others who think Abel drew first and Frank killed him in self-defence. But me, I'm goin' with the theory that someone stepped out of the closet, knocked Frank out, shot Abel, planted a gun on both men, then skulked off into the night. I know that sounds bizarre, but this was a well-considered frame-up.'

Patricia stared at me in horror, her cling-film skin stretching to snapping point. 'Abel had one gun, Mr Shale, a licensed weapon which he bought to protect our home. But that wasn't the gun the police found beside him. That gun was here, in our safe, and that's been confirmed by the police. The loaded gun they found at his side, well, that was obviously planted on him by Frank Ellis after the shooting.'

'But the gun at Abel's side had his prints on it?'

It was a question, a supposition, yet Patricia's downturned gaze told me the answer before she opened her mouth.

'Frank obviously thought his plan through,' she seethed. 'He must have squeezed Abel's palm around that particular gun after... afterwards.' She gulped back the remainder of her drink, then sneered at me. 'Of course, that perhaps never crossed your mind, Mr Shale, seeing as how you're the type who seemingly forms a conclusion as soon as he gets tired of thinking.'

I ignored the smarty. 'Well, I *have* actually been thinkin' since I met up with Maria Ellis, and this is what I came up with. There's a single bullet-hole in the wall beside the door of room 18A – the door through which both Frank and Abel entered – but your husband was lyin' in the centre of the room. To account for the trajectory of the bullet, this means Frank was either standin' in or around the closet area when he fired at Abel, after which he then walked back to stand directly over Abel's body, where the janitor found him only seconds after the shot was fired. The problem is, it's a big room and it would've taken five, six seconds for Frank to make that return walk. We then have the added problem of Frank supposedly plantin' the other gun on Abel, but again, due to the fact the janitor entered 18a almost *immediately* after the shootin', that doesn't add up. And frankly, lady, Frank was frozen in shock when the janitor entered the room.'

I paused and regarded her with something bordering on post-coital arrogance as she attempted to digest my salted pearls.

'Then what does it mean?' Patricia asked softly, slumping onto the arm of Joe's chair. He recoiled as if she were a jungle snake, and I smiled thinly. Joe was the eternal boy-scout who should've gone scouting for the unfairer sex much earlier in life. Thing was, he hadn't, and I got the feeling that, just then, he'd rather have been sitting in a tunnel alongside another boonie as it rained rockets. 'Do you truly think someone else was involved, Mr Shale?'

'Now we're readin' from the same hymn book, lady. That's what I've been tryin' to tell you since I got here.'

Joe nodded a serious. 'Abel didn't secure his flank, lady. He should've put a decoy on point, then lurped the outlyin' areas, maybe tossed in one or two frags. Instead he bought it from sniper fire...'

'Jeez, Joe!' I snapped as Patricia gazed at him dumbfounded. 'Why don't you go outside and check our outlyin' area? See if we've got a tail or somethin'.'

'Kit Carson the area?' Joe grinned like a loon on a triple dose of Thorazine. 'You serious?'

'Serious as a heart attack, Joe.'

Joe liked that idea. He left the room and eagerly took to the mansion's grounds.

As Patricia and I sighed in relief at his departure, I said, 'But this is where I have to ask some serious questions, Mrs Shirinski. If this was a frame-up, we have to look at *why* someone would've wanted to do that. We also have to re-examine the time-frame of the shootin', but first things first. So, revenge is usually a good place to start. Do you know anyone who may've hated both men?'

Patricia eyes were lost in the past for a moment, but then she shook her head. 'No. It's very likely they both had professional adversaries, but the only person I can think of to connect them is their old business partner Jim Harrison, though he parted with both of them on good terms many, many years ago…'

'Fair enough. And are you certain that – apart from the prints – Abel can't be connected in any other way with the gun they found at his side?' I raised my palm-heels as she attempted a frown that sprung near-instantly back into place. 'It's just that he's in the security business, and in that business guns are easily accessible. And if it's proven that he owned the gun, or that he brought it with him, well, that blows my theory out of the water.'

Patricia shrugged uncertainly. 'Abel could probably have gotten another weapon if he wanted. And I can see why he might have taken it with him, Mr Shale, because those letters we were getting contained nasty threats. But if it's proven that he did…'

'Then what?'

Patricia straightened in her chair, took a deep breath, then averted her gaze. 'Then…his reputation, the business we built together, it will all have been for nothing.'

I scrutinised her intently, aware that she'd been about to say something else before changing her mind at the last moment. I wanted to turn the heat on there and then, to tell her I'd been taken in by a girdle once but that hadn't lasted long either, yet I held back, realising that it was way too early in the investigation to play hardball. Maybe she'd talk more freely when things were a bit more comfortable between us: Maybe after I'd sent her some new underwear in the post and asked her out to dinner. After all, she was attractive, single and she'd smiled politely at me the first time she'd answered the door. Obviously, somewhere way deep down, she actually liked me.

'So, these letters your husband was receivin', could I see a few of them?'

'I never actually saw them. They were sent to his office. He kept them in his safe.'

'Right, but if he was gettin' nasty letters, why didn't he go to the police?'

'My husband genuinely believed Frank Ellis was sending him the letters, Mr Shale, and he thought he might eventually get him to see reason.' She rose and went over to pour herself another drink, then offered one to me. I took a brandy as it was free and the most expensive drink in the cabinet. 'Besides, Abel was a very private man, and the more people involved, the more chance there was of a scandal.'

'Well, if both Abel and Frank were receivin' letters, the same person was obviously sendin' them out. Are you sure you can't think of another common denominator?'

'Mr Shale,' Patricia sighed. 'I don't know that many people here in the city. I don't even know many Americans – I'm Canadian, thank God! I met Abel in Toronto about fourteen years ago. His business dealings had wound up in the States, and soon afterwards he hit upon the idea of selling surveillance equipment to ordinary members of the public.'

Just then I recalled the piece of metal I'd found in room 18c. I'd examined it once, but hadn't been able to determine what it was. Now an idea began to form in my mind. Usually, when I start getting original ideas, I take an aspirin and they go away. But this was one I planned to develop long past the chrysalis stage. I didn't say anything to Patricia, however. I simply nodded, before getting up and pouring myself another drink, though I didn't offer one to my host as she hadn't offered me one earlier. Through the window, I espied Joe chasing someone elderly across the lawn. Still, as it was Joe, I really wasn't too surprised: The guy had no inhibitions about causing an exhibition, and every time you saw him you could almost hear the theme of Loony Tunes going off in the background.

'Y'know, Maria Ellis reckons Abel set that meetin' up because he was a sore loser in an old love triangle,' I said, returning to my seat and temporarily switching track. 'She also said Abel had a bit of a temper, and that she was takin' the mutton dagger from him long before you were. What's your take on that?'

'They say one man's lady is another man's whore, Mr Shale, and Abel once told me Maria was no lady, so you do the math. That said, I'd nothing against her.'

'But your husband only moved to Canada because he got tired of Frank floutin' his fling with Maria, isn't that right?' I said candidly. 'He couldn't take the fact his affair with Maria had started off as puppy-love before goin' to the dogs.'

'Maybe,' she reflected moodily. 'Whatever the reason, Canada was our home and we were happy there. Then about two years ago, Abel suggested moving back as he was homesick. But we didn't tell Frank and Maria we were returning. We thought it best to let the past remain in the past. Then, a few months ago, we started getting the letters.' She raised an open palm. 'That's all I know. Abel had no other enemies that I know of, and he only ever considered Frank a lost friend, never an enemy.'

I nodded, finished my brandy and stood up. A scream in the garden had caught my attention. 'Well, you've been more than helpful,' I told her quickly. 'I'll see myself out. No, really, sit back down. I'll, uhm, keep in touch.'

I urged her back into her seat and rushed into the garden. Joe was there, lying face down and spread-eagled upon the gravelled drive, the irate gardener holding a pitchfork tight to the back of the veteran's neck.

I flashed my badge at the old man and said, 'I'll take him off your hands.'

'Next time he comes around here,' the elderly gardener spat, 'I'll tear him apart like a Thanksgiving turkey!' He removed the pitchfork from Joe's neck

Joe rose up from the gravelled path, spat out some small stones, then said through gritted teeth, 'You couldn't fight your way out of a bingo hall!' He wagged a finger after the old man. 'And if I ever see you in one, I'll prove it.' He made a pretence of going after the gardener, though only after I'd taken him firmly by the arm and led him towards the Buick. 'Bastard!'

I drove off before the Ham could secure an image of the man in his mind for future reference. On the way back to the office my eyes were somewhere between the road and Heaven, and I wondered why most people seemed to spend their lives going down hills while I seemed to spend an inordinate amount of my own going up them.

SEVEN

We left Specksville close on 3-00pm, and, feeling slightly peckish, I had Joe treat me to pre-dinner in an uptown restaurant where the food was so good you'd have been happy enough to have eaten the menu.

Still, even though I'm usually a regular appetite with the skin pulled over it, my urge to peck had been slightly dulled by the fact that the Shirinski case was leading me up all sorts of blind alleys. But because Joe was paying – and as he was just another person squatting in the dung-heap that was my life and adding to it – I ordered two expensive starters and swished them around my plate. In truth, he didn't seem too concerned about that; and so, as he scoffed his Chicken Surprise, I found myself darkly wishing that a wishbone from that fowl surprise would give him a foul surprise and end to our shotgun-wedding once and for all.

Sadly, as I often point out, wishes don't do dishes. So, as Joe pecked at desert, I lit a cigarette, blew some smoke in his face and consoled myself that at least Doc Edgars would be proud of me come our next meeting down the local anorexia unit. No more would I have to astound him with nutritional science and tell him I always ate from the five basic food groups – tinned, alcoholic, frozen, take-away and ice cream. And no more would he be able to snidely suggest that I should be fitted with a nosebag, or that my idea of a balanced diet was a burger in each hand. Now, he'd see that it was only a matter of time before a flock of slavering hyenas started following me around on a regular basis.

Some forty minutes later, we made our way down Dahmler Row amidst a throng of blue- and white-collars, the sweltering sun high in a cloudless sky. Marcie was filing her nails into dagger-like points as Joe and I entered the office.

She rose like a wolf in puppy-dog clothing to hold open the frosted glass door that separated her working-area from my resting-area. It was a manly thing to do, yet the smile upon Marcie's face was primeval and for once she was no gentleman. I averted my gaze and entered warily, all too aware of her usual modus operandi.

'It's Friday,' she informed me testily as both Joe and I moved past her. 'My relatives are arrivin' from upstate tomorrow. So, do you think...?'

I faked a cheesy. 'Thanks for the update, Marcie. Those night classes are payin' off big time. You, uhm, know Joe, don't you?'

Marcie held up a letter-opener, pointed the sharp end in Joe's direction. 'Yeah, I do. And if he ever pats my ass again, he'll be drawin' back a stump!'

Joe raised his palm-heels and moved meekly behind me. He and Marcie had met twice before and talked of many things, all beginning with the letter V. Understandably, Marcie had tried to mutilate Joe with the fax-machine the second time around. Now, before she considered doing something similar to me, I asked her to give Joe a slice of her coffee and a sick-bag, told her I'd a few urgent phone-calls to make, then urged both her and the Ham out of my office into the reception area, closing the door fast behind them.

I was relaxing in my swivel chair minutes later when Marcie came in, shutting the door softly behind her. She approached me with all the coyness of a wolf in a sheep-pen and pretended to tidy up my unorthodox filing system. In turn, I began opening my mail to show her that I too could feign the art of work when necessary. But suddenly, Marcie's stance was that of the Great White Hunter. And, sitting before her, I felt like the Great White Hunted. 'It's Friday, Marty,' she reiterated firmly. 'You told me I was gettin' paid.'

I tapped my watch with a pedantic digit. 'What time is it, Marcie?'

'Nearly four.'

'Right. And at what time on the last Friday evenin' of the month do you *normally* get paid?'

'Four-thirty,' Marcie replied. She added hurriedly, 'That's on the days I *do* get paid, which aren't as regular as they should be.'

I shook my head slowly. 'Marcie,' I smoothed. 'You've been workin' your butt off for me for over six years, but you still can't see the doughnut for the hole. Now, I've already told you you'll get paid, and I'm a man of my word. And may God strike everyone in that street down with thunderbolts of fire if I lie!'

Marcie managed the sort of smile you instantly wanted to fix with a wheel-brace and three months of corrective surgery, yet I'd no way of knowing if it was for real. She'd probably heard the man-of-my-word joke before. Either that or she still couldn't pick out the approaching storm-clouds beyond their faint frame of silver.

'Alright, Marty, I'm a believer. You need anythin' else? You, uhm, maybe want me to go down the bank and draw out the cash?'

I raised an index and wagged a strenuous no-no. 'Uh-uh! What I'd like you to do is get me the name of the attorney who's workin' the Frank Ellis case. Get me an appointment with him this evenin'...'

Marcie glared sourly at me: She'd stick her hunting hat on at a moments notice.

'Any time *after* four-thirty is fine,' I added, quickly. 'Because, naturally, I'll be here in the office until then. And then get me an appointment with Maria Ellis. Oh, and get me the address of Abel Shirinski's office here in town as well. I might have to go over there eventually and see if I can dig anythin' up.'

Marcie's eyes glinted with hope, and for a moment she reminded me of a lamb knocking on a slaughterhouse door, asking what time they opened. 'Go on, Marcie,' I grinned. 'Get at it. That's what I'm payin' you for after all.'

She made to leave with that half-smile drawn onto her mousy face. 'What about that sociopath in the waitin' area?' she asked dryly. 'You plannin' on leavin' him there until I take his nose apart and see what makes it run?'

I'd almost forgotten about Joe. You read about the mind doing things such things in traumatic situations. It's a survival mechanism, apparently. 'Uhm, Joe, ah! Listen, you just keep him there for a second, will you? I just, uhm, want to get a little rest. I've had a hectic kind of mornin'.'

'You know I don't like him!'

I waved a hand dismissively, and got the feeling that, if need be, she'd use that excuse in court. 'No one does, Marcie. That's normal. Just nod and smile when he talks. No sudden movements. Don't give him anythin' sharp. You'll be fine.'

Marcie nodded grimly and exited the office. Moments later she phoned through the name of the attorney working the Frank Ellis case. I knew the guy already and didn't need to ask for an address. His name was Chester Hardcastle and I'd only met him once before on that Triad-Mafia case I was telling you about, though even then I'd taken an instant disliking to him just to save time. The guy was a snake-oil salesman, the sort who believed wills were dead give-aways, and he gave me the impression that when the meek eventually inherited the earth, he'd be there slapping them with Inheritance Tax.

He had an office at the end of the street, something I hadn't realised until last year. Maybe that's a city thing, y'know, where your nearest neighbours are often strangers until a calamity brings them together. Or maybe it's a reputation thing, whereby mediocre types are bypassed for more accomplished sorts. I know that feeling alright. Sometimes, I feel there are weeks on end when my death would go unnoticed in my office, even if Marcie was in the next room. Come pay-day at the end of the month, however...

Which reminded me – I had to get out of here, and fast.

I turned on the intercom, ruffled a pile of papers about as if I was working on something, then turned it off again. Then I rose gently from my seat and moved towards the window, opening it very slowly. I was on the 2nd floor, but every building hereabouts has a fire-exit, which is very handy at times. I'd just go see Chester, then slip back before 4-30pm, and neither Marcie nor Joe would even know I'd been away.

The mind certainly is a funny thing at times, I mused, as I paced down the street towards Chester's office, hoping all the while that God wouldn't take me up on that bolt of lightening joke. I read somewhere once that of the 1440 minutes in a day, the average person spends 1300 of those in a fantasy world, asking 'What if'?

It's the same with me at times. As I'd ventured out onto the fire-escape, I'd momentarily convinced myself I'd be back in my office by 4-30pm. But, even as I'd opened the window, I'd known deep down that Marcie wouldn't see me again until Monday morning. With a bit of luck, Joe Sinto would have returned to his own 'hooch' by then, too. Still, I must admit that luck and I are relative strangers at the best of times, and we usually only meet up when one of us is in a foul mood and unable to appreciate the finer qualities of the other.

Chester has a 1st floor office close to the main street – which means, basically, that he has more money than me and half the locality. He saw me coming and tried to lock the main door. It was an attempt to create a diversion to alleviate his aversion, but he had a conversion as I threatened –

through the mailbox, and in view of the whole street – to subject his nose to a hard and bloody inversion. He told his secretary to let me in as he disappeared into his main office. She asked me to sit and wait for him to finish something he was working on. But I knew that trick because I'd just used it. I stormed into his office before he could get out onto the fire-escape.

'Waterin' the flowers, Chester?' I sniffed loudly. 'No, definitely no flowers around here. But I am gettin' a strong whiff of somethin' that smells pretty much of sulphur and brimstone.'

Somewhat exasperated, Chester stepped back inside. I ignored him and looked around, trying to figure out the difference between his office and mine. It was much the same but cleaner, though, unlike me, Chester didn't seem to view his desk as a wastepaper basket with drawers. 'Mr Shale,' he said through a slitted smile. 'To what exactly do I owe – how would I put it – the *pleasure*?'

'Lets cut to the chase, Chester,' I told him as I deliberately threw myself into a seat that strained under that vicious assault. 'I'm not here on a social. The first time we met was one time too many. In my opinion you couldn't defend an earthworm from a chicken, and you've probably as much between your ears as you have between your legs. Speakin' more plainly, I don't really like you, but I think we're goin' to have to co-operate on this Frank Ellis case.'

'Well, Mr Shale, I hold you in the same regard. You possess an inverted Midas Touch, whereby everything you handle turns to shit, and you couldn't find your pecker with a hand-mirror and a photograph of the deceased...'

'Your wife never has any trouble findin' my pecker, Chesty. Only, she's the one who's always tryin' to hide the damned thing!'

'I'd love to sit and trade insults with you, Mr Shale,' Chester returned sourly. 'But I don't have a low enough IQ for the job. Now, if you're here to discuss the Frank Ellis case, you're wasting your time. We're talking first-degree murder, and the best I can do is plea-bargain for diminished responsibility, or even temporary insanity, considering his so-called alibi. But then, Frank's around fifty-seven years old. I reckon I can get him out of the slammer in three, maybe four at most.'

I snorted derisively. 'Four years as a rock-breakin', mailbag sewin' degenerate in Iron Bar city for doin' nothin' at all? Sure, Frank will lap that offer up, big time.'

'It's an open and shut case,' Chester snapped. 'He won't have much choice.'

'You're forgettin' that I'm on the case, Chesty, and I'm the best P.I. in the state.'

Chester laughed contemptuously. 'If you're the best in the state, then we're all in a very sorry state. Now, tell me something you think I *don't* know about this case, or get the hell out of my office.'

I gave him my bullet-hole theory and he laughed snidely. Then I fiddled around under my jacket to let him know I was carrying a friend. And my friend, I hinted, didn't like anyone laughing at either him or me.

Chester clammed up soberly.

'That theory of yours doesn't mean a thing, Mr Shale. There were two people in the room and two guns, yet only one weapon was fired. Do you really think the police are going to act on that ridiculous assumption? People don't just go into rooms to stand in one spot. They move about and then, if so inclined, they shoot at each other. Your theory is as shallow as your intellect.'

'Talkin' about shallow, hasn't it crossed your mind to at least forward a self-defence plea on Frank's behalf? After all, Abel also had a gun, so Frank could say he was just a little quicker on the draw.'

'No, Mr Shale. If a self-defence plea fails and the jury finds Frank guilty of homicidal intent, he could receive a life-sentence. An early plea of diminished responsibility or temporary insanity has a better chance of success.'

'I have other evidence,' I said coldly. I produced the small metallic object I'd found in room 18c. 'You wouldn't recognise this, Chester, but it's part of a small receiver. An ear-piece to be precise, and I found it in the adjoinin' room.' I held it out to him, then pulled it sharply back as he made to take it. 'Oh no you don't! I keep this. You go tell Malone the plea-bargain is off, and that you want a more thorough investigation of the second conference room. I think we're definitely dealin' with a third party on this one.'

Chester stared at me blankly. He was thinking of something smart to say when his blonde-haired secretary burst into the room in quite a fluster.

'Mr Hardcastle,' she said quickly. 'They want you down at the State hospital. Frank Ellis has just been admitted with a suspected coronary. He asked for you as they took him in.'

'He must be fuckin' delirious!' I muttered. I turned to Chester's secretary. 'Has Maria Ellis been informed?'

She regarded me blankly, then turned to Chester, who simply asked the same question with a raise of his head

'No. but I'll get on to it straight away.'

I regarded her momentarily. She was as mousy as Marcie, but much prettier. Some day, I mused, when the money was rolling in, I was going to get myself a pretty little thing like that. They cost a bit, the better looking ones, but then that was why I had Marcie, I supposed. And probably why I hadn't had her as well, come to think of it.

She left hurriedly and Chester followed after her. I got up from the chair and it collapsed into a heap.

'Even the furniture can't bear you, Mr Shale,' Chester sighed. 'You're leaving now, I take it? Never to darken my door again until the end of the world, amen?'

'Oh, I'm leavin' alright,' I smiled. 'Funny thing is, Chester, I'm goin' over to the hospital with you. Frank, lest you forget, is also *my* client.'

'You're an insensitive jackass,' Chester snorted. 'If I take you there, I want you to go away as soon as we exit the car. Maybe you could use a different entrance. You could, couldn't you, if I gave you, say, ten…no, twenty dollars?'

Chester pulled a tattered bill from his pocketbook, dangled it under my nose like a carrot. I nodded, took the bribe, and he smiled contemptuously. As he hurried from the office into the street, I trailed after him, staying Siamese in case he considered driving off without me. He had a shiny blue Mercedes parked kerbside some fifty feet away.

I stared at it jealously.

'Seems I got into the wrong profession, Chesty.'

Chester grinned sanctimoniously. We got into his car and he pulled out into the traffic. It was 4-35pm and the build-up along the avenue was starting to take hold. As we moved, Chester revved his engine and honked his horn at every car driving under 60mph. It was as if he believed the city owed him a private lane.

'You drive as if you're in a hurry to get your accident over with,' I said, as he laid out a stream of well practised invective at every passing motorist. 'You want me to drive? I've actually got a licence to do that as well. And, unlike you, I didn't find mine in a box of Wheaties.'

Again, Chester ignored me and eventually got us onto the freeway. From there we had a clear run at the hospital. I tried winding him like an alarm clock all the way, but he didn't bite. He did pass one comment when I asked him why he was so quiet. 'I'd rather people wondered why I didn't speak than why I did,' he told me in his dull and unenthusiastic manner.

Just then, I suspected that he was trying to tell me something, though I couldn't quite figure out what.

Still, I should've remembered the old adage: The man who smiles when everything is going wrong has thought of someone else to blame it on.

But it was only when we entered the sliding doors of the hospital and Chester slipped off to the nearest phone booth that it all clicked into place. However, as was now usual in my life, by that stage it was just a tiny bit late for me to do anything about it.

EIGHT

You ever notice how some people remind you of animals? To me, Chester was like something half-slug and three-quarters rat, with nine-tenths of something slimier cast into the mix. It wasn't just a physical thing, y'know, because I never judge anyone by appearances unless I don't like the look of them. And so what if he had tight beady eyes that made him look as if he'd just ruptured his spleen, or glistening skin that made him resemble an otter straddling a hot-plate? No, I was more repulsed by the way he walked, talked and breathed. And, less than ten minutes after arriving in the hospital, I sure wouldn't have minded seeing him bleed!

At Admissions, we got directions to the Cardiac Unit, only to arrive amidst a confusion of doctors running hither and thither. I slowed one with a choke-hold and lectured him about running in a built-up area while there were built-up people like me in for a leisurely. Somewhat hypocritically, he then violated his Hippocratic by swearing to violate me with a hypodermic if I didn't get out of his way.

Flustered, I walked on.

In the next corridor, two badges stood guard outside a room, and I knew we were in the right place. After checking in with the ward nurse, who told us they were still working on Frank, Chester excused himself and went to the Ladies, but I should've guessed something was afoot. By then, however, my appetite was starting to return a little, and so, with thoughts of food heavy on my mind, I found a candy-vending machine and bought a soda and six snack bars before moving casually into the waiting area.

The waiting-area had all the atmosphere of a funeral parlour without the benefit of a focal point. I sat beside a lady with a face like a catcher's mitt and scoffed my candy until I espied Maria and Tommy Ellis rushing into reception in a flurry of worry. Recalling our working arrangements, I lifted a magazine and shielded my face, figuring I'd talk with Maria when that inconsequential ruckus died down. Unfortunately, as distracted as I was by a voluptuous nurse at the front desk in my sugar-spiked haze, I failed to notice the arrival of Tork Malone.

Now, I've already mentioned that Tork's the sort of cop who'd skin a bear for its fur and then charge it with indecent exposure. What I may not have mentioned is that he's also the kind of African-American who acts more like an American on holiday in Africa. He's also an ex-marine – which ultimately means that if you get kerbside of him, you go in as a pig and come out as sausages. All of that aside, I'm sure he's the reason why Congress has recently been lobbying for policemen to be used in scientific experiments, namely because you can't form any emotional attachments to them.

Needless to say, I didn't want to run into him at that or any other juncture. As fate would have it, however, he noticed me before I noticed him, and he was all over me like a badly knitted sweater.

'Ah, Marty Shale, it's a small world, isn't it?'

'Yeah, but I sure wouldn't like to have to vacuum it.'

Tork smiled wanly, ignoring my scathing wit. 'So, what has you out from under your rock this fine evenin'?' Before I could utter yet another inane reply, he added, 'And you happier than a pig in a brown place, too, stuffin' that bore-hole of yours with Nature's best.'

'Ticker's on the flicker,' I sighed, patting my chest. 'One step from a diabetic coma. Need sugar.' I made to get up, the hospital door and freedom heavy on my mind. 'Maybe I should go lie down in the guest-room for a while before I, uhm, shuffle off this mortal coil, as it were...'

Tork pushed me back into my two seats, stared at me carnivorously. He has this habit of getting in close and breathing wreaths of halitosis over you, which is fine if you like that kind of thing. I don't. I like fresh air, cigarette smoke and the heady waft of green-backs. Furthermore, the only people I want invading my body-space at any time should have big breasts and a look of wanton abandon on their faces. Tork didn't qualify here on any account. Truth was, he'd be doing us both a favour if he went and chewed on a couple of Odour Eaters.

'You're not waddlin' off this mortal coil until I've spoken to you, Marty. I hear you're investigatin' the Ellis case. And a little bird told me you have somethin' on you that might help my enquiries.' He extended a hand expectantly. 'Get it out, now, or I'll charge you with obstruction and withholdin' information that may be relevant in the investigation of a murder.'

I peered behind Tork and noticed that Mo was standing further down the lobby. Mo's the cliché ever-faithful assistant you read about in five-dollar wood pulp. At that particular moment, I could've faked an innocent, but Mo was shaking me a no-no. It was his way of telling me to come across with the goods if I didn't want Tork to start playing hide-the-size-ten.

'A little bird didn't tell you about this,' I snarled, producing the ear-piece and slapping it into the detective's hand. 'It was that chicken-shit stool-pigeon, Chester.'

'He's just a decent citizen goin' about his duty,' Tork smiled, slipping the ear-piece into his jacket pocket. 'You should take a leaf from his book, instead of runnin' around like a professional decoy. Every time we get near somethin', in you come with twenty insane leads that have us all saunterin' down the Road to Nowhere with blinkers on.' He sighed heavily. 'And you can't keep doin' that, Marty.

You're makin' yourself about as popular as a turkey on January 2nd!'

'You just see my faults through a microscope, Malone, and your own through the wrong end of a telescope. I'm close to the truth on this one, its obvious.'

'Sure it is. Obvious as two tears in a bucket of water.'

'Well, I'm the, uhm, one comin' up with the new theories, aren't I?'

Tork pushed himself down next to me on the bench, and I suppressed a fart that could equally have left my boxers full of stogie.

'Tell you what I'll do,' he smiled. 'Now, usually I wouldn't dream of tryin' to pick a grain of reason from the philosophical manure of your brain, because no matter how hard I chewed it over, I'd never end up swallowin' it. But this time, I'm goin' to listen to you.' He noticed the surprise on my face, raised a hand. 'I know, I know, it's like explorin' the cuttin' edge of insanity. Still, I've always believed that, should a wise man discover 99% of the answer to a given problem, you may rest assured a heaven-born idiot will discover the other one. So, what's on your mind, *Whale*, if you'll pardon the exaggeration?'

I regarded him dimly, uncertain whether or not I could trust him. Then, deciding I'd nothing to lose except my dignity – and perhaps my freedom for tainting a crime scene – I ran my theory by him, seeking to gauge his reaction as he firstly nodded me a positive, before shaking me a negative. In hindsight, I probably should've kept that particular ace up my sleeve, especially as I wasn't dealing the cards.

'That's some concept you got there,' Tork said, his gaze focused upon the ceiling. 'Only thing is, if I tried to run that up the precinct flagpole, no one would salute.' I feigned a dopey and he sighed, realising he'd have to elaborate. 'The door to 18C was locked between 7-00pm and 8-00pm on the night of the murder, and Rick and that other dipso, Victor, had the only keys. Yet Victor was home at the time and swears nobody could've gotten his keys without his knowledge. As for Rick, he saw nobody else on the 18th floor at the time of the shootin'. And, as he was directly outside the door of 18a, he couldn't've missed a thing.'

'Skytowers is a big place,' I wheedled. 'Anyone could've waited for Rick to turn his back, slipped in past him and hid themselves away. Let's face it, the guy's two rungs short of a stepladder! And as for Vic Fellows, he should be livin' in a fuckin' swamp!'

Tork slapped his hand down hard on my shoulder. 'You're a hot-air balloon, Marty,' he said with a cruel smile. 'And, as much as I hate to see the slayin' of a beautiful hypothesis by a set of cruel, ugly facts, the kind of thing you're talkin' about only occurs in newspapers.'

'And what about the ear-piece?' I said as he rose from his seat and led Mo down the corridor. 'Is that somethin' I made up too?'

'Industrial espionage is big business, so it could've been lyin' there for ages. *You* may even have put it there to make things harder for me. Still, the case is closed. You're weavin' a merry tale on a worn-out tapestry with broken needles and invisible thread, and if you keep on jumpin' all over the bandwagon you're goin' to break the fuckin' thing.' He glared sourly at me 'Now stay out of my way. Or else!'

Somewhat surprised by his superior use of mixed clichés, I didn't react, just to confuse him. Tork, however, seemed unfazed by my silence. He just shook his head and laughed derisively as he made his way in to visit Frank Ellis. As he entered the room, however, Chester was on his way out.

Upon espying me, the Attorney to the Damned took a bulbous whitey and retreated even further up his own backside. 'You want your thirty pieces of silver now?' I snarled as he approached me. 'Or can you hold out until the day of the crucifixion?' I suddenly noticed the two badges further up the ward had their obsidian-like beadies all over me. I took a deep breath. 'Alright, Chesty, just tell me how Frank is and we'll let it go. For now.'

'It seems news of the plea-bargaining upset him a little,' Chester slithered. 'Seems it triggered some, uhm, heavy palpitations. But they say he'll be fine in a few days.'

'Unless you speak to him again, and maybe tell him more good news, eh?'

'At least I'm trying to help him. What have you achieved so far?'

I was debating whether to give Chester a smarting riposte or an equally smarting punch in the face when Maria and Tommy exited Frank's room. I uncurled my fist, and Chester – seeing that I was about to go with the last resort of the exasperated – chose that particular moment to hastily exit the hospital.

'Yeah, run Chesty. You're like a Christmas tree – your balls are for decoration!'

Despite my less than cheerful mood, I greeted Maria and Tommy with a cheesy. Maria's skin was alabaster, vitamin and make-up deprived. She was also wearing a red dress that made her look as if she'd been poured into it and someone had forgotten to say when. In contrast, Tommy was dressed as if nobody owned him, which was standard teenager style. Both were obviously a bit shaken, so I decided to lighten the atmosphere with some light and airy shit-chat.

'Don't worry, kid, your father will be up and doin' his whack in no time.' Maria shot me a stony, so I feigned a helpful. 'You want me to take the kid away for a while, get him a few beers, maybe get him laid? You could give Frank a *stretch* before he does his stretch, y'know, calm him down a bit.'

I considered adding a few Italian hand-signals but didn't bother, figuring that if a girl like that didn't know what it was all about by now, she never would. My attempts at levity, however, went down quicker than an Air India jet.

'No, thank you, Mr. Shale,' Maria replied, fixing me with a cream-curdler. 'Tommy is going home, and I'll be staying with Frank to make sure no one bothers him. You should go and do some work – that's why I hired you!'

'I'm gettin' results as we speak,' I exaggerated. 'Firstly, I've informed Chester in no uncertain terms the plea bargain is off. And secondly, I've nearly convinced the local P.D. into openin' a fresh investigation.'

'I won't hold my breath,' Maria said, curtly. Her nose lifted and she reminded me of a Concorde taxiing down the runway. She turned to Tommy, then pointed at me. 'Off you go, son. And remember, *that's* what happens when you lose all drive and ambition.' Tommy nodded pensively, then left the hospital at speed. 'Now, if you want to earn yourself some money on this one, Mr Shale, you'll have to work the case from a different angle. Just keep trying.'

'I am tryin', lady.'

'You are, Mr Shale. *Very* trying! Now, go! I'm paying for your services, and I expect you to work all-day, every-day, until this case is solved.'

As I was about to mutter an inane, Malone exited the room and called Maria over. I knew they were discussing me from their guttural tone and the way their eyes narrowed when they occasionally scanned me from head to toe. As that verbal assassination concluded, Maria nodded happily before walking towards me. Grinning, Tork walked away.

'I've just had some good news, Mr Shale. Well, actually, it *isn't* good for you. You may be interested to know that Detective Malone is reopening the case, which means I don't need you any more.'

It was like taking a kick in the eggs, and the bitch couldn't have hurt me more if she'd raided my icebox. Still, I rallied: 'Look, lady, you're makin' a big mistake here. You shouldn't be listenin' to him and his pointy views – he's only sayin' stuff to get at me. He doesn't care less…'

But she'd gone off to join Frank in his ward, and I was left standing there as alone as a lonely thing. I sighed a deepy, realising just then that I couldn't have been under any more pressure if someone stuck me in a pressure cooker and lowered me into the Marianas Trench.

It was 6-10pm when I went outside, the sky was as dark as a hog's eye, and it had begun to rain in abandon. I stood in the doorway, inwardly raw as a clubbed seal, and hailed a cab. Not even when the driver charged me over the odds could my mood have been worse.

It didn't matter to me that Malone's investigation would be half-assed or whether Frank spent his next few years in the slammer – the sad fact was that Maria Ellis had just condemned Yours Imminently to Death Row.

NINE

Years ago, a girlfriend told me that we're all whores in a way, because in order to feed our addictions we've got to trade off soul, hole, mind or kind. After short-changing that skank-whore and tossing her out of my motel room, I'd smoked a post-coital and begrudgingly admitted that she had a point: We're all taking it from someone in some way – it's all about learning to lie back and maintain your dignity.

As the cab pulled up outside the brownstone, it struck me that I'd been Maria's piss-poor whore, whom she'd used, abused and violated in an all-too-familiar way before kicking to the kerb. Again, it was karma, I supposed: Life's way of telling me that sometimes we're the crapper and sometimes we're the turd. So now I needed to change my soiled clothes, scrub myself clean and drink myself into a stupor until people like Happy Valentine, Maria Ellis, Joe Sinto, Gus Diamond, Tork Malone, Greta and Marcie became a subconscious blur. More importantly, I needed to think of myself for a change, which basically meant going out on the town and doing the sort of things to others that had just been done to me.

Nevertheless, as the cab drove off, I got the sort of tingling in my veins I usually only get when life's about to take a dump and I'm the only thing around to clean its ass with, and it warned me to keep a weather-eye out for unwanted visitors. Thankfully, the last owners of my new abode had much the same idea as me where gardening is concerned – they didn't! My current yard is a regular Garden of Weeden, and, if not as yet crying out for a Game warden, there are pockets of it in which I wouldn't be all that surprised to find a few Japanese soldiers still hiding out the war.

As it turned out, my suspicions were confirmed by my first furtive gaze in through the kitchen window from behind a heavy build-up of weeds. Joe and Greta were in there performing a series of torturous physical exercises that would've exhausted a super-model. I shivered at the sight. I hate exercise, and I've always believed that if God wanted me to keep touching my toes, He'd have stuck them on the end of my nuts. To be honest, I'm happy jumping to conclusions, pushing my luck, stretching the truth and running up bills. Still, I wasn't too surprised to see the physical jerk doing his physical jerks in my house, though I've always felt that Greta should've been exorcised in a different manner altogether.

Needless to say, I wasn't for hanging around. Cursing under my breath, I drove over to Ramon's, where I moved wearily through the half-filled diner and slumped into my favourite seat. As Ramon's harassed wife flung me a menu, I grinned a diamond-white minus the carats and – because I'd rather buy a torch than eat carrots – asked her to throw me up something minus the carrots that looked as if it hadn't been thrown up. As I ate, I reminded myself that it was Friday night, my main night on the town, which perhaps differs only from any other night in that I don't spend all my time in the Gutted Moose.

No, Friday night is my night for sourcing what I'm supposed to be missing in the way of *les belles femmes*.

Naturally, I have a set of rules which I try to adhere to on those nights when my pecker has a lead over my brain, and these apply whether I'm trawling the city's dimmer streets looking for some equally dim Wendy Whoppers upon whom to sate my lust for the lowest price possible, or cruising the best strip-joints on my one man Crotch-Watch.

The first thing I try to remember is that I'm only looking to exercise my love muscle in a broad-minded broad – I'm not looking to court or marry her. Y'see, to me, marriage is a bit like getting a licence when the hunt is over, and the Mexicans say it's the only war in which you get to sleep with the enemy on a regular basis. If you add this to the fact that many beautiful women are like the Venus de Milo – in that they're well formed, but rarely all there – you'll see why I think deep and meaningless relationships are better for everyone.

Still, I'm drifting here.

And I was drifting just then. Thing was, I was gut-full and content as a virus in a hospital ward, when I should've realised that, even though Camp Shale hadn't been under fire for an hour or so, there was a good chance it would turn into the Alamo again real soon.

So I'm sitting there, ready to go on a low-fat desert or two and planning my night on the tiles, when who walks in through the door? The Ham, of course. And the look upon his face told me he'd turned from plain Joe Sinto into Billy-Joe-Bad-Ass.

I paled instantly, guessing my scent must've drifted down past the brownstone. 'Joe,' I feebled. 'I've, uhm, been lookin' everywhere for you. Where were you?'

Joe nodded darkly, sat across from me and fixed me with his recently adapted Two-Yard Glare. He clicked his fingers at Mrs. Ramon, ordered a bagel and coffee, then stared at me as if we were the only two people in the world. His world – The World – where anyone with olive-skin who wasn't wearing olive-green fatigues was apt to find themselves getting unsavourily stuffed with the olive branch of peace.

I swallowed uneasily, aware that Joe had smoked long on the pipe of peace since the end of the war but had rarely inhaled. A waitress brought Joe's order over, and, for a few seconds, she played a servile Eve to our testosterone-imbued Cain and Abel.

'Saw you leavin' the buildin',' Joe told me inanimately, his eyes black as tar. 'Saw you enterin' Hardcastle and Lee,

Attorneys of Law. But the hospital was harder to infiltrate, so I skirted the perimeter and waited in the tree-line.'

'You followed me as I left my office, is that what you're sayin'?' Joe nodded a Grim Reaper. 'Yeah, well, my, uhm, latest client's rev-counter went into overload, so I...'

Joe raised a palm-heel to let me know my excuse was slowly being worked through the shredding-machine of his reasoning department. I nodded warily, stopped speaking and wrapped my tongue firmly around my upper lip.

'Then I saw that detective you're always cursin' out,' Joe continued bleakly. 'Knew him instantly. Heard of him back in 'Nam. Saw photos of him collectin' his gongs end-of-tour. He was in the braid, way up the ranks, and we boonies never saw eye to eye with those guys. They thought they were better, y'see.'

'We goin' any place with this conversation?' I hedged.

But I didn't really need to ask. We'd just hiked across two continents and we were boarding a landing craft, skirting a bamboo-infested stretch of the Mekong, and looking for some place to disembark.

'You'll see where we're goin' here, Marty.' Joe glared me a big-eye. 'If you let me finish talkin'. Now, these guys thought they were better. Like, they got non-specific urethritis, y'know, whereas we got the clap. Like, they stuck us on point durin' every patrol, so that at every step we were waitin' to tread on a toe-popper or get gutted by some well-hidden punji stakes. Christ, best thing we had to look forward to at times was a colostomy bag and maybe some shoes to match.' Joe shook his head, his hand as yet raised defensively to ward off any incoming. 'Not that I mind wars. God, I've fought in places where there so many coups goin' on that the rebel leaders often did their inauguration speeches from the back of a getaway truck! Thing is, you can't have those guys takin' liberties in the name of liberty.

Nor can you have them tryin' to take a piece of the Free World without firstly payin' the price.'

'Look, Joe, I've heard of Vietnam, and I'm sure it was like a fuckin' jungle over there, but you were talkin' about Malone.'

'I *am* talkin' about him,' Joe said thickly. 'And I'm talkin' about *Vietnam*, Marty. Just to re-irritate here, I had a bad fuckin' time in that bamboo market. Buddies of mine cashed their tickets in over there because of guys like Malone. Their switches were flicked and they were waxed fightin' their turf by those slant-eyed sons of...'

'Jeez, Joe, hang with the programme here!'

Joe took a deep breath, then another. 'I've got my feet firmly on terra cotta, Marty, always have had. It's just that sometimes recallin' that stuff sends me fugazi in the head, y'know, and I can see and think of nothin' else.'

'Yeah, well, when your feet are on the ground and your head's in the clouds, you're stretchin' it somewhat, caprice? Now, you were talkin' about the hospital.'

'Yeah, I was sayin' that when you went AWOL, I heard Malone mention your name in-between a heap of curses to that other detective out on the steps. Then he produced this.'

Joe held out his closed palm, then slowly opened it. In his hand was the ear-piece Tork had taken from me.

My heart sank quicker than a punctured dinghy, and my mind's eye developed a sudden nervous tic as I inwardly envisaged the carnage Joe must have wrought to get the ear-piece back from Malone. I was all too aware that where Joe travelled buzzards usually gathered, and my next words were laboured.

'Tell me you didn't kill anyone, Joe, please?'

'I'm not totally insane. Malone just dropped it, and I just happened to find it.'

I didn't believe either of those statements, but I took the evidence from him anyhow. 'That's, uhm, good work. But seriously, say you didn't smoke him.'

Joe shook his head and got in close. Too close. 'You were testin' me, weren't you?' he grinned. 'When you went AWOL, you were just seein' if I'd follow?' Before I could reply, he added, 'you got me real good!'

I nodded a cowardly. 'You're an astute guy, Joe, and you passed straight off. But that aside, I also wanted to ask you about Marcie. She, uhm, say anythin' about me leavin' the office in such a hurry? She make any rash statements you might find yourself repeatin' in court should I fail to turn up some day soon for my work?'

Joe grinned a cheesy with relish, then nodded. 'Sure, she passed one or two remarks, but I'm too much of a gentleman to repeat them. Then she asked me to lend her a gun. She didn't say what she needed it for, though.'

'And you gave it to her?' Joe nodded and I suppressed a dark urge to rip chunks from his throat. 'Yeah, 'course you did. Uhm, tell you what, you wanna go out for a drink later? Celebrate your initiation into the business, as it were.'

'Wouldn't mind,' Joe beamed. 'Actually need a brew after all of that recon.'

We didn't leave Ramon's until dark, and, when we did, I stayed as close to Joe as is considered decent here in Vesperville before sloping into the car and driving off into centre city. As we did so, I put all thoughts of the Shirinski murder out of my mind – after all, it isn't good to take work home, and everyone needs a social. But no matter how hard I tried to forget, my mind kept drifting back to the mad killer whom I now knew to be out there stalking the streets.

Still, I suppose I should've paid her her wages.

***

I wasn't taking Joe with me for a drink out of any social grace, you understand. I was using my smarts, and, simply put, he was to be my decoy. My old High-school teacher used to tell me that a little knowledge could be a dangerous thing, and that I should always avoid small men on balconies as well as the man of one book. I never did figure out what the hell he was talking about, although I do know now that a little knowledge, if used properly, can actually save your life.

Joe and I were hardly of the same size and stature, but that didn't matter: He'd be big enough to confuse the issue when the shooting started. And the little information I speak about concerned Marcie. I'd taken her down the range once to let her try out my Magnum. She couldn't have hit a gable-end at five yards with a rocket launcher, so that was handy to know. But I also know that every pistol, should it be in the hands of a champion marksman or a newcomer such as Marcie, pulls a little to the right when fired. So all I had to do was lean a little to my left and keep Joe on my right. That way, a few of my ever-mounting problems would soon be resolved. Joe would also come in handy for buying drinks when I refused point blank to do so, which I would do at some stage of the evening.

Probably when I got my indignant head on after the first gallon.

So we toured the city's red-light area, eyed up a few bargoyles, took in a few strip-joints where it was common enough to find one or two foxes sitting amongst the hounds, and, in-between drinks, we picked up the odd meat-sauce sandwich. In truth, we had ourselves a skinful, an eyeful, and – when I'd finally had a bagful – we also got around to having ourselves a few domestics. It was your normal Friday night on the tiles in every respect. In fact, at one point I was getting it on with a rather attractive young thing in a seedy dive off Giancana Boulevard – who, prior to my arrival, had been using her saline buoys to attract some sailor boys – and it looked very much like no money would be exchanging hands later that evening. Then in steps Joe and asks the young lady if she had any friends.

'Human, you mean?' She looked as if she was about to gag. 'For you?'

Well, what with the light and everything...

Still, Joe didn't take that too well. I had to drag him out of there by the scruff of his flak-jacket just as he was about to give the doorman a little one-on-one. The police were nice enough, though, when they showed up. They did hit us a couple of slaps with their nightsticks, but at least they had the decency to dump us off outside my place shortly afterwards.

Once inside, we drank a few bottles of anaesthetic for an hour or so, after which I let Joe sleep on the settee as I ambled uneasily to my room. It was – according to the many hands on my alarm clock – either 6-30am, 4-10pm, or 42 degrees in the shade.

***

I am, however, quite positive about the time Greta began vacuuming my bedroom carpet: It was 7-22am precisely, and I knew that was the time they'd state on the coroner's report if she kept it up. Now, I've mentioned that Greta is my 'maid', which isn't strictly true, so here I'll have to digress a little.

Y'see, in my youth, I was a bit of a delinquent. Thing was, I was born the youngest of two sons, and my older brother Henry turned out to be the athletic, blue-eyed academic apple of my father's eye. Sadly, my father only had room for one apple in his rather un-spacious eye, and so, even though I was quite proficient at school, my every success was a comparative failure. As a result, I began skipping school and running errands for my uncle Don, who was a far better role-model for me in that he liked to rest long before he got tired, and in that he believed luck was responsible for the success of people he hated. Not too surprisingly, I ended up rather poorly educated and working in the P.I. business, which, as you may have now gathered, is the kind of game where you're continuously sticking your neck out to keep your head above water.

And what has this got to do with Greta? Well, she worked for my uncle at the time. How they hooked up, I'm not sure, yet I'm near certain that Greta arrived stateside around about the time a certain Eva Braun allegedly got smoked in a bunker alongside another infamous kraut. What I do know for certain is that Greta helped my uncle out in his office and at home, and he sort of liked her, whereas I wasn't too fussed on her at all. Still, some two weeks before my uncle Don mysteriously vanished, he'd been chatting to me about looking after her if anything happened to him. At the time, I'd thought little of that conversation and put it down to the maudlin effects of gin and cocaine. Nevertheless, because he'd always kept me straight, I somehow felt I owed it to him and so I'd kept her on.

There were times when I regretted doing so, of course, and now was definitely one of those times.

As yet in somewhat of a drunken haze, I lifted my gun carefully from the bedside table and pulled back the hammer. Greta dived to the floor in a panic.

'Greta, you fascist swine,' I seethed. 'Don't you know that nature abhors a vacuum cleaner – that's a scientific fact. Now, what the hell are you at?'

'But, Herr Shale, early to bed, and early to rise...'

'...is the motto of people whom I despise! Now, give me one good reason why I shouldn't fuckin' shoot you, you son of a Hun!'

I placed the .45 Magnum – a gun I favour above others, because, like me, it's noisy, hard to handle, and often well off the mark – between my legs and slowly drew back the hammer. And when I say slowly, I mean carefully. My dawn-horn was down there, too, and at the moment it was at half-mast, like a wrestler's forearm clutching a bowling ball. One balls-up now and I'd be two balls down, and I wasn't turning eunuch for anyone

'You wanted in hospital,' Greta stormed. 'Geh zum teufel, Herr Shale...volbescheissene!'

'Tellin' me to go to the Devil and that I'm full of shit is not – I repeat *not* – the way to earn my respect, Greta!'

I heard her shuffling about beneath me and tried to guess exactly where she was at: One clean shot would more than likely do it.

'Tommy   downstairs,'   Greta   whined,   the   panic increasingly evident in her voice. 'You get off fat ass! Him in trouble.'

Sighing irately, I sidled out of my reinforced bed, pulled on my robe and went down to the sitting room. I passed Joe on the stairs. He'd been sleep-crawling – no doubt sidling up a bunkered hill in Da Nang – and his trigger-finger was jumping about with a life of its own. Tommy was in the sitting room when I entered, pacing up and down as if his world had collapsed in around his ears.

'Right, Tommy, what the hell has you botherin' me in the middle of the night? And this better be good, kid, or they'll be puttin' me in the same cell as your father.'

'Something h...happened,' Tommy stuttered. 'I think you better g...get down to the h...hospital at once.'

Tommy didn't say much more. I plodded drunkenly upstairs, pulled on some wrinkled clothes, then plodded back down again. I didn't even think about waking Joe – sleeping dorks, and all that.

'Tell him I'll be back sometime,' I told Greta. 'And tell him *not* to follow after me – again. That's an order. Caprice?'

Greta scowled at me, then gave me the finger, a balled-fist salute, and then a load of German insults that I hadn't as yet got to grips with. I left with a shake of my head, wondering just what I'd done in my past life to deserve what I was getting in the present.

Tommy was just about to climb into the Buick. Before he'd half a chance to rip open the steering column and hot-wire the engine, I stopped him, handed over the keys and nudged him over to the driver's side.

Still, if Tommy was surprised I was actually letting him drive, he wasn't showing it. I also threw up on the way to the hospital, all over the front of my own car, and that didn't faze Tommy either.

Whatever was wrong with him, I knew then that it must have been real bad.

TEN

Due to the ongoing effects of the sauce, my vision was still a little fuzzy as we drew into the hospital lot, so I heard Mo Breasley before I saw him. He was leaning against an outside pillar, dragging on a cigarette and spitting like a camel into some nearby flowerbeds. Mo's own vision was less flawed. As I staggered towards him like a new-born foal, he cursed loudly and kicked those same defiled shrubs into nothingness. 'What do you want, Whale?' he snapped. 'Hell, look at you! Every time you walk down the street, the kids must think there's a fuckin' parade! Someone should be walkin' in front of you wavin' a red flag.'

'What do I want, you say?' I stopped, steadied myself against a nearby tree and took a few deep breaths. 'Same as everyone, Mo, I guess – life, liberty and the ability to freely engage in the happiness of pursuit. That, and to maybe know exactly why I've been fuckin' dragged down here.'

Mo didn't reply. He frowned as Tommy raced past him into reception, regarded Yours Unevenly as if I was something under his shoe, then stuck his arm solidly across the door as I attempted to lurch into the building's interior. 'Not you, Marty. We're in the middle of *another* investigation and don't need the fun you're certain to provide. And you're drunk.' As I breathed on him, he moved his cigarette quickly out of range. 'Don't fuckin' do that, unless you want to turn into Freddie the fuckin' Flame-thrower!'

'I'm not drunk. My inner ear's just playin' me up somethin' awful lately, and it's affectin' the hell out of my balance.'

'I don't think so. If I'm right, you were out on yet another booze-cruise. I know you – don't forget that!'

'I'm tellin' you, Mo,' I grinned, 'I'm sober as a juckin' fudge!'

'Yeah, well, how many fingers am I holdin' up?'

I regarded him and his hazy doppelganger for a few moments, counted the digits they were waving about in front of me, then divided by two. 'Twelve?'

'Yeah, close, but no cigar. So, you can stay out here until you're stable enough to climb on board the next train into reality-ville.'

I shook my head forcefully and, within half a mo, only one Mo remained.

'Don't I even get to hear what's goin' on?' I asked, pedantically. 'I was halfway through my quota of zees when Tommy showed up and told me I was needed here. It's still the middle of the night, for Chrissakes!'

'I suppose it can't hurt,' Mo grinned. 'Seein' as how you've got the recall of a fly bouncin' off a windowpane, you'll forget it in ten minutes anyhow. Well, it seems that while you were out gettin' your nose wet, Maria Ellis decided the best way to Frankie's heart wasn't through his stomach or his groin, but through his chest with a scalpel. Then, after playing hide-the-knife five or six times, she flaked it on the ironically named 'Recovery-Room' floor. A doctor found them both some twenty minutes later and called the police.'

I whistled a wet and noiseless. 'Christ, I wasn't expectin' her to do that!'

'Yeah, well the unexpected sure has a way of happenin' when you don't expect it, and that's a fact.'

'And so, uhm, has Frankie's clock stopped tickin'?'

'Not altogether. He's in surgery as we speak, where – just as ironically – they're now goin' at him with more scalpels. Of course, he's old, so there's no guarantee he'll pull through. Though if he does, he'll sure end up hatin' fuckin' scalpels!'

I felt a little queasy, yet it had nothing to do with the news I'd just heard. I was tired, needed to get back to bed, and the searing ache in my shoulders and my back reminded me I'd recently been a testing zone for three truncheons. Still, I tried to show an interest. 'Say Mo, why d'you think Maria would want to do such a thing?' I shook my head and Mo wobbled. 'Let's toss a few ideas up in the air, because two heads are always better than one.'

'Try tellin' that to Siamese twins.'

I feigned a giggly. 'Aw, go on, Mo. I haven't the time to think this thing through for myself. I'm sore enough as it is.'

'You really don't know?' Mo fixed me with a lofty. 'Alright, I'll tell you. Just shortly after Abel returned from Canada, he and Maria re-kindled their affair. But Maria's husband was obviously in the way, and so, between them, they devised a scheme to kill Frankie – a scheme that was supposed to make it look as if there was a third-party involved. As we now know, things didn't go the way they were supposed to in Skytowers and Abel ended up taking a bullet instead. A short time afterwards, Maria realised she'd been left with chump instead of prime, so she attempted to carve Frankie up like a twelve-ouncer because he'd killed the only man she ever loved. It's as simple as that.'

I shook my head wearily.

As usual, Mo's theories were wending their weary way to his mouth via his ass. He hadn't a clue about women, that was obvious, and he'd probably been married to his job so long he'd forgotten he was also married to his wife. Alright, so women often boiled at nothing and froze for no apparent reason, but they also melted if treated correctly. It was obvious to me that Frank Ellis had put Maria upon a pedestal; and, even though everyone knows that men who put women on pedestals rarely knock them off, Frank had done just that, and more. He'd buttered this girl's parsnips from day one, and you could tell that from the way she spoke of him, the way she softened every time someone mentioned his name. Mo was definitely clanging the wrong bell there. Maria didn't want Frank dead – it wasn't like that at all.

Mo also seemed to have forgotten that, for this particular theory to hold any weight, Maria and Abel would also have needed to get rid of Patricia Shirinski. Still, there was no point in saying this to Tork's water-boy just then, as he was the sort who put great energy into idle rumours, and he'd inform his boss as to my way of thinking long before I could shout Grass!

So, unable to think of a suitable reply, I threw up over Mo's trousers. He stared in disbelief as my up-chuck dripped down his pants, and, only for a few passing nurses, I reckon he'd have hit me a kick or two in the gongs.

'Look what you did!' he stormed. 'If I don't get this stain out, Marty, I swear, I'm goin' to make sure that's all that's left of you!'

Mo was obviously a little angry. So, out of respect, I didn't actually enter the hospital until he was halfway to the nearest john. Tork Malone was standing in the lobby when I stumbled in through the revolving door, no doubt debriefing his men on this latest twist in the case. He turned as I entered, and he looked set to round on me like a Doberman that had cornered a rat.

'Right, who ordered the Pavoroti-o-gramme?' Tork stared around him, only to be met with a host of drooping heads and shuffling feet. 'Well, I want it out of here. Come on, shoot the fuckin' thing!'

As his uneasy associates drew their weapons, the senior detective held up a hand. 'No, wait, leave this to me.' He lurched towards me, his hands tightening into clumps. 'Weren't you dismissed from this case, Shale?' he barged. I was mustering a reply, when he retreated two steps and placed his hand over his nose. 'Christ, you smell like downwind of a landfill!'

Which was rich coming from death-breath – very rich!

'You're, uhm, very offensive,' I told him, from under a corrugated frown.

'Yeah, well *I'm* tryin' to be. *You* just can't fuckin' help it!'

'I'd like to, uhm, see my client,' I feebled, closing my eyes in case he did a Mo and split into two. 'I've got rights too, y'know. I'm human, like most people.'

'Yeah? Well, would this be the client on the operatin' table, or the one suckin' on her seventh Valium? You'd probably get as much sense out of either.'

'Maybe Mrs. Ellis,' I shrugged. 'Frank's probably a bit busy tryin' to learn how to, uhm, breathe again and stuff.'

Tork nodded grimly, gritted his teeth, then clicked his fingers and summoned one of his men over. 'Vic, take my *good friend* Shale here over to the waitin' area and let him talk to Maria Ellis for twenty minutes, that's all.'

I couldn't be certain but I think he winked at Vic. I winked at Vic anyhow, though more to gain credence with Vic than for any other reason.

Seconds later, Tork put an arm around my shoulder in his strangely unfraternal way, then walked me towards the elevators. 'Y'see, Marty,' he grinned. 'I am your friend after all. Who else would let an inebriated sot with a mouth as big as the San Andreas Fault in to see his client, eh? Who else would let a puss-filled boil in the butt of life...?'

'You're hurtin' me...'

Nodding sadly, Tork released me a little. 'Right, you've got twenty minutes, so try not to fuck it up by doin' or sayin' somethin' stupid, y'hear me?'

'Hey, you could trust me with uncounted money. Seriously!'

'I wouldn't trust Jesus, and you'd have to go a bit to fill his sandals. Now, you've got nineteen minutes left, so move it!'

As Tork walked back across the lobby, Vic pressed the lift button and watched the light descend through the floors. As we waited, it crossed my mind that Tork had an ulterior motive for letting me see Maria Ellis, his sly wink being the giveaway. Still, if I made a good show in the next few minutes, I'd be back on the case. Or maybe I was being over-optimistic on that score. If what Mo had said was true, Maria would be doing life in the Big House real soon, I'd be working for zilch, and both Happy Valentine and Marcie would end up fighting it out over which one of them had the right to ventilate me good and proper.

My heart was beating a tattoo as we exited on the 5th floor, yet I was somewhat heartened by the fact Maria was sitting there in the waiting area looking like a B-movie star who'd just run four miles through a dark forest only to meet up with the beast at the far end. The truth was she'd once been a vision, but now she was a sight. Of course, you have to be tactful with women where their looks are concerned. You can tell them they look out of this world, but you can't tell them they look like nothing on earth. And it's one thing to tell them that gazing into their eyes makes time stand still, but something else to tell them they've a face that would stop a clock.

Like I say, I know all about women, that's why I'm single!

Anyhow, I don't think Maria would've caught on just then if I'd told her she'd won the state lottery. It was starkly apparent, even to a semi-inebriated sot like me, that she'd so many uppers in her she should've been levitating higher than a Yogi in a vacuum. As I sat beside her, I asked Vic to leave us alone, but he insisted on sitting less than ten feet away. He pretended to read a newspaper, while glancing furtively between us. It became obvious to me then that he was only called Vic because he got up people's noses on a regular basis.

'What the hell happened?' I asked Maria quietly. 'Is it true what they're sayin' about you?' She stared at me for a moment, then through me, so I shook her bodily before slapping her face hard. Vic dropped his newspaper and made to rise, but Maria began to awaken from her stupor. 'She's in shock,' I told Vic. 'Could you go get her a glass of water or somethin'?'

Vic stared at me coldly. 'I've been told to shoot you if you try anythin' funny.' He patted a bulge under the right hand side of his coat. 'Actually, Malone's hopin' on it. He gave me a set of lead-tipped dumdums especially.'

'Yeah, well that aint happenin' now,' I said thickly. 'But you fetch me that water and I'll see what I can do for you later.'

Grumbling, Vic rose and left us alone. I turned and hit Maria a few more slaps across the chops, then watched her flicker slowly back to life.

'Look, this is no time to go Helen Keller, lady,' I told her sharply. 'The supplementary eyes and ears of Ed Malone will be back soon, and he's been led to believe you're a latter-day Ma Barker. Now, last night someone tried to slice Frankie up good. So, if you've anythin' to say for yourself on the matter, you'd better say it now.'

Maria sobered instantly and pinched her nose as if someone had just revived her with salts. 'You smell as if you spent all night in a brewery, Mr Shale,' she replied haughtily. 'You really do need a wash.'

'Yeah, I'm under the influence, lady, but you're obviously still under the affluence! Now, are you goin' to help me out, or what?'

Her eyes went all watery and feminine. 'I was sitting there with Frank and he nodded off,' she said softly, still in somewhat of a daze. 'So, I drank a cup of coffee, but I suddenly felt very tired. When I woke, Frank was gone. The doctors told me he'd been stabbed several times and that they'd rushed him to surgery.' She cupped her face in her hands. 'There was blood everywhere. It was horrible. There's no way I'm capable of doing that. Unless I did it in my sleep or...'

'Unless nothin', lady,' I soothed. 'Someone must've slipped you a Mickey.' She looked mortified for a second, then raised her hand as if intending to slap me hard across the face. 'A Mickey, lady, a *mickey*! Christ, you'd think you'd know the difference by now!' She dropped her hand and went at the Japanese eyes. 'Anyhow, whoever tried to frame you must've had a grudge against you, Frank and Abel.' I went to put an arm around her shoulder, but she recoiled, snakelike. 'Yeah, whatever! Anyhow, I'll get to the bottom of this thing if it kills me. I might have to use my brains a little...'

'Really, Mr Shale, do you think that's wise?'

I willed my own eyes into venom-filled slits. 'Maybe not, lady, but that's how bad things are gettin'.' I rose from my seat, sicker now than when I'd joined her. Maria Ellis was a snooty little cow, yet I'd little choice but to butter her up so I could milk her dry. As Vic returned with the water, I made my way over to the elevator.

Before the door closed, Maria Ellis said, 'You'll keep in touch?'

Against my better judgement, I replied, 'Yeah, lady, you'll hear from me real soon. I promise.'

***

Greta and Joe were sitting around the dining room table when I arrived back home. I hurriedly crossed the rubble strewn hallway and made for the stairs, trying to pretend that those two misfits didn't exist.

'Where the hell did you go?' Joe asked, loudly. 'I was about to go look for you when Greta relays the command. You'll notice I didn't move a muscle.'

I came back downstairs. It was 9-00am – virtually the middle of the night–but I was ravenous and needed to eat before I got back into bed. I regarded Joe – now dressed only in pyjama bottoms – and grinned as I noticed the series of night-stick marks across his torso that made him look as if he'd been heavily char-grilled. If he was in pain, though, he didn't show it, and he was eagerly chomping on something grey and greasy that would've made a dung-beetle retch, yet seemed content enough doing so. Greta was in the midst of cooking her own Cordon Noir, so I clicked a finger at her, ordering up some for myself.

Joe pointed to the heap of charred inedibles upon his plate, then piled some into his mouth using a knife. 'Good C-Rats, Marty. Best I've had for a while.'

I sat down and muttered a quick prayer, the way I always do before attempting Greta's cooking. Just then, however, I was in the mood to eat anything that didn't bite back, so I hovered a little over Joe's plate and poked at some sausages with a finger, then the bacon, before sticking my finger into his egg and licking it. 'Yeah, it's not the worst. You already eaten that bit, Joe, or are you just about to?'

Joe seemed to go off his food all of a sudden. He slipped it across the table and I took a fork to it. Whatever it was, it wasn't too bad, so I got stuck into it straight away, with no immediate regard for the consequences. Minutes later, Greta fired a second plate of gunge across at me, sat at the table and got stuck into her own breakfast. I polished off Joe's, then went quickly to work on my own.

'So, what's on our agenda today, Whale?' Joe asked, wiping his hands all over the white tablecloth. 'You find out who the bad guys are yet?'

I shivered. I wasn't telling him who the bad guys were or he'd be off on a crusade, the result of which would perhaps leave an entire nation listening in as the word 'atrocity' was used several times over by those covering it on CNN. 'We're the bad guys, Joe – well, accordin' to Tork Malone. You eatin' that, Greta?'

'Nein.' Sourly, Greta shifted her plate towards me. 'I work on hall closet.'

She went to rise, but I grabbed her wrist solidly: The woman was a jackass of all trades and an Obenfuhrer of none. 'I'd appreciate it if you didn't,' I told her, satanically. 'I'm goin' to my room to do sleepy things, caprice?' She glared at me darkly. 'I've a lot of Zees to catch up on, so the closet can wait.' She pulled free and made for the sink, snorting a bunch of Germanic comments that I instinctively felt didn't concern beer-festivals and dancing.

'So,' Joe smiled, 'we're not workin' the case today?'

I ignored him, ate the rest of Greta's meal, then licked the pool of grease from the plate. Native Americans used to rub the grease of cooked meat onto their bodies, believing it kept their skin moist and wrinkle free. I'm no real perfectionist in those sort of cultural matters, so I usually make do with wiping the excess on my vest. Moments later, I left the room, slogged slowly upstairs and made for my bed.

'Remember, Greta, no renovation work,' I called back. 'And Joe – just stay put. Wake me in about eight hours. *Then* we'll go do some work.'

***

Joe woke me shortly after the crack of midday, obviously having no real concept of time in this, the real world. He offered me a bottle of lunch, but I didn't want it, so I let him drink it.

Greta – for once clued into the fact that her maidly duties involved doing things I wanted – passed me some freshly ironed slacks and a clean shirt. I showered and met Joe at the bottom of the stairs shortly after 1.00pm.

'See you later, Greta,' I said, on the way out. 'Anyone comes lookin' for me, tell them I'm out of town. Way out of town. Tell them I'm followin' a lead and may not be back until Monday. Maybe. Or even next week, I don't know exactly when'

Greta nodded disinterestedly, slammed the door after us, then returned to her own version of the New Mexico Caverns with her big noisy toy.

'Where we goin' anyhow, Whale?' Joe asked as we climbed into the car. 'You got a lead on somethin'?'

'We're going to stop off and make a few phone-calls,' I told him. 'And I need to get talkin' to Patricia Shirinski again, because things just aren't addin' up!'

ELEVEN

As Greta often makes it her business to find out things which aren't her business and turn a tidy profit from them soon after, I called the Shirinski household from an outside line and instantly recognised the elderly gardener's voice on the other end. Recalling his last meeting with Joe, I sincerely hoped he wouldn't wake up some night soon under six-foot of topsoil to find himself feeding the flowers on a more personal level than he'd ever imagined possible. 'She went out,' he told me curtly. 'She's down the crematorium seein' Abel off.'

Very briefly, I found myself envying Abel the certainty of his fate. For him, getting smoked was now just a harmless procedure, while for Yours Worriedly getting smoked was going to hurt real bad.

'They're torchin' him already?' I gasped, loosening my noose-like shirt collar. Outside, it was thirty in the shade, and, across the way, one guy was opening his car door with a set of oven-mitts. 'But they can't. We might need another autopsy to determine the trajectory of the bullet and...'

I heard a voice in the background, and then Patricia Shirinski suddenly took the line. 'What exactly do you want *now*, Mr Shale?'

As quickly as I could, I filled Patricia Shirinski in on the latest news. And, in truth, what with Abel's upcoming barbecue, I wasn't expecting her to be overly concerned at Maria Ellis's latest predicament, yet her sharp snort of derision made even my blood run cold as liquid oxygen.

'Well, I hope she gets the chair, but I doubt they'll keep her legs together long enough to strap her into it. They'll have to bury her in a Y-shaped coffin!'

I laughed dryly. Christ, this girl was a regular slave to contention, and holding so tightly onto a grudge that her fingers were probably bleeding all over the phone. 'Listen, lady, I'm glad you're happy, but I need to ask you a question about...'

'It's a nice change to see her paying for someone else's services,' she continued, ignoring the self-serving path I was rapidly trying to lay down and following the trail of her own spite. 'The bandy-legged little whore!'

'So, she's the type of girl who does for money what you do for pleasure – I get it in wide-screen! But now I need the address of your husband's downtown office. Somethin' in those letters might point me in the direction of the *real* killer.'

'There's nobody there at the moment,' Patricia returned coldly. 'We're all on our way to the crematorium, in case you've forgotten!'

'It's just that I have a theory which might help both you and Maria Ellis out of this mess. Couldn't you at least have them put Abel on a low gas for a while?'

Patricia slammed her phone down, and I frowned a deepy, wondering what had her in such a fluster. By working against me, she was working against herself. Still, because she was the sort of girl who didn't worry about spending money beforehand if she could do it afterwards, her lack of finances would soon have her clambering back into my side of the bed. I just prayed that, when she eventually decided to do so, I'd be in slightly better shape than either Abel or Frank. With that dim thought in mind, I slammed my phone down and rejoined Joe in the Buick. As my blood-pressure soared in the noon sun, I wiped at my forehead, ground the car up through the gears and took the freeway back into centre city

'So where we goin' now, Whale?'

'I need the address of Abel Shirinski's office, so we'll probably have to go over to the crematorium and see if we can get Patricia to lighten up a little.'

'Hey, I know that address.' I raised an eyebrow and he grinned a cheesy with relish. 'Marcie got it on the horn yesterday. I heard her repeatin' it as she wrote it down. It's at 273, Milan Avenue. You know it?'

I nodded a relieved, wheeled the car across two lanes amidst a series of screams and screeching brakes, then took the next exit in the direction of Masseria Park. As I did so, Joe smiled broadly. 'You know how I retain info like that, Marty? Three years in Recon, that's how!'

'Three years, eh?' He nodded, and I feigned a thoughtful. 'Any experience?'

'A little. Say, here's a thing' that's been gnawin' chunks from my ass for a while. You never did tell me why you weren't in 'Nam.' Joe's cheesy melted ever so slightly, and my woman's intuition told me that I, too, was just about to be grilled. 'Why was that anyhow?'

I swallowed hard, realising Joe was right: Until now, I'd avoided telling him why I'd dodged the Draft, because, well, Joe hears what he wants to hear. Sure, I could've mentioned that, in my opinion, people fighting for a national identity rarely have a personal one to fall back on, but that might ultimately have led to Joe standing in an identity-parade and to my corpse being barely identified. I could also have told him I was a conscientious objector, but conscientious and cowardly were the same thing in his language. Anyhow, strictly speaking, I'm not sure that run I'd made for the Canadian border during the Draft strictly constitutes a voluntary spinectomy, as it had taken a hell of a lot of nerve to swim down Niagara Falls with the Coastguard in hot pursuit.

Besides, cowardice can, at all times, also be called self-preservation.

'So, I never told you, eh?' Joe shook his head so hard the sawdust nearly fell out. 'Must've slipped my mind. Well, I've nothin' against war, Joe, as you know, because in this densely overpopulated world, I'm all for the odd cull. Just so long as it's abroad and we're talking foreigners, and plenty of them!'

Joe fixed me with an indecently wry smile. 'I hear you barkin', Big Dog!'

I nodded sagely. 'I know we all die at some time in our lives, too, usually some time near the end of them. And in my mind, a bullet is as quick a way to go as any.'

Joe slapped me on the back and laughed wildly. He was Curly, Larry, Mo and Charles Manson all baked up in the one banana fruitcake. 'So how come you never ended up in-Country, Whale? Sounds like you had the cookies for it alright.'

'Religion, Joe,' I replied humbly. 'Oh, I was up for it alright, and I had cookies so big I had to walk as if I'd rickets, y'know. I mean, I *wanted* in on that turkey-shoot as much as the next man. But religion – that was the problem.'

'I thought you weren't a fuckin' Conchy!' Joe suddenly wore a corrugated frown, and his haunted look returned to haunt us both.

'It's spooky the way you pick up on things so quickly, Joe. But it isn't the same thing. Y'see, I didn't dodge the war. It's just that I got whacked with the same God-stick as Cassius Clay. We both turned Muslin, for Chrissakes! And he's a brave man – you tryin' to say he isn't a brave man?'

At times, I can hit Joe with a paradox. Clay – aka Mohammed Ali – was a hero of his; and, like many lunatics, Joe tended to dismiss things that weren't strictly black or white. For example, he could never understand how Cassius could ignore the war, yet climb into a ring with some of the fiercest men on the planet. Still, saying that, religion as a sole explanation was way too ethereal for Joe. With him, if you couldn't break it or make it bleed, it didn't exist. He frowned heavily.

'I've heard of your God,' Joe informed me, seriously. 'Chinese isn't he? But you aren't Chinese, Marty. You're a honky like me, so what's the deal?'

'You heard of Muesli?' I asked in surprise. He nodded uncertainly, and I faked a diamond-white toothy. 'Of course you have: Little bald guy with wings, fat as a poisoned pup, fires arrows at people and makes them fall under the Big Delusion? Yeah, that's Muesli alright. Sure, he's not white, but he's powerful.' Joe nodded again, and I smiled thinly. 'Not as powerful as your own eternally-angry-yet-immensely-forgivin' white God maybe, but, yeah, powerful enough to make things happen if you make enough craven idles of him and maybe dance around a bonfire naked for him every now and then. Sure, I'll admit I don't practise as much these days. I'm sort of a lapsed Muesli-ite, as it were. Stopped goin' to bar-mitzvahs, takin' communion and everythin'.'

Joe stared deep into the build up of traffic for a moment and nodded a thoughtful, before suddenly chuckling wryly as he spotted some guy in a wheelchair getting mugged at the junction of Geist and Mackey by two kids. I smiled wanly. With a few well-chosen words, I'd short-circuited Joe's reasoning processes, and he was back enjoying the simple things in life again.

Ten minutes later, we reached Milan Avenue, which was situated in a small warehouse district east of Hooch Creek. The Shirinski's Industrial Investigation and Home Security unit was a dingy little office with barred windows and cameras above the door. I knocked, not really expecting an answer as Patricia Shirinski had told me there was nobody here. I knocked again, then peered in through several windows, yet nothing was moving.

At the third knock, however, the door was opened by a strikingly pretty young lady of about 21 years of age, the type who'd have looked equally good pursing her lips suggestively at you from the centre-spread of your picture-book educational. She wore a smart low-cut blouse and a grey business suit, and her auburn hair was tied into a neat bun. She also wore a little gold chain around her neck with a tiny gold aeroplane at its centre. I found my eyes drawn instantly towards the landing strip.

'Can I help you?' she asked, trying to draw my gaze up to meet her own. 'We're actually closed at the moment, but I could give you a brochure.'

'Am I hot or is it you?' I asked, feigning a bashful. 'You have to excuse me here, lady, but the better a woman looks, the longer I do.'

She smiled, blushed and drew her blouse in tight in an attempt to put that little plane in its hangar, yet there just wasn't enough material. 'So, uhm, how may I help you?' she continued, still attempting to catch my eye. 'Or *can* I actually help you?'

I willed down my Horn of Plenty, pushed all carnal thoughts aside and raised my eyes to meet hers. Then I told her who I was, and she introduced herself, in turn, as Anna Delaney, secretary and sole employee in the retail end of I.I H.S.

'Patricia Shirinski told me this place was closed,' I said evenly. 'I thought everyone was at the funeral.'

Anna dropped her gaze, clearly embarrassed. 'I wanted to go,' she replied softly. 'Abel was the kindest boss in the world and he used to call me his Little Plum...' Her voice trailed off, and for a moment I thought she was about to cry, yet she took a deep breath, heaved her mammaries once or twice and composed herself. 'But Patricia's financial affairs need to be kept liquid until the insurance money comes through, so it's business as usual until then.'

I raised an eyebrow. 'The insurance on her husband?' Anna nodded evenly. 'She never mentioned that.' Instantly, something clicked into place: If Abel was found to have been carrying a weapon with the intention of using it for nefarious purposes, it was almost certain his life-insurance would be voided. Now I knew why Patricia hoped the police couldn't connect Abel with the gun they'd found at his side – if they did, she was getting squat. 'Of course, you must remember, Miss Delaney, we all know money talks, yet it doesn't always tell the truth.'

She frowned heavily. 'Whatever are you trying to say, Mr Shale?'

I sighed deeply. 'I'll cut to the cheese here, lady, and you should brace yourself, because sometimes the truth has a way of hittin' you hard in the gut like a pointy stick. What I'm sayin' is Abel and Patricia were making a lot of money, but makin' money and keepin' it are different things entirely. Moreover, Patricia's insurance claim can't be wrapped up until this murder case is done and dusted. And that might take a very long time.' I looked her square in the chest. 'Now do you understand?'

'I think so.' She nodded glumly. 'You'd better come in. And why don't you invite your friend in. He may see something he likes. I'll have to presume that any business we receive from here on in can only be good business.'

I called Joe over – reluctantly. We entered the small office and the Ham took on a big-eye, amazed by the array of spying goods on display in the locked glass cabinets. He moved slowly from shelf to shelf, studying each item in turn. Anna was right: Joe was the sort who'd mortgage his house to keep up with the latest in Do-It-To-Others-Yourself gadgetry, yet he was also the type to sell his television set to buy a video recorder. She might get herself a sale here yet.

We left Joe in the display area and moved into an inner office. I looked around. There were a few pictures of Anna in a skimpy bikini on the desk, and on the wall a few more of Abel and Patricia attending some wedding. Once again, I found myself bitterly wondering just why all the beautiful secretaries loved their bosses. I'd seen a photo of Abel in the Shirinski household: The guy had a phiz like a prize-fighter who'd fought his last six fights in the one night, yet he'd been dipping his pen into Maria and Patricia's ink-wells to no end. Whether Little Plum here had also been letting him pluck cherries from her fruit basket remained to be seen, yet here she was, all dewy at his memory.

Then there was Chester – his secretary was probably giving him all sorts of loving as well. Me, I had Marcie, a persistent assistant whose eyes were filled with termination determination, and the only thing she went about jumping on was my case. Where in the name of Lucifer's fucking fork was I going wrong?

Anna told me to take a seat, then asked how she could help.

'I'm interested in lookin' at some letters that Abel keeps...kept...in his safe. Can you get them for me?'

'I don't know if I should. I haven't had any word from Patricia.' She wrung her hands together, frowned. 'I'd like to help, really, but...'

'You don't want to mix business with pleasure,' I said, winking at her. 'Sure, you're havin' a good time chattin' to me, and you think that if we let business get in the way, it mightn't go anywhere from that...'

She regarded me quizzically. 'I don't understand, Mr Shale. This visit is purely business, isn't it?'

I blushed, mentally letting go of the shitty end a stick. 'Uhm, yeah, business, sure. I'm just testin' you to see where your loyalties lie.'

'Hmm, I think I know what you're saying,' she replied uncertainly. 'Anyhow, that aside, I really don't know if I should help you. I may end up losing my job'

'Your job isn't safe anyway, lady. I've known insurance agencies keep cases on a thread for even a hint of a discrepancy, and this case smells like a trawler in a heatwave. You have bills the same as the rest of us, I presume?'

Which was the argument that swung it: From the disturbed gaze upon Anna's face, I knew then that at least some of her loyalties were as liquid as mine. She opened the safe that was cleverly secreted in the floor under her seat. As she did so, I espied a used typewriter ribbon in the bin. I picked it out carefully so as not to gain her attention. Anna rifled through the safe's contents, then handed me six thick envelopes. I didn't bother to scrutinise them there and then. There'd be time for that later.

'I'll get these back to you,' I told her as I pocketed them. 'And now I need a little information on this.' I produced the small earpiece I'd found down in Sky-Towers. 'You know what it is?'

Anna took it from me and examined it carefully. 'It looks like an earpiece from one of our discreet surveillance receivers,' she replied evenly. 'The 22mm model, if I'm not mistaken.' She rose from her chair. 'We have a complete unit outside in the display cabinet. Follow me and I'll show it to you.'

If Anna saw Joe trying to prise open the sealed cabinet which contained the pen-cameras she didn't say anything. And Joe at least had the sense to put his pocket-knife away as we exited the smaller room and entered the office proper. I nudged him hard in the ribs and whispered, 'You'd be helpin' yourself more, Joe if you helped yourself less.'

'Just lookin', Marty, nothin' else.'

'Yeah, well, I'd rather be partnered up with the sort of person who's content enough to leave their footprints in the Sands of Time, not their fingerprints.'

As I spoke, Anna unlocked one of the cabinets and brought a tiny recording device over to me. It was about the size of a matchbox. 'You could put this anywhere in a room and listen in from the next,' she told me. 'And you can clearly hear everything being said within a radius of thirty-feet or so of the transmitter. No static, no muffled sound. It's the latest in aural surveillance. The range is greater with our larger models, of course.'

I nodded. 'And how is it powered?'

'By battery. A tiny nine-volt cell that lasts about four-months at a time.'

I nodded again, wishing I could probe her more deeply, and maybe ask her a few more questions too; though in the latter regard, at least, my expertise was severely lacking.

'Well, you've been very helpful, Miss Delaney.' I shook her dainty hand and she smiled. She wasn't too comfortable with Joe's warrior grasp but, again, her professionalism showed through.

She led us out towards the door. Before we exited the store, she said, 'Do you really think Frank Ellis was consumed with jealousy about his wife's past, Mr Shale? I mean, the affair happened so long ago. Why would he kill Abel now?'

I smiled, pushed Joe out the door and stepped outside into the near-debilitating afternoon sun. Anna moved after us.

'There's a few things you should know about men, Miss Delaney – they all want to marry the sexually experienced virgin. Oh, and no man minds a girl havin' a past, just so long as they don't have to meet up with it in either the present or the future. Anyhow, time will tell.'

Anna nodded undecidedly, fixed me with a pale smile, said goodbye, then moved inside and closed the door behind her. I led Joe back to the car.

'Wow, Marty, that sweetheart is stacked!' Joe smiled. He went at a clenched fist and forearm, and I nodded. 'Looks like a dead-heat in a zeppelin race! Wouldn't mind gettin' it on with her for a while.'

I laughed thinly, aware that Joe's idea of a dirty weekend more likely involved changing the oil filter in a T62. 'Yeah, wouldn't mind pressin' her buttons myself. Girl's got a regular breast-fest goin' on.'

Joe grinned and continued talking at me for a time. I keyed the engine into life, then drove off without really listening to what he was saying. It was something inane about how he'd love to aurally investigate Anna, then something else about the latest in Snoop-a-Vision pens, about compasses that pinpointed your whereabouts in the world at any given moment, and watches that relayed your position via satellite back to Command Headquarters.

None of which would've been of any use to Joe, of course. Truth was, he was Grade-A schmuck and chances were he couldn't have found his own ass with a hand-mirror and an atlas.

TWELVE

I was sitting in my car – about fifty-yards from the brownstone, with the engine idling over and the bonnet pointed in the general direction of Mexico – when Joe relayed the news I so wanted to hear: Marcie was nowhere to be seen. Naturally, as that same message was first relayed in Morse and guttural woodpigeon, it took a bit of decoding, yet all became clear as soon as Joe leapt from the hedgerow, beamed a 100 watt and thumbed me an A-OK. What Joe had sadly failed to add, however, was that my home currently provided sanctuary and succour for another set of itinerants, namely Clay and Muddy Rivers.

Inside Chez Shale, I peered momentarily into my now elongated hall closet and winced, wondering how Greta's *lebensraum* revival was affecting the neighbours, before shrugging unconcernedly and ambling into the kitchen after Joe. There, Clay and Muddy sat at the table sipping on *my* beers as if they belonged, and Greta was cooking a stew on the hob, which wasn't simmering, more festering. Again, we're talking about Greta's own version of nouvelle cuisine here, whereby the less food you get, the happier you are. That said, my three uninvited guests refused to be outdone by sight, smell or experience, and, moments later, they got stuck into the lot as if they'd got word of an imminent famine.

'Hi, uncle Marty,' Muddy grinned. 'We were just passin' by. We're drivin' down the coast to the casinos, and we were wonderin' if you'd like to tag along.'

I felt like saying, 'The next time you're passing, I'd be grateful if you would.' But I held off, realising this might be a good time to off-load the Italian Scallion. Or then again, I mused brightly, I could also hit the casinos and try to win back the money I owed Gus Diamond – providing someone staked me some stake-money.

I casually de-tabbed a beer, fingered Joe's stew, tasted it, then winced. 'Yeah, I might do that. Sayin' that, you need moolah to make moolah, and I'm moolah-ed out.' I willed my eyes funereal and turned to Clay, making a silent request for a large bequest. 'Might have to borrow a few bucks from you though, buddy.'

Now, Clay's meaner that a skinned baboon in the midday sun, so his response was hardly surprising. 'I've nothin' on me at the moment, Marty. *Not a cent!*'

'Yeah, you have,' Muddy cut in, innocently. 'I gave you the fifty I owed you just before we came in.'

'That'll do fine for now, Clay. I'll get the other 450 later.' I looked away before he could mutter a response. 'Well, grab the rest of that beer and let's go!'

Joe scooped up the rest of the brewskies as if they were of woman born. 'Fuckin' A!' he said happily. 'But, hey, Marty, could you do me a favour?'

'If you need to borrow money, Joe, Clay's the man.' I winked at Clay and he near faded Caucasian.

Joe waved a quick hand. 'Shit, no, I get a small fortune off the government every month for keepin' my mouth shut about the conspiracy. No, I'd just like to be the one to drive us down the shore. And in my own vehicle too, if that's alright?'

'Is that the, uhm, armoured car thing I saw you in the other day, Joe?'

'Yeah, the Humvee. It's all-weather, land *and* terrain. So, how about it?'

I could have asked him to backtrack a little, to tell us more about the conspiracy. Him and Oliver North? Him and Lee Harvey? Still, it didn't matter. I needed horse-power, not ass-power, and he was only getting behind the wheel of my ride over someone's dead body.

Not mine, of course. But his, sure. Or maybe Clay's.

'Ah, can't let you, Joe,' I weaselled. 'You're insured to drive T2's, and my Buick doesn't crunch things beneath it, doesn't float, has no roll-bars, and is built for one side of the road only – minor details like that.'

Joe didn't reply. He just gave me the Japanese eyes, crushed his empty beer can in one hand, then rose and stormed out the back door without a word. Which was good, in one sense, in that I thought we were getting rid of him, but not so good in another, in that I'd rather have Joe offend me verbally in the present than attempt to off-end me physically sometime in the future. Anyhow, as it was, I didn't have time to consider whether Joe was going to vent me or his wrath, because, at that moment, two things happened. Firstly, there was an urgent rapping on the back door; and, seconds later, there followed the unmistakable report of a low-calibre gunshot.

The shot, as a matter of record, merely served to reinforce my suspicions about the knock on the door, in that I knew it wasn't Opportunity standing on the doorstep, because in my life it rarely is. Still, my primary instinct wasn't to dive under the kitchen table and grab a mouthful of carpet, unlike Clay, Muddy and Greta, all of whom went pancake instinctively. Instead, I crawled behind the thickest kitchen wall and stared out, as best I could, into the dense Everglades which passed as my yard. Yep, I mused sourly, the Marty Shale Camp was under fire once more, yet this time it was under fire for real.

Still, just then, I wasn't all too concerned. Y'see, I know Joe can be very childish if he doesn't get his own way, and when that shot rang out, I thought he'd finally creamed himself. Of course, one bullet wasn't going to be enough to penetrate that head, and he sure wouldn't have been blowing brains out of there, but at least he'd have been showing an interest. So, you can imagine my dismay when Greta finally opened the door and Joe ran back inside again, clutching his shoulder and cursing like a born-again Christian in a brothel.

'You're bleedin',' Muddy gasped in horror.

Joe started to fumble around in his belt for a handgun – and an extremely big handgun at that! 'I don't have time to bleed,' he replied in John Wayne-ese. 'And remember, kid, anythin' that doesn't kill you only makes you stronger.'

'Or leaves you susceptible to gangrene,' Clay muttered from under the table.

'Yeah,' I hedged. 'Listen, Joe, I knew a guy took three wounds like that once: He only recovered from two of them. Might be best to quit while you're ahead.'

Joe frowned a corrugated. 'I knew I shouldn't have talked. Knew it!'

I nodded pensively. In Joe's mind, this was a CIA plot to take him out before he unveiled Sinto-gate, and it would've been far too easy for this to be the work of a crazed secretary or a frustrated gangster.

I pulled out my Magnum, checked the chambers and drew back the hammer, even as I tried to catch Joe's gaze. 'C'mon, Joe, you're scarin' the doo out of everyone. Did you even *see* the shooter?' I watched in horror as he pushed a bloodied clip of armour-piercing into his sawn-off elephant gun. 'Was it a male? Or maybe even some sort of a female, even?'

Joe shook me a Grim Reaper. 'Nope! But then, no one will be able to actually tell when I'm finished, will they? Now, are you goin' out there with me, Marty?'

I shook him a no-no, not really in the mood for doing a Butch and Sundance. 'Look, Joe, this isn't the right time to go swannin' out there and singin' your swan-song, caprice?' He nodded uncertainly. 'Good. Now, who's to say the person who fired that shot is after us? After all, around here, people shoot at each other all of the time simply because they're too lazy to stroll down the range!'

Which wasn't exactly a lie: In fact, there are some places in the city where, if you aren't home by 10-00pm they declare you legally dead, and if the coroner finds any less than four bullet wounds on your corpse he writes it off as natural causes.

'Look, tell you what, I'll go out there and reason with whoever it is.' I raised my palm-heels. 'In a while, that is. Let's all do a spot of *very* easy-breathin' first.'

'You're right, Marty,' Clay rasped. 'Besides, it's probably you they want anyway.'

I shook my head. 'You're some friend, Clay. One minute I'm the mutt's nuts with you, next thing I'm in the mutt's hut. Good job you're with me, not against me!'

Now Clay Rivers was doing his impression of a river – small at the head and big at the mouth. I sighed angrily, then edged the door open a little. Suddenly, Joe raced past me and threw himself through the small gap into the dark yard. Within seconds, we heard the sound of five cannon-like reports. Moments later, a single shot was fired in return, this one low-calibre, very much like a firecracker going off in a tin can. Then I heard Joe scream. I knew it was him as it sounded way too feminine to be coming from anything as small and feeble as your average woman. Instinctively, I slammed the door fast, stuck a foot hard against it and got down low to the floor.

'Open it open,' Greta cried in her nonsensical version of English. She waved her arms about, tried to crawl out from under the table. It took the combined strength of Clay and Muddy to keep her in place. 'You get him back in here. Now!'

'He'll be fine,' I snorted. I eased the door open a little, peered outside and saw Joe's lifeless body on the tarmaccadamed driveway. 'Tell you what, Greta, *you* go get him. There's an Iron Cross in it for you if you do. What d'ya say?'

'Is he alright?' Muddy whispered as Greta went into a strop.

I shook my head dolefully. 'He was never alright, kid.'

'Is he...dead?' Muddy's mouth was agape.

'If you want the truth, kid, I've seen more life in a tramps vest.' Another shot rang out and I slammed the door shut, then moved in tight to the wall. 'Yeah, shame, but that's the way he would've wanted to go. Either that or takin' it straight through the rear-door of a dogship flyin' low over Happy Valley. Still, he was a stand-up kind of guy before he finally laid down his life, and I can't recall him ever sayin' or doin' anythin' of real worth, but I swear I'll never forget him.' I waved a dismissive hand. 'Still, that's enough of the mushy sentimentality...'

'Yeah, you're sure takin' it hard,' Clay rasped. 'You should try not to get so emotionally involved in things, Marty.'

'I'll sob later, Clay,' I snapped. 'And, alright, he was a good sport for doin' what he did, sure, but the trouble with bein' a good sport is you have to lose to prove it. Now, there's a shooter out there, so why don't you phone the police while I keep the door covered.' As an afterthought, I added, 'Oh, and you better get an ambulance over here too, I suppose. Just in case it's too early to hope.'

Clay called me a few unflattering names, then sidled crab-like into the hall and got on the phone. I got in close to the door. 'Hey, you out there!' I shouted. 'I don't know what your problem is, but the cops are on their way. Why don't you go back to your gamblin' den, or even your office, or, y'know, wherever it is you're from?'

I slammed the door shut as another shot rang out. Wood splintered in the top left hand corner of the frame.

'Why are you tellin' them to do that, uncle Marty?' Muddy asked hotly. 'Don't you want the police to catch them?'

'No, well, yeah, of course.' I shot him a doubtful. 'It's just a preventative measure to ensure *they* – whoever *they* are, and none of us know for sure who they are, even if we see them – don't storm the house. Know what I'm sayin'?'

Muddy nodded and frowned simultaneously. 'I don't know what you're sayin', uncle Marty, but I think I know what you mean.'

'Good. Maybe you're not a chip off the old blockhead after all.'

As it turned out, that was the end of the shot-fest. Mo Breasley arrived some minutes later in a squad car, an ambulance in tow, sirens blazing and tyres screeching. I peered out the front window. Tork Malone was sitting in the car next to him. 'Shit!' I snapped at Clay. 'Ten bucks says I get the blame for this.'

Still very on edge, Clay shrugged me a whatever, then sat and finished his beer.

Tork beat a tattoo on my front door with his fists, then hit it a kick with his size-tens before Greta opened it for him and his merry men. Then the senior detective stormed in as if it was his country and he was king. He stopped in the middle of the hall, pointed to a spot on the carpet where he probably wished they were doing a portrait of me in chalk, and said, 'Get over here, Shale.'

As I walked meekly towards him, Greta led Mo Breasley into the yard. 'There's a stiff out here,' Mo shouted back seconds later. 'Accordin' to the maid, the guy's a war veteran. He bought it tryin' to defend the place.'

Malone's ears pricked at that statement, then he glared at me accusingly, hoping to prick my conscience. But he'd have no chance of doing that, the prick, and the sooner he got his prick out of my conscience the better! Still, I feigned a subservient. It was only right after all, because I'd gone and killed one of *them*.

'Someone take a bullet for you, Marty?' Tork sneered. 'Yeah, well, maybe it's as well, because if you ever got shot we'd have to slaughter dozens of chickens for the blood transfusions.' I feigned a cheesy, but Tork leaned in close, all halitosis and ice. 'Don't grin at me, Marty. We're goin' downtown, and, unless you talk, you aren't comin' back. Y'know what I'm diggin' at here?'

I nodded feebly, raised my palm-heels. 'Fine, just so long as you know I had a series of X-rays done recently, so everyone knows where all my bones were up until today.'

As Tork was about to reply, Mo came in from the yard. 'It's alright,' he grinned. 'The guy's alive. Seems he fell and hit his head on a rock.'

'I hope he hasn't put a hole in my fuckin' driveway,' I muttered, sitting down.

Malone pulled me up by the lapel of my jacket, not an easy task by any stretch. 'Get a paddy-wagon over here,' he told Mo. 'A strong one.' He threw me as best he could in his deputy's direction. 'I want all of them locked up until they're ready to talk. Especially this one.'

'You heard him, Mo. He's havin' a go at me over my proportions.'

'Just sit the fuck down, Marty, and watch you don't break the fuckin' seat!'

As Tork then left as if he'd never been, Mo sat down beside me and shook his head. 'Does anyone like you, Marty?'

I sighed a heartfelt, dropped my head. 'My mother – I think. But if you're takin' an opinion poll, I suggest you maybe start in a sewer and work your way down into the bowels of the earth.'

***

131

Unfortunately, Joe's wounds turned out to be little more than scratches. He was returned to our cell an hour later with a bandage on his shoulder and one on his arm, looking barely the worse for his adventure. We were in the darkest cell in Administration – I knew that because the No Smoking sign was in Braille – and Tork was standing there staring at Joe through slitted eyes.

'Don't I know you from somewhere?'

'Maybe I saved your ass back in 'Nam,' Joe replied seriously.

Tork laughed scathingly. 'This isn't a good time to start flingin' monkey dung,' he said acidly. 'No, I'm talkin' about a bit more recent. From down around the State Hospital, maybe?'

Joe shook him an innocent. 'To the best of my recollection, I can't actually recall.'

Tork nodded complacently. 'Maybe after a bit more time in here it'll come back to you.'

Joe raised his head defiantly and crossed his arms. He was wearing a look that said he wouldn't speak if you took a blow-torch to his parts.

'You can't hold us here,' Clay protested. 'We didn't do anythin'. The only thing that we're guilty of is bein' Marty's friend.'

'You wouldn't know a friend if they threw themselves on a fuckin' frag-grenade for you, Clay,' Joe cut in, vehemently. 'Friends don't rat each other out. We'll do our stretch, standin' on our heads if necessary.'

Tork laughed dryly again. He signalled to a nearby police officer 'Tell you what, they can all go except for Shale. Me and him have a bit of talkin' to do.'

'See you soon, uncle Marty,' Muddy said as the police officer opened the cell door and urged him outside. 'But, if not, we'll write you every week.'

'Thanks, kid. I'll be in Lubyanka. Salt Mine No.9, third set of manacles on the left.'

Before he left, Joe stopped in front of me, took my arm in that familiar warrior's grasp. 'Remember, Marty, stone walls do not a prison make, nor iron bars a cage.'

I sighed wearily. 'Sure, Joe, not unless the architect has it down on paper that they do.'

Moments later, Tork and I reached the holding room and the senior detective closed the door behind us, effectively sealing us off from the outside world. 'You just can't keep your nose clean,' he sighed. 'But this is your chance to get into my good books, Shale. I want you to tell me exactly what Maria Ellis told you. Y'see, as much as it pains me to admit this, you may actually be on the right track.'

THIRTEEN

Tork didn't make mistakes – or, at least, he didn't think so. So, an admission that I *might* be right meant he *might* be wrong. It was a lot to take in, yet I didn't ask him to repeat himself, content just then that he wasn't going Ahab at this particular Whale. It was only when he told one of his men to fetch us some coffee that I began to suspect this was a trap. It had to be – why else was he being nice? I sat there at the interview table in that holding room sweating like a hog on a griddle, certain he was trying to set me up for a fall. And, of course, he got into the small-talk first, trying to soften me up a little. But mentally I'm tougher than a rhino's instep, and he didn't fool me for an instant.

'You're lookin' good, Shale. You on some kind of a diet?'

'Yeah, I eat as much as I want, but I don't swallow. It's a new concept in weight loss, and apparently it's all the rage with us catwalk types.'

He nodded disinterestedly, took to pacing the room. 'That's nice. Anyhow, I'm real busy right now. As well as this case, I've got two suicides, a gangland hit and a host of misdemeanours to look into. One of the suicides is a John Doe, though I suspect he's a doctor as I can't read his suicide note. The other guy was at a bachelor party and jumped off a high-rise, so it seems his last fling was just that. As for the gangland hit, well, that's par for the course in this city. But the Shirinski case has me bugged. What are your thoughts on it?'

'I still think a third or even a fourth party was involved,' I replied sagely. As the coffee arrived, I drew my jacket lapels in closer. There were six letters in my inside pocket which I didn't want Tork getting his heavily-callused paws on. 'And

I think I know who they were.' I adopted a smuggy, stared him straight in his obsidian orbs for half a second, then quickly relinquished my gaze.

Tork circled me, shark-like, nodding. 'Well, if that's the case, we can do business here.' He took out a packet of cigarettes, offered me one.

I took several, lit one, and sipped at the coffee. It was industrial strength, with the fluidity of setting tar. A pleasant enough distraction, considering.

'So,' Tork said easily. 'This theory of yours, I'm waitin'...'

'Well, the upshot is that Patricia Shirinski is the main perp,' I told him with a self-satisfied grin. 'The bitch is in it all the way up to her reconstructed neck!'

Tork nodded, but his eyes didn't. 'Alright, let's go with that for now. Why?'

'She has a motive for killin' Abel and for slicin' up Frank Ellis. Y'see, she figured her husband was back puttin' the meat in Maria's sandwich soon after they arrived back in town. So, she waits in Skytowers, bumps off Abel and frames Frank, figurin' she'll cash in on the no-claims. You're talkin' bereaved *and* relieved.'

'All right, say that's the case. That means she's in for a big pay-day soon. So, why would she want to jeopardise that by goin' after Frank Ellis?'

'To make Maria suffer – jealousy, pure and sinister! And when she hears Frank is hospitalised, she figures she can put a cherry on the icin' she's already slapped on the cake. So she dresses as a nurse, enters the recovery room when both Frank and Maria are dozin', slips a mickey into Maria's coffee, then carves Frankie up like a Sunday joint. Money and revenge – prime motives.'

Tork ceased nodding, shook me a no-no. 'That's all very well, *if* we discount the witnesses who can account for Patricia's movements on the night of each crime. On the night of Abel's murder, she was in Bogart's restaurant uptown in view of fifty witnesses. And last night she was layin' on a post-funeral bash at home for thirty more. Are you suggestin' she slipped out of there and over to the hospital with the bread-knife in the middle of makin' the sandwiches?'

'Maybe.' I shrugged uneasily, dragged deeply at my cigarette.

'Or maybe it was her doppelganger, right? Or a long-lost twin sister, who then skipped town on a freight-train shortly afterwards, but returned to shoot at you today because you're gettin' too close. Is that it, *Sherlock*?'

This was more like it: Classic Tork! Any minute now he'd shout something about having a Big Game licence, his cheeks would inflame like a set of mandrill's buttocks and he'd go at me with a soft-edged phonebook or a hard-edged baton until I ended up squealing louder than the last lobster in the fish restaurant.

I shrugged a non-committed. 'Again, you, uhm might be onto somethin'.'

Tork sat on the edge of the table, staring at me coldly. 'Then, if it *was* indeed someone other than Frank Ellis who fired the fatal shot, we have a rather absurd timeline. Frank says he was knocked out by the real killer, that Abel was then shot dead, and that a gun was supposedly planted upon both him and Abel before the killer absconded through the central closet, all of which would've taken at least a minute or two. After this, Frank supposedly came to, got up – gun in hand – and found himself standing over the body of his former associate, wonderin' what had happened. But the janitor swears he walked into the room only *seconds* after the shot was fired. Does that sound in any way strange to you at all?'

'It's a big buildin',' I hedged. 'Time is relative, sounds can get sucked in by Black Holes, then re-emerge in alternate dimensions, and, uhm, things and stuff...' I trailed off lamely and sucked an inch out of my cigarette. Tork had blown so many holes in my theory it couldn't have held water in a monsoon. 'Look, you aren't hearin' me out,' I said defensively. 'There was a fourth person – the gardener – and maybe...'

'That old guy?' Tork snorted. 'He's so slow that if he went down there to kill you in the evenin', he'd come back that same mornin'.'

'No way! He's a regular fuckin' Ninja – I've seen him in action!'

'You're the one livin' in an alternate dimension, Whale,' Tork laughed. He waved a hand towards the door. 'Get the fuck outta here. I'd get more sense out of the National Enquirer.'

'You haven't told me what you think I may've been right about,' I said, rising. 'I thought this was a two way-street. Instead, you've run me head-first and blinkered up a blind alley and given me zilch in the way of squat-shit!'

Tork nodded his approval at my use of untamed metaphor. 'Alright, Marty, but, unlike you, I'll have to rely on facts to pad my story out. So, firstly, one of the hospital nurses says my officer was sleepin' when he should've been guardin' Frank Ellis, which means anyone could have walked in sliced him. And secondly, when Mal Brennan took a sample from Maria's coffee, he found traces of a sedative. Seems Maria could've been tellin' the truth after all.'

'Could've-smood've! So, did you release her yet?'

'I can't. She still has probable cause. She *smood've* tried to kill her husband, before druggin' herself to cover her tracks.' He sighed deeply. 'Don't you get it, Marty? These days, your average murderer is a cold-blooded no-good who plans things in detail. Also, Maria Ellis said young Tommy was visitin' a friend on the night Abel was murdered, so she was home alone. Therefore she has no alibi for both murders, and thus she stays put for the foreseeable future.'

'Well, no offence, but it sounds a bit wishy-washy to me.'

'After the fairy tale you spun me?' Tork gasped. 'My own stories sound nothin' if not reasonable in comparison. Go forth, Whale. Go forth and multiply!'

I rose indignantly from my seat, put the cup on the desk, stubbed my cigarette butt on the stone floor and watched him revelling for a few seconds in his own wit.

'Yeah, well, I'll tell you somethin' else for nothin',' I said caustically.

Tork shook his head and smiled broadly. 'What's that, Landslide?'

'I must be thinkin' along the right lines. Someone thinks so, or they wouldn't have been tryin' to blow me away this afternoon.'

Tork stopped laughing, suddenly lost in thought. I slammed out off the holding-room before he could think of a reply, a small yet hollow victory tucked under my belt. The way things were going, however, he'd have another gangland hit on his plate real soon, and Yours Fatally would be playing the Corpse in the Copse as part of a Happy Valentine's Day massacre.

Jeez, it didn't even bear thinking about!

Still, as luck would have it, I ran into Tork's senior forensic expert, Mal Brennan, in the corridor. Or should I say that, half-blind as he is, Mal ran into me. As I bypassed him, I reached into my inside pocket and pulled out the typewriting ribbon and twenty dollars. With Mal, there's no real need for talking when money is present, and he accepted my offer with a grin. 'Monday?' he said. I nodded, the transaction short and sweet. This was one guy whose fillings would never come down with metal fatigue.

That done, I made my way through the bowels of Administration. After thirty warm and uncomfortable hours in that hole, it sure felt good to finally pop out onto the sidewalk. There, as steam rose from my soiled clothes in the heat of the morning and a malodorous smell hung around me like a wraith, the true and good regarded me as something they'd rather not step in and hurried on by. And so, feeling more or less the way I looked, I opted for as many back alleys as I could find to lead me back home to the brownstone.

***

I quickly discovered that Joe, Muddy and Clay had returned to my place after their short incarceration, and Greta was the first to pointedly inform me that Marcie hadn't either phoned or dropped by. I tried to get her on the line at her apartment but there was no answer, so I hurriedly dead-bolted both my front and back door before grabbing a beer and sitting at the kitchen table.

'Wasn't that long, was I?' I asked the assembly of lunatics who joined me there seconds later. It was 5-20pm by the clock on the wall.

'Not in God's great scheme of things,' Clay agreed, dryly. 'What did you do – squawk like a parrot?'

'Uh, uh! I ran my theory past Tork and he was extremely impressed.'

'And he took you seriously?' Clay asked, incredulously.

'Hey, I get asked to read encyclopaedias in public, that's how seriously I'm taken.'

'They any idea who was doing the shootin'?' Muddy asked, pensively.

'There are a lot of people out there who'd consider my death a mercy killin',' I replied grimly. 'Serious people with serious attitudes.' Muddy smiled, yet everyone else regarded me seriously. 'So, uhm, are we still goin' down the shore?'

'Sure we are,' Joe said, transforming his serious into a freaky. 'We'll hang out in my aunt's hooch, spend all day Sunday playin' the crap tables, then get back up here by Monday mornin' before the trail runs cold.'

I shrugged lamely, figuring that as good a plan as any, then we bundled out into the car. Our first stop was a mini-mall, where we bought a heap of pepperoni sausage. Then we stopped at a liquor store, where we bought several crates of cheap beer and potent wine. After that, we skipped town, roaring along the coast road at 90mph with Clowntown radio racking up the latest hits. An hour later we were at the shore, with the warm evening wind blowing in across the ocean. Crowds gathered on the boardwalk, lovers sauntered in and out of the little open-faced store-fronts, and the entire place was lit by a blaze of gold, purple and white neon.

But we weren't there for the sights. So, I reminded Clay about the money he'd promised to lend me – indefinitely, as he so rightly feared, yet no words passed on the subject – and he slipped me another 450. Before leaving the car, we tanked up on beer, ate a sausage or two to fill upon healthy carbs, then entered the Albino Casino, a smile on our faces and possessed of a strong feeling that Lady Luck, if not on our side, might for once cast her lust-filled eyes on one or two others first.

After cashing in our money for tokens and chips, however, I veered off in a different direction to everyone else. Thing is, I don't like people hanging over me when I'm gambling with their money – it makes me feel as if I owe them something.

'See you all back here in a few hours,' I grinned. 'And don't think I won't treat you the same as always when I win – you still aren't gettin' anythin' from me.'

They laughed, avarice in their eyes, and left me to my own vices and devices. As Joe made for the poker room, Muddy and Clay hit the blackjack tables. Me, I sauntered casually into the gaming room and took a seat between a few aging slot-jockeys at a dollar-chomping machine that outsized me by 150 pounds. There, I piled my tokens high in the tray, before whistling over a pretty young bit of fluff in a bunny suit. 'You shall be my waitress for this evenin',' I informed her pleasantly.

'This is Jane's area,' she replied, as if somewhat relieved. She pointed to Jane – who was like a bad photograph, in that she was overdeveloped and overexposed – and I shuddered. Still, when she came strolling over to join us, that didn't deter me from taking a handful of sandwiches and a few Martinis off her serving tray.

'You get your ass back here when you hear this thing payin' out,' I told the first young lady. 'Then we'll go somewhere and make a night of it.'

She smiled wearily, as if she'd heard that promise before, then wiggled off down the aisles.

'You want me to get a few dozen more bread rolls for you?' Jane asked, as if bored. 'Something to maybe tide that waste disposal unit of yours over until you return to your nosebag in the barn.'

I slipped my first dollar into the machine and crossed my fingers. 'I don't think you're in a position to run me down, young lady. You look as if you spent all afternoon workin' two beds in Madame Harlot's fun-time emporium.'

She nodded, not a bit impressed 'Tell you what, pork-storm, you're definitely a gifted social critic, but do you see that big guy over at the bar?'

I glanced over at the counter. A security guard with hands like Mighty Joe Young stood chewing on a pizza. I nodded. 'Uh huh!'

'That's Tiny,' she told me with a thin smile. 'And as soon as you're done pumpin' your hard-earned into that machine, he'll have you doin' the sidewalk shuffle and bounce. So you keep eatin' and drinkin', big guy, because you're gonna need all the extra paddin' you can get.'

'Well, that would be fine, lady, if I was a loser, but I'm not. Now, as Greta Garbo once reportedly said when she wanted to get back to nature, I vant to be a-lawn!'

As she sidled off, I gave her the finger, then stuck another token in the machine. By now, of course, you'd've imagined I'd have learned my lesson where gambling is concerned: Don't! And maybe George Washington was right when he said that reckless financial speculation was the child of avarice, the brother of iniquity and the father of mischief – though, I personally think that he forgot to add that it's also the mother of all rushes. Still, all that aside, I have my own rules – two of them in all – when it comes to gambling.

The first is: Never tell all you know.

Anyhow, I'm rambling again. So, there I was sitting at my machine and, for a split second, a million-dollar symbol promised to end every worry I'd ever had, before disappearing amongst a million duller symbols. Thing was, that mangy machine had the appetite of a Chilean Air crash survivor after four months in the mountains. It also had me in a Vulcan mind meld, whereby, out of the earshot of everyone else in the room, it was silently promising me the earth and half the universe besides. I slapped it a few times as soon as I ran out of sustenance, then hit it a kick or two because it shouldn't have lied to one as gullible as I. Then I heard Jane on the radio shouting out for Tiny. He came by a few minutes later. By that time my machine, despite being the larger of us, had stopped its brash flashing.

Tiny apologised to Jane about taking so long – his radio was out of range. Then he lifted me with consummate ease, and deposited me onto the sidewalk with a not so consummate ease. I thanked him digitally and made my way down the shore.

A cool breeze blew in off the ocean and the night-lights of the city's Golden Mile were subdued beyond the boardwalk. The sand was soft and wet beneath my feet, and, for some reason that made me think immediately of Clay. From a pocket full of dreams to a pocket full of nightmares – imagine him trusting me with money. Christ, the guy was so thick he couldn't have won a one-man game of snap on Fantasy Island.

FOURTEEN

It was calm at the water's edge, the only real noise to be heard that of couples making out beneath the stanchions or the ocean breaking on the shore. Meanwhile, I'd grabbed some booze from the car and lit a cigarette, and I was just about to get into the Shirinski letters by moonlight when a foreign noise broke the tranquillity of the night. It was the sound of shouting somewhere outside the casino, yet it only counted as a foreign noise in one respect, though not in another, because I knew the voice. It belonged to none other than the Ham.

'That a glass eye you got there, buddy?'

I trained my eyes on the casino's main door and saw Joe – tanked up on duel-fuel, and thin as a matchstick with the wood shaved off – standing before the over-sized Tiny. As usual, Joe was leading with his chin, arms at his side. I shook my head wearily. Some day I was going to have to show that little guy how to fight.

'Actually, it is!' Tiny snapped. He hovered over Joe like a grim delusion, his fists clenched into footballs. 'What of it?'

'I knew it,' Joe told him boldly. 'That's the one with the fuckin' sympathy in it!'

'You got anythin' else you want to say?' Tiny growled, his stance declaring he was just about to go gorilla at the chimp to his front.

'Yeah, I didn't know they could stack shit so high! Bring it, big nuts!'

I stepped up onto the boardwalk and sat in the shadows, smoking and sipping on my beer. Sometimes it's just as nice to watch a fight as get into one.

Had Joe been before an Olympic panel just then he would've earned a 9.9 for the double-Sukahara and half twist Tiny urged out of him. The Italian Scallion skipped the boardwalk, tumbled over the sand and landed at the water's edge. Tiny didn't hang around to watch the end of that complicated manoeuvre, however. He went back inside the casino, probably having seen it a dozen times over. I chuckled a while, dragged on a fresh cigarette and allowed Joe time to regain his composure. Then I sauntered slowly across the beach to join him.

'Any luck?' I asked him as I stepped out of the shadows. 'Hey, keep your nose away from those jellyfish – they'll slurp it off!'

'I tripped, Marty, nothin' else.' Joe sat up, shook his head groggily and leaned heavily against a stanchion. 'Think I might have a bit of concussion.'

'Hey, maybe you should lie down and have a nap.' He regarded me uncertainly. 'Yeah, honest, best thing for it. Read that in National Geographic.'

Joe stood up, stretched out. 'Nah, I'll be fine. Guess it's not my lucky night.'

'Ah! Well, did you see Greta, Muddy or Clay in there? Bet they're rakin' it in.'

Joe waved a dismissive hand. 'Seen nobody. Anyhow, gamblin' aint my Jones. There's more to life. What did money ever buy anyone except things?'

Joe the philosopher. If ignorance was bliss, he'd be happy forever. I moved back down onto the beach, where I sat on a dry patch of sand and began reading the Shirinski letters. Joe came over, sat at my side and peered over my shoulder. I pulled away, so he grabbed a beer, sauntered down to the water and gazed into the receding tide. 'I thought we were fuckin' partners,' he called back in a huff.

'We are,' I told him. I sighed a dismal, got up and went and sat down beside him. His cold, murderous heart was in the right place after all. 'I'll get a read at them first, then give you the low-down.'

As Joe nodded a satisfied, I got stuck into the first letter. He strolled to the water's edge, stared off into the blackness of the ocean, and whistled softly to himself every time another rolling wave eased slowly onto the shore. 'You believe in mermaids, Marty?' he asked me moments later in a subdued whisper. 'Women who are maybe half-female, half-pilchard?'

'Do you want to know what's in these letters or not?' I lifted my gaze, fixed it on the rolling tide. 'No. Yeah. Maybe. Hell, I d'know!'

He didn't speak for a time afterwards. Not to me anyway. He sipped at a beer and spoke to something beyond the shoreline in a low murmur.

I ignored him.

The first letter to Abel Shirinski had been postmarked the previous December. It was succinct and neatly typed onto un-headed paper by a standard typewriter. The sender had begun with a rather inappropriate 'Dear Abel' before bluntly suggesting the businessman had rekindled his affair with Maria upon returning to the city. The sender then declared that, if Abel didn't stop, he'd get filled with so many holes they'd be using him as a colander. I scanned the other letters and quickly realised their contents were much the same. Abel's love-thermometer was given a verbal trashing in each, after which threats were dispensed in volume. Joe chuckled wildly as I read certain paragraphs out to him. I didn't actually blame him for doing so. This was hate-mail with a capital F.

Joe put up a hand to stop me after the fourth letter. 'I've a theory,' he said suddenly. He was on his fourth beer and I was on my seventh. I was actually surprised he'd taken so long to come up with something, to be honest. Me, I'll give you my opinion on anything at all after three drinks, whether you want it or not.

'It's a penis-envy thing,' he told me, between sips. 'We're lookin' for a guy with no dick. Or, maybe just a little stump of a thing.'

'Or a bit of skirt who isn't gettin' her oats,' I told him with a shrug. Mental images of Patricia Shirinski, Maria Ellis and Anna Delaney came quickly to mind. They all wanted me bad, and I knew it. Like many women, however, they just hid it real well.

Joe shook me a no-no. 'It's a guy. Frank Ellis sent those letters, I'd bet my shirt on it. If I was a gambler, which I'm not...'

He paused as Muddy came trailing across the beach, shoulders sagging and his hands buried deep in his pockets – his empty pockets, by my reckoning. The kid grabbed a beer and threw himself onto the sand. 'There should be a limit as to how much you can lose in those places, uncle Whale.'

Joe grinned a demented. He pulled out his elephant gun from the small of his back. 'Don't worry, kid, I'll get our money back in another hour. With interest.'

I pulled the gun sharply out of his hand. 'I don't want to rain on your parade, Joe, but this is a fun weekend. You want to pull a heist, you do it when I'm two cities away.' I pushed the gun into my own belt. 'I'll keep this. In case a shark creeps up on us. Or a mermaid, whatever.'

'Hey, only jokin',' Joe said easily. He unplugged a bottle of wine with his Bowie knife, passed it around. 'Now, read out that last letter, Marty. I want to run my theory by you again.' As I was about to begin, however, he held up a stalling hand. 'Incomin',' he said, nodding back towards the shore access. 'Twelve o clock.'

Greta was doing a subdued goose-step across the sand. Another sore loser, she sat down beside Joe and went at the indignations in German. He sympathised with her for about twenty seconds, then threw her a bottle of solace. She downed it in one swallow, before tucking into the wine.

'The letter,' Joe reminded me.

The night was blurring, so I took a swig of beer and lit up a cigarette to steady it. '"Dear Abel"', I read aloud. '"You bastard! What did I tell you about dippin' your half-inch into my wife? Your time has come, blah, blah, blah... It's time for you to learn your lesson, and time for the world to discover our little secret, blah, blah, blah... Yours, with more than a hint of sincerity..."' I scrutinised the bottom of the letter. 'No signature,' I told them. 'Wouldn't be, I suppose.'

'I'm tellin' you, it's Frank,' Joe said with the conviction of a raving zealot.

'No, no!' Muddy interrupted with a shake of his hand. 'It's Maria Ellis.'

'It's Patricia Shirinski,' I said loftily. 'Maria Ellis was framed. She's as free from sin as the Virgin Mary.' I considered her past sexual exploits. 'Well...nearly.'

'I knew a virgin called Mary once,' Joe slurred. He had a vague look in his eyes that could only mean one thing. Or one ving, whatever. 'Well, she wasn't a virgin, and I don't even think her name was Mary, come to think of it. But she was a looker, y'know. I was goin' to marry that girl, too.' He sighed heavily, his vision 900 yards out and moving fast. 'Only had her once, but it was enough. We both knew it was right and fell in love. We had plans, dreams for the future.' He nodded coldly, clenching his jaw muscles so tight a spasm of knots stood out hard his neck. 'But she turned out to be a Hanoi Hannah and I had to shoot her. Yeah, a gook spook! In Vietnam it was...'

'You any dreams, uncle Whale?' Muddy interrupted. Which was both timely and nice.

I put my letters back into my inside pocket. 'Yeah, I got dreams, kid,' I told him, wistfully. I lay back on the sand, tucked my arms under my head, closed my eyes and allowed the salt air to wash over me. 'I want to open up a home for wayward girls aged between eighteen and twenty-four. I want to empty Detective Tork Malone with a sledgehammer. I want to be free to do what I want to do, to be what I want to be. I want to get twelve cheerleaders in a hotel room with a bucket of cream, five pounds of strawberries and a batman suit. I want to...'

We didn't make it to Joe's aunt's place, succumbing, as we did, to the soporific effects of the drink, and as engrossed as we became in building castles in the air upon Cloud Nine. I was the first to dish out my pie-in-the-sky dreams, then Muddy dished out his, and by the time it got around to Greta and Joe all sense had deserted us. That said, the sand was soft and warm, and it's not the first time my bed has been alive with crabs, so I slept like a corpse.

Several hours later, I was awoken by the morning sun's warming rays, and when I'd sobered enough I quickly drew my feet out of the incoming tide, a sudden memory resurfacing of a time years before when I'd awoken from a similar session on the beach to find six guys rubbing me down with lanolin and trying to roll me back into the water. After a quick yawn and stretch, I then squelched up the beach to shake the still-stewed Greta awake.

Joe rose out of the ocean some ten minutes after I'd revived Muddy. There was an entanglement of seaweed on his head which made him resemble Neptune on a bad hair day. He had a knife between his teeth, four sea bass in one hand and a small squid in the other. He stacked some dry twigs beneath one of the wooden stanchions, then rather thoughtlessly set it alight by using two rocks and some dry seaweed as tinder. I offered him a cigarette-lighter, but he didn't want to know. I took a walk along the shore with Muddy. I'd a feeling we were the only half-sensible ones on the beach.

'You see your father anywhere?' I asked.

Muddy shook his head. 'No, don't know where he is.'

I nodded easily. The kid didn't seem too worried, as strange behaviour figured as normal with Clay. The drink in the casino was free, but Clay had probably hung around for Happy Hour. In my opinion, that man's priorities were definitely way up the left.

Muddy laid himself down on a stretch of dry sand after about five minutes of walking. It definitely wasn't a suntan thing, probably more a dehydration thing. 'You know where there's a church around here?' he asked as I lay down beside him. 'Dad always likes me to go pray on a Sunday.'

'Can't say I do, kid. To me, religious freedom is somethin' that allows you to choose what kind of churches you avoid on a Sunday, y'know.'

'Don't you believe in God then?' Muddy rose up onto an elbow and cupped an eye from the sun. 'My dad says you should worship your maker.'

I shrugged easily. 'That's because your father is a self-made man, kid. But with me it's personal. Y'see, I got to wonderin' years back why you're allowed to talk or sing to the Big Guy in church, yet you try talkin' to him on the street at two in the mornin' and everyone thinks you're off your horse. Worse still, it's alright for you to talk to Him, but if He talks back to *you* and *you* tell everyone, then *you* are in one hell of a load of shit! Schizophrenia they call it.'

Muddy lay back down on the sand, pursed his lips in a thoughtful. 'You're right, uncle Marty,' he agreed, eventually. 'And why has he only got two arms and legs? Why can't he have four claws and the head of a Mutant Ninja Turtle?'

'Yeah, kid,' I pouted. 'Now you're catchin' on. Y'see, people think He created us in His image. But, I mean, he *must* have wings, armour and lasers if He's a god of any real note, so why don't *we* have any?' Muddy smiled and I continued sagely. 'And why wouldn't he put one eye in the back of our head and one in front, all topped off with reversible knees, so we wouldn't have to turn in a narrow alley? Nah, kid! If God is like us, He must have *real* problems!''

Muddy smiled dreamily. 'Yeah, I think you're right, uncle Marty. I don't think I'll go to church any more. Never liked it much anyhow.'

'Be your own man, kid,' I told him with a wag of my finger. 'Make your own decisions. Oh, and don't tell your father I've had any influence on you. I've enough people chasin' me down as it is.'

Joe's voice drifted down across the sand. Breakfast was ready. Sea Bass in its jacket. Octopus, two legs each. And warm, sandy wine. Still, it was better than Greta's cooking any day.

***

Clay came wandering over the sand into our Robinson Crusoe encampment some time after 10-00am. He was grinning a fifty-six-toother, kitted out in an expensive tailor-made suit, and had a short-haired blonde bimbo on his right arm. I stopped sucking on my octopus leg as he approached, thankful for the brief respite.

'Hey up, boys!' he smiled. His eyes were double-glazed and I wondered just who was holding who up. 'Thought I'd come pay my respects before I jet off to Monte Carlo for a turn on the tables.'

I eyed him sceptically, then smiled magnanimously as it all clicked into place. 'You won a heap of moolah, didn't you, *buddy*, eh?' I got up and enthusiastically shook his hand, slapping his back to let him know we'd always be friends until either great adversity or something small and inconsequential drove us apart.

Clay stepped back, and it may have been a trick of the light but he appeared to be counting his fingers. 'Not so fast, Whale. I might be drunk, but I still have my senses about me. I'm not signin' any release papers, no matter what you say.'

'Don't be like that,' I said, accusingly. I feigned a pained that I usually save for dinner at home. 'You're my friend, so I'm happy for you, nothin' else.'

Clay lowered his head and took my hand solidly. 'Thanks, Marty. And sure, I had a stroke of luck, won a couple of dollars. So...' For one agonising moment his hand wavered close to his pocket, but then he must've sobered slightly. 'So, uhm, I'll be off then.'

As he turned to walk away, Muddy said, 'When will you be back, dad?'

'Sometime,' Clay replied seriously. 'I'll ring you, kid. Sometime.'

I placed an arm around Muddy's shoulder as Clay and his new found friend, each the other's crutch, ambled up onto the pier and off, I presumed, towards the nearest airport. Seconds later, I grabbed a bottle beer and struggled up the beach after them. I was panting as I reached them.

'F... for you, my friend,' I said, handing the beer to Clay. 'May...you be lucky...in your new life.'

'Didn't you bring one for Judy?' Clays face was a solemn mask, and I shrugged sorrowfully. He suddenly broke into a smile, slipped a hand into his pocket, and drew out a bank-heist of bills. 'Here,' he smiled. 'There's about 1200 dollars there. Give Muddy 500 and get yourself somethin' nice. Tell the kid I'll be back in a week or two.' He turned, grinned manically. 'See ya!'

I wished him well, then strode back down the beach. I'd pocketed the money at that stage, of course. Some of that belonged to Gus Diamond.

'What did he say?' Muddy asked.

I slipped him a bill. 'He gave you this. Said he'd see you in a few days.'

'Twenty bucks?' Muddy sighed. 'Is that all that he thinks of me?'

'Don't sweat it, kid. He didn't win that much. He's just tryin' to impress his new friend.' I made a balled forearm, winked, then called Joe and Greta over. 'C'mon, we'll head back home and I'll stand us a few beers in the Moose. I got out of that evil den last night before the Devil corrupted my soul, so I've still a few dollars to play with.'

'You've got willpower, Shale,' Joe smiled. 'I admire that. Now, can I drive? I'll be careful. Swear.'

Joe had me figured all wrong again. To me, willpower is only eating seven bags of pretzels when you have eight.

'No,' I told him. He glared at me, his eyes filled with approaching storm-cloud. 'Hey, you said you admire willpower,' I hedged. 'So, I'm sayin' no. You, uhm, have to admire me for it. Uhm, don't you?'

Joe nodded and wagged his trigger-finger playfully. 'You're a joker, Shale,' he smiled. 'You're just testin' the tiger again, aren't you?'

'So, now you're the tiger, eh?' He nodded and slapped me playfully – if a little too roughly – on the back and I cursed inwardly, suddenly recalling something about having a tiger by the tail, and something else about the man who rides the tiger never being able to dismount.

It was all a bit vague, to be truthful. And, again, I don't know why those particular proverbs came to mind just then, but it perhaps had something to do with my instinct – as always, muffled and straining to be heard – trying to inform me that Joe was definitely more Shere Khan than Tigger.

FIFTEEN

They say there's no sounder sleep than that of the just or the just-after. Thing was, I'd had to travel down the shore to get the only decent sleep I'd had in a week, yet back here in the city I was once again sleeping the sleep of the just-in-case, which entailed keeping one eye open, one hand on my gun, going to bed when I wasn't tired and getting up when I was. Still, when Monday morning came around, I knew a fresh run at the Shirinski case meant firstly getting Marcie off my case, so I took Joe with me to my office, hoping he'd serve either as a witness or a shield.

As we went upstairs, Joe took point while I fixed together two wraps of money, one of 50 dollars, the other of 100. Marcie wasn't in reception when we got in, yet from the mess of the place, it was clear we'd either been burgled over the weekend or my irascible secretary had used something unbreakable in there to break everything else. As I waded through a sea of scattered paper, Marcie exited my office, crab-faced and seemingly taller, the way bears are when they're posturing up for a claw-fest. She also wore a holstered gun at her side, and from the way she'd eased her jacket behind it, I got the feeling she wanted me to draw first so she'd look good in court.

'We have visitors over the weekend, Marcie?' I hedged. 'I always imagined that if we had burglars, they'd break in and leave stuff out of pity, but obviously not...'

'No one likes you, Marty,' she sniffed unconcernedly. 'It's not hard to see why.'

I clicked a finger as if suddenly recalling something. 'Jeez, now I know what it was, I forgot to pay you Friday, didn't I? I got an urgent call from Maria and had to leave quickly.' I reached into my pocket, withdrew the 100 dollar bundle and handed it to her. 'There you go – the first part of your wages. I'll get you the rest when I wrap this case up in the next day or two, swear. You, uhm, happy now?'

Marcie snatched the money from my hand. 'Sure, Marty, happy as a sack of wet kittens.' She tugged lightly at her jacket, her skirt, her blouse. 'Why wouldn't I be? I'm wearin' last year's style and look frumpy enough to be my own grandma.'

'Be reasonable, Marcie. You hadn't a rag on you when you started workin' for me.'

'No, but I've plenty now!' She seemed to grow taller. 'You, you're a fuckin'..!'

I shook her a no-no and tried not to show fear – animals can smell it a mile off. 'Now, Marcie, less of the potty-mouth – the Tourettes crowd over the hall will think they're invectively inadequate!' She feigned a mopey and I came right back with a dopey, even as I withdrew the 50 dollar bundle from my pocket. 'Right, take my last few bucks.' She took it in a cobra-strike. 'Yeah, I'll, uhm, just go without.'

As Marcie tucked the money into her purse with a wry chuckle, I craned to get a proper look at her gun, but she sat hurriedly at her desk. I moved alongside her and pretended to be scanning the mail, though I was actually checking out her fingertips for powder-burns. 'So, uhm, any particular reason for the sidearm?'

She glared me a frosty as she eased a stack of unopened bills and other junk-mail by rote into the shredder. 'I heard there was a shootin' at your place, so I'm wearin' this in case anyone associates me with you and I don't get a chance to plead insanity.'

'Uh huh? Hmmm!' I nodded uncertainly, but decided to change the subject. 'Right, so is Maria Ellis still down in Administration?'

'They're shippin' her to the Big House at three o clock accordin' to Chester Hardcastle.' She lifted a bulky envelope and handed it to me. 'Oh, and Mal Brennan left this for you.'

'Ah, the typewriter ribbon!' I pocketed the envelope. 'Right, c'mon, Joe, let's go see Maria.' I was about to leave. 'Say, Marcie, any word from Tommy Ellis?'

'He checked in with me an hour back, wanted to know if you had any new leads. I told him you were probably in a brothel somewhere workin' on your fetishes.'

I nodded tolerantly. 'That's nice. Well, tell him to call at my place sometime after six, or, if I'm not there, I'll be in the Moose. Oh, and could you maybe tidy this place up? At the moment it looks like the sort of place elephants come to die.'

Marcie raised her eyes heavenward as we made to leave, and I suddenly recalled the last time I'd seen a face like that on CNN they'd had to destroy the whole herd. Still, I was smiling as I left.

Alright, asking Marcie to tidy up was maybe expecting a bit much: After all, if your secretary keeps the sugar in a coffee jar marked 'Tea', how tidy is the place ever going to get? But, the main thing was, Marcie and I were back on track. Now, for another month at least, she'd have to at least subconsciously accept she'd always be expendable when she wanted anything rightfully hers, and indispensable when helping me go after anything rightfully mine.

***

Many retired policemen will tell you that years on the Force forced years on you, and Mo Breasley was a fine example. When Joe and I entered Police Administration, he was frowning like a Pug, chugging on coffee, and chest-deep in paperwork. Needless to say, I felt about as welcome as the Captain of the Enola Gay at the post-Hiroshima get-together.

156

'What the fuck do you want now, Marty?'

'Just lookin' to see my client, Mo. I may have a fresh lead in the case.'

Mo chuckled so demonically I could see his tonsils beating a tattoo on his palate. 'Wow, another one? That sixth *non*-sense of yours must be ready for a breakdown, competin' as hard as it does against your other so-called five!' He sighed wearily and clicked his fingers at the desk sergeant. 'Wallis, take Laurel and Hardy here down to see Maria Ellis.' As the sergeant nodded – and as everyone else in the office laughed snidely at Joe and I – Mo stood, pulled on his jacket and made for the revolving doors. 'And Marty, make it quick. Malone will be back in a few minutes, and y'know how he gets when you're around.'

I shot him a lofty. 'Yeah, if he had his way I'd be ringin' a hand-bell and shoutin' "unclean" for the rest of my days. But he knows I get results where he gets consequences. I've got a reputation...'

'Yeah, well, some people don't get a reputation until they lose it, Marty, know what I mean?' Mo laughed snidely, gave me the finger, then left as if he'd never been.

Moments later, Wallis led Joe and me down to the holding cells. I had Joe remain outside in the aisle, warned him not to interrupt, then entered Maria's cell. She was wearing a blue dress suit, standing at the barred window and staring out into the yard with such a tragic look upon her face you'd've needed a heart like a swinging brick not to laugh. Wallis stood close by, watching our every move.

'You can go now,' I told him. 'I can defend myself.' Thankfully, however, he didn't move a muscle, so I gave him the thumb and a wink, then focused upon Maria. She turned towards me, all dewy-eyed, though I wasn't falling for that schmaltz because it's common knowledge that even a block of ice sheds tears when the heat's turned on.

'So, uhm, Maria, any word on how Frank's doin'?'

'They say he's still critical, but that he'll come around in time.'

'Sure he will, lady. With you in here out of the way...' She wiped her eyes and raised an eyebrow. 'Well, he'll know exactly where you are, that's all I'm sayin'.'

She nodded uncertainly. 'Yes, maybe you're right. Anyhow, what's with the black eyes and the red centres? You look like an albino rat with runny mascara.'

'I've been fightin' the good fight, lady,' I replied soberly. 'All weekend. For free. In fact, to quote some famous juggernaut, never in the history of mankind has so much been done by so few for no money.'

'You need money – I get it!' Maria retorted sharply. 'And you *will* get it. In fact, I'm only sticking with you because you were the first person to believe me when I declared my innocence. Saying that, now that Detective Malone has reopened the original murder case, we might have a *real* chance.'

I sighed in exasperation. Don't get me wrong, I'm used to going from retarded to regarded, and as often to being the flavour of the minute, but it was now all too obvious that Maria had a habit of switching horses mid-race, and she seemed to be in this thing for herself. I had to set her straight, to let her know that if she didn't stick with me it would be the biggest mistake since every major margarine manufacturer failed to sign up Marlon Brando after Last Tango in Paris.

'Jeez, lady, Malone doesn't believe you any more than I...' I paused, shook my head. 'I mean, Chester's probably just draggin' this case out so he can hit you for more money. Seriously, I'm the only one around here you *can* trust.'

Maria's next sigh seemed to come right up from somewhere around her ankles. 'You're right, Mr Shale. I'm sorry. Ask me whatever you want.'

'That's better. Now, you told me Frank and Abel originally set up in the microchip business with a third man. I'd like you to tell me a bit about him, if you would.'

Maria's eyed skipped to the past. 'Jim Harrison, you mean? He was a poultry farmer originally, though he was involved with Frank and Abel for only about a year before he left and went straight back into that line of work. But you're definitely barking up the wrong tree there.'

'Perhaps, but I have to follow every lead. So, do you know where I can maybe dig out somethin' about him?'

'Over at the Free Library, probably. I'd imagine they have back editions of local agricultural journals. Jim used to own a sprawling farm outside the city, and he supplied a large section of the community with produce.' She studied me intently for a second. 'I don't want to sound indelicate here, but you *can* read, I presume?'

'Not the joined up stuff, but I'm good with pictures,' I grimaced. 'Say, are you sure you haven't any of those anonymous letters Frank got a few months back? Perhaps they're stashed in a secret place at home. The place he keeps his porn, maybe.'

Maria averted her gaze for a second, then shrugged lamely.

'Look, lady, I didn't come down in the last shower. Y'see, I read over the letters that Abel received, and the sender said he'd be shown-up if he didn't show up for a showdown. Now, the way those letters were phrased makes me believe that particular secret had nothin' to do with the menagerie-a-trois you guys were involved in, and that it was maybe somethin' else.'

Once again, Maria seemed on the verge of crying. 'Look, I keep telling you, Mr Shale, Frank didn't keep any of those letters. Secondly, I wasn't involved with Abel – our affair ended many years ago. And thirdly, I know nothing of any *other* secret.'

She was lying. It was all in the eyes: They shifted east for recollection purposes, west when you were feeling inventive, north when you were doing calculus and south when you were getting all evasive. Maria's had just done a world-tour minus the Antarctic, and I knew then she'd have given a polygraph a nervous tic. Still, what was the point of having it out with her? I'd no proof, and women always have the last word in an argument – anything you say after that is just the beginning of another argument. I nodded evenly, moved towards the cell door.

'Fair enough, lady. But just remember, as it stands, you and Frank are lookin' at so much time your parole officers haven't been born yet; Tommy is lookin' at a future of drunken foster-parents and drive-bys; and, some time after 3pm today when you team up with your new cell-mate in the Big House, you'll discover the alternative meanin' of the phrases 'tongue-in-cheek' and 'don't-do-dick'!'

I allowed Maria a few moments to chew tentatively on my gems, then exited the cell and whistled Joe over. Outside, it was hotter than an Alabama cheerleader, but, as we made our way down the precinct steps, my blood chilled in my veins. Across the lot, sitting in the driving seat of a golden Mercedes was Happy Valentine; and, beside him, sat the silver-haired and perma-tanned Gus Diamond. Upon espying me, the normally inscrutable Gus screwed up his face as if struggling with the beast inside, after which he fashioned his hand into a gun and pointed it directly at me. Beside him, Happy rolled his eyes heavenward, then shook his head, before feigning a grim for his boss.

Instantly, I was on Brown Alert – which is similar to Red Alert, if not as pleasant on the nose – and I moved towards the Buick at speed, urging Joe to do the same.

Joe looked between me and the Mercedes. 'You know those guys, Whale?'

'Yeah, I, uhm, hung around with them once.'

I keyed the engine to life and eased the Buick in behind a police cruiser that was leaving the lot. As I did so, I kept a keen eye on the rear-view mirror. Happy wasn't following us, yet I still felt a week's backlog of food moving swiftly through my colon, so I clenched my parts, hoping I'd make it to a restroom in time. On a positive note, of course, the adrenaline-surging events of the last week sure had eased my once perpetual constipation, so I could now say in all truth that with friends like mine, who needed enemas?

'Yeah, well, they don't look so friendly,' Joe returned sourly. 'If you want, I'll go over there and have a word with them, teach them some manners.'

I smiled gratefully and dropped my head, humbled by that sudden and unexpected show of loyalty. It was then, in that rare moment of tranquillity, that I was able to see Joe for the thoughtful, astute and very misunderstood little guy that he was.

'Y'know, Joe, Maria Ellis is damn lucky to have us *both* on this case,' I said warmly. 'Damn lucky! Though she'd better hope we turn up some new clues soon, or the only way she's gettin' out of this one is if she imports herself in an L.A. jury.'

***

I may've already mentioned that, often, when things are going pear-shaped in my life, Lady Luck occasionally likes to round on me like a rabid badger. Take, for example, when Joe and I exited the Skytowers elevator on the 18th floor. Just then, the corridor was still in lock-down, dimly lit and devoid of life, the only clue to its enforced hibernation a yellow banner-tape across the door of 18a reading 'Police Line: Do Not Cross'. So, reaching room 18c should've been easy. Unfortunately, due to the haunting shadows, the tropical 'music' in the back-drop, and the rich canvas of palms and fronds, the atmosphere was a couple of continents west of where it should've been. And when Rick stepped out suddenly from a doorway clutching a set of pruning shears, I guess that neatly compounded the situation.

'Jeez, Joe, get off him and stow the knife! You'll give him a gangrenous ear!'

As Rick screamed louder than a demon at an exorcism, Joe took on a big-eye, shook his head wilfully, wrapped a hand around the janitor's mouth and dragged him deep into a lair of fronds. 'I'm stowin' nothin', Vince!' he replied in a low whisper. 'I've caught me a god-damn General! Just take point, keep an eye out for the rest of the patrol, and we'll be back in the LZ in no time for the dust-off.'

'Vince? Who in the name of Beelzebub's fuckin' cat is Vince?'

But I didn't need to ask. We'd skipped back over two decades in time and were now somewhere three clicks west of Da Nang on Hill 309 flanked by hundreds of NVA and VC. Tracers, Willie-Petes and Whizz-Bangs were lighting up the backdrop, a flight of Hueys were trailing in from the south, and scores of M16s and Ak47s were shredding the early morning mist.

It was all there in Joe's eyes, which were now as soft as diamonds with the hardness extracted and told a story, half-fact, half-friction. Worse still, the Ham had found Ho Chi Min and he was now all over the guy's trail.

'Joe, seriously, did you take your fuckin' medication today?'

Joe emerged from the fronds and stared coldly at me. I'm near sure, in that heart-stopping moment, he visualised me wearing a conical hat, a black muumuu and carrying a little pig to market, all trussed up in a basket. I farted, checked out my slacks for lumps, then began sweating like a 60% burger on a griddle.

But then, half-cocked and ready to go off, Joe cocked an ear and continued talking cock: 'You hear that, Vince? The old marty-arty two clicks west of here. Maybe you should get on the horn and have them throw in a Bouncin' Betty.'

'C'mon, Joe, you're freakin' the doo out of me! Ease up for Chrissakes!'

For several time-wrenching moments, it seemed as if I'd lost Joe and he was never coming back. But then, as suddenly, a small embryo of enlightenment worked its way into the two pinpoints of darkness that served as his eyes. He shook his head once, twice, and then stared at Rick as if he was an unsavoury prosthetic before casting him coldly aside.

Clearly embarrassed, the Ham then said, 'Wow, man, that was a trip! I, uhm, didn't take my meds today, sorry about that.'

I moved towards Rick, whose face was now whiter than the Lone Ranger's conscience, and helped him up from the floor. 'Sorry about that, little guy,' I squirmed. 'I really don't know how to explain that, so I won't. But, uhm, any chance you could lend me your flashlight again?'

Rick cursed under his breath, rubbed hard at his neck, then left to get a flashlight. He returned a minute later, handed me the torch, then warily led Joe and I into room 18c. From there, we all moved into room 18a, where I turned off the lights and shone the flashlight around the carpet. But there was no sign of the luminescent trail I'd seen on my last visit.

'Say, Rick, did you vacuum this place recently? It's just there was some kind of stuff on the carpet the last time. It's not here now though, and I wonder why that is.'

The janitor pouted angrily, shook his head. 'Personally, I don't give a monkey's fuck, Detective. Can I go now?'

I nodded, thinking him a little rude, then returned my attention to the floor, trying to remember the exact direction of the trail. Now that I recalled, it had stopped rather abruptly about three-feet from the furthest wall. I stood there thinking for a time, then realised the trail had actually led in the general direction of a ventilator duct high upon the wall. I moved towards it. The duct was positioned just above head height and slightly dusty, yet I noticed fresh scratch-marks around the screws. Using the sharp edge of my key-ring, I unscrewed the hood, took it off and probed about inside the vent until my hand came into contact with something.

'What is it?' Joe asked.

'Looks like a booster of some kind.' I examined it for a time, then pocketed it. I took a brief look at the carpet directly beneath the duct, after which I moved to the central closet door, which I checked out for thickness. A sudden memory resurfaced as I did so, of Tiny and his earpiece in the Albino Casino, and I nodded to myself as another piece of the puzzle clicked into place.

'Is that a big clue?' Joe asked.

'It sure is,' I told him, darkly. 'But it's one I'd rather not have gotten. In fact, I now think it's very likely that Maria Ellis is our murderer!'

SIXTEEN

It may've been the octane-laden smog blanketing the city in the muggy afternoon heat, the slow grind of traffic on the overburdened grid, or the fact I'd discovered something that promised to ruin my payday, but less than two blocks from Skytowers my mood tombstoned into a pool of shit.

Y'see, certain people here in the city will tell you I'm as loyal as a hound under a banquet table, or that I don't mind my clients laying their cards on the table so long as they're plastic. But that's not entirely true. Fact is, once bought, I stay bought; and, so long as my clients are paying, I'd rather they told me the truth, even if they're guilty as sin. That way, I don't have to saw against the grain, I can feign a fair day's work for a fair week's pay, and I can probably befoul the waters of even the clearest investigation.

Unethical? Maybe. But then, in what way exactly do I differ from your standard defence attorney?

Thing was, the evidence against Maria Ellis was mounting daily, yet I had to conduct my investigation upon the premise she was innocent. Which meant looking for other suspects, of whom there were few, and alternative evidence, of which there was little. And that, basically, meant a lot more work. And they can say what they want about hard work – it might not kill you, but the damage is often irreparable.

'So, what's chewin' your loaf, Marty? Tell me what you're thinkin'.'

I sighed a deepy. 'I think we're lookin' for a woman,' I told him. 'Chances are, it's Maria. I guess I was tryin' to fool myself into believin' otherwise.'

'Wow, Marty, are you sure?' Joe seemed genuinely perplexed. 'I mean, you once told me women have smaller brains and think emotionally, so why would you now think one of them had the savvy to pull off something this big?'

'I know, it makes absolutely no sense. But that's the way the evidence is pointin'.'

Joe nodded a ten-watt, then shook me a thicky. 'Right. So, uhm, what evidence?'

I sighed, realising I'd have to explain. 'Y'see, the luminescent trail I found in room 18a was broken every 12 inches or so, meanin' that, whatever the substance was, it was stepped into the carpet. The repetitive pattern of the trail also showed a main indentation followed by a smaller, circular indentation, which signifies our perp was wearin' high heels. The fact the trail stopped so far from the duct confused me at first, but then I realised it was because the perp was small and needed something to stand on to unscrew the duct lid. She had to wheel a table out of the closet and across the carpet to set it under the duct so she could stand on it. That's also confirmed by thickly imprinted coaster marks on the carpet just under the duct.'

'Mmm, alright! But why did this dame need to hear what was goin' on?'

'She had to know the precise moment to pull off her plan. For the first part of the set-up, she needed someone unobtrusive yet nosey enough to witness Frank and Abel holdin' a furtive, after-hours meetin' on a deserted floor in Skytowers. Rick's perfect in that regard: He works the 18th floor each night at the same time, he's thick as month-old shit, and he's a regular Neighbourhood Watch. Next, our perp had to kill Abel, then frame Frank for the murder. So, she entered room 18c, moved into the central closet, then waited until Abel and Frank engaged in a heated argument that'd be overheard by the janitor. And that's where the spyin' equipment comes in: The closet door is thick, so it's hard to overhear what goes on in any of the rooms, yet you can't leave it even slightly ajar as the automatic light stays on. Thus, the need for an earpiece and transmitter. So, when the two men begun arguin' – leavin' an indelible impression on Rick – our killer sprang from the closet, knocked Frank out, shot Abel, then took to her heels – or her high-heels, whatever – only seconds before Rick entered the room and saw what he was supposed to see.'

Joe shrugged undecidedly. 'Mmm, maybe, but there are several women in this case, Whale. I've a different theory if you're interested…'

I nodded as if I was, then switched off mentally.

Still, Joe had a point: The killer could have been any of several women. Not only that, my theory had a major flaw in it, namely the time-line. Rick had sworn he'd entered room 18a only seconds after Abel was shot, yet it would've taken the killer much longer to not only knock Frank unconscious and kill Abel, but to then plant a gun solidly in each of their hands, before making her escape.

Still, I'd have to work on that one later. For now, I had to reconsider the movements of every woman involved in the case, and that meant utilising a scientific method my Uncle Don called the Theory of Relatively Ugly.

Now, the Theory of Relatively Ugly dictates that, the uglier a person is, the worse crimes they're likelier to commit; and, while this may sound like stereotyping, it's a view long-esteemed by sociologists, policemen and bigots the world over. Thing was, in the Shirinski case, there were no truly ugly broads to throw the blame on. Sure, Maria Ellis was dragging forty and gravity was tugging at her ass, yet she'd a chin I'd rest my nuts on any day. My difficulty lay in the fact she'd no alibi for her whereabouts during the Abel Shirinski murder, and she'd also been at the scene during the attempted murder of her husband.

Of course, alibis are often overrated, as most people can't recall where they were on any given night if you ask them, and it's more often the guilty party who has the soundest alibi. Still, speaking as one who knows how easy it is to be fitted up by the local filth, I always know where I've been the night before, even if I'm pickled as a gherkin and suffering more blackouts than your average war-torn city. Leave a trail of destruction, that's the answer. Go through life like Genghis Khan with a toothache because there's one sad truth about our fellow man which can rarely be disputed: When you're good they never fucking remember, but when you're bad they never fucking forget!

Still, I'm rambling again.

So, then we had Patricia Shirinski, who actually fitted in with my theory slightly better. I was willing to bet that she'd been pug-ugly with a neck like a komodo dragon before she began having herself recast in plastic. I was also willing to bet that she wasn't even biodegradable anymore, and I'd stake my life she hadn't ventured too near the furnace when Abel was getting crisped, just in case she melted. But the thing was she could recall exactly where she was on the night of her husband's murder or the night of the attempted murder of Frank Ellis.

Which made her even more suspicious in my view, for reasons I've already mentioned.

Lastly, there was Ann Delaney. Now, to be fair, Mal Brennan's examination of the used typewriter ribbon hadn't proven much use: None of the poison-pen letters had been typed on that particular scroll, nor were there any individual letter defects on her typewriter that matched to any of the letters I'd taken from Abel's office. Still, Anna was female and had access to lots of spying gear, all of which she was familiar with, so did this Little Plum have a heart of stone? And yet why would she kill her boss, a man she clearly admired, or attempt to kill Frank Ellis, someone whom she'd never met?

I shrugged, unable to think of an answer, before glancing at myself in the wing-mirror and thanking the Big Guy in the

Sky that no one would ever be able to apply the Theory of Relatively Ugly to me. I could literally get away with murder. It was then that Joe nudged me back into surreality and back onto the correct side of the road.

We'd reached the Free Library, so I exited the car and abandoned it in the only parking space available, beating the invalid who had legal access to it by merely seconds. Still, I did limp up the library steps, because if nothing else I'm tactful.

Joe trailed after me, and, inside, we made our way to the Commerce section. There, with some help from a young assistant who was so pedantic she could've told you the time in seconds, we eventually found quite a lot of material on Jim Harrison. It seemed that on Jim's 30th birthday, he'd inherited 20, 000 acres of land from his parents that he'd used for initially raising poultry. He'd developed that business for about eight years, then sold up and gotten into computer export. As Maria Ellis had then so rightly stated, he'd stuck with that for just over a year, then sold out at a profit and moved to Honolulu, where he intended to raise a family.

Several grainy photos followed in which Jim and his wife – then at the height of their local celebrity – were viewed alongside the city's mayor at fundraisers and charity functions, and they were seemingly your ordinary, everyday middle-aged couple: Fat, dull-eyed and teed-off, with all of that hidden beneath grins and chins. And the more I read into Jim Harrison's life, the more ordinary he seemed. He was a normal, faceless businessman, who'd swindled as much as he could from the gullible public without attracting the undue attention of the law. Then, much like every philanthropist, he'd stuck on a tie and given a little back publicly of all he'd stolen privately, thereby crystallising into a solid, everyday citizen

But it was another newspaper article from the same year that caught my attention, and it read: Death of Local Businessman in Plane Crash.

It seemed Jim Harrison had popped his clogs in a freak aeroplane accident west of Honolulu. I shook my head in dismay. My latest theory – perhaps my only saving grace – had just plummeted to its death with that banner headline, taking a dump on me as it passed by. I refolded the news-sheets and looked around for Joe.

I found him in the history section between U-W.

'Let's get out of here!' I told him. 'I need some air.'

We got into the car, and we were driving nowhere in particular when Joe began to speak: 'Hey, Marty, I was tellin' you about that theory of mine...'

I took a deep breath, bracing myself. 'Yeah, go ahead, I'm listenin'.'

'A midget. Maybe even two or more,' he said. I nodded as if carefully considering his proposition. 'They lift a table out of the closet...'

'On a forklift, right?'

'Maybe. Now...'

He went at it, and I drove, going nowhere in particular and only half-listening. I heard talk of a conspiracy in the background, one that probably went all the way to the top, which involved not just ordinary midgets, but secret-agent midgets with licences to kill who'd formed contacts in the Cuban underworld. I shook my head, my mood darkening. Christ, Joe was a regular Spielburg in Ed Wood clothing!

'So what do you think, Marty?' Joe grinned finally.

'Mmm, well, as you maybe know, Joe, there are no grassy knolls in Skytowers that anyone's aware of...' He nodded eagerly and I shrugged. 'And all those midgets escapin' in a trail of laundry baskets through midtown would've been way too conspicuous, so we won't hang our hats on that one just yet, eh?' He seemed slightly dismayed.

'Still, that's not to say it's not worth considerin' as an option.'

Joe beamed a proud smile. 'I'm here for you, Marty.'

I nodded sourly. 'You're here with me, Joe, I can't argue with that.'

Just then, however, my mood had begun to brighten, if only a little. I'd driven the car, totally on reflex, to the Gutted Moose, yet I can't explain exactly how that happened. Was it coincidence? Had my mind, now so finely attuned to my body's nutritional needs, subconsciously directed me here so I could fill up on my daily quota of B-vitamins? Or did it all have something to do with the fact that, because my every last lead had trickled into nothingness and my imminent 'whacking' was now heavy on my mind, I now felt like drinking myself into a fucking coma?

It was hard to know. Yet I hoped it would all become much clearer – or, actually, much unclearer – after a vicious onslaught of beer.

***

As usual, the Gutted Moose was about as atmospheric as anyplace you'd go to drop off ransom, with most of its customers looking as if they were there solely to provide each other with an alibi.

I weaved through the crowded bar towards a free booth. 'Get me a pitcher, when you get a moment,' I called back to Joe. 'And a double-double Mac from next door with sauerkraut, relish, mayo, cheese, gherkins, pickles, salami, liverwurst and tomatoes.'

'Ugh!' Joe snorted. 'That's disgustin'!'

'Yeah, you're right. Hold the tomatoes.'

A small time later, someone leaned into my booth and tapped me on the shoulder. My heart did a double-flip as I turned and noticed Clay standing there. He regarded me so lamely that I immediately felt like handing him a crutch.

'Well, well, if it isn't the Cincinnati Kid!' I snorted. 'How was Monte Carlo, *Omar*? You win much on the crap tables?'

He shrugged, clearly embarrassed. 'Not exactly. That bitch, Judy, ripped me off at the airport. She took my wallet after we boarded the plane, then hightailed it out of there before we took off, leavin' her luggage behind. Of course, the other passengers thought there was a bomb on board, I was arrested by an air marshal, and then I got whacked with a bill for a 1000 bucks because the flight was delayed.' He regarded me expectantly. 'So, I was thinkin' that the, uhm, money I gave you...'

'What money?' I stared at him as if he were a reggae singer at a Ku Klux Klan convention. It's a funny thing, but you can make anyone doubt their own sanity if you try hard enough. And I was about to do that. The only witness to our transaction down the shore had been Judy, and she was as crooked as a four dollar bill, so she didn't count. 'Uh-uh, Clay, no way! You gave me twenty bucks, and I gave that to Muds, as you requested.'

'But I could swear...' Clay's eyes were mining the past and coming up with little but chunks of fool's gold. 'Or maybe it was all that herb I was smokin'...'

'That's *exactly* what it was!' I out-turned my pockets to show him I was carrying about 60 dollars and change. By this stage, of course, I'd deposited most of his money in my sneakers, the way I always do in case I get mugged, so that I'll only ever end up losing my life. 'And this is all I have. Due to all the red-tape in this Shirinski murder, I haven't received a red cent from that Ellis broad, so my red-letter day...Well, let's just say I'm slightly in the red.'

Clay dropped his gaze and nodded sheepishly. 'Yeah, but I could've sworn...'

I patted him on the shoulder, told him to take a seat. 'Tell you what,' I smiled easily. 'I've give you 50 bucks, you can knock it off the 500 I owe you, and you can pay it back to me anytime you want. That ok?'

Clay nodded gratefully. 'I don't know what to say, Marty.'

'No problem. But you'll have to stand me a few beers as I've no money left...'

'Thanks, Marty, I really don't deserve a friend like you.'

I didn't know if he was being serious, though I feigned an aw-shucks in case he was, after which I snapped my fingers at Bernard and ordered a few pitchers.

Soonafter, Joe returned and we spent the next few hours drinking like drains. Of course, as the night progressed, there was no getting away from certain subjects and I grew well-versed in the topographical layouts of both Hanoi and that cheeky little scam-artiste Judy. Which would obviously have come in handy if I ever got to set foot, or half a foot, in either. By about 8-00pm, however, some of my own problems had resurfaced in my memory, and these were less-than-subtly revealed in my tendency to pick fights with everyone and anyone thereabouts. Clay, being the most sensible of our group, decided that was probably the right time to leave. He went outside and hailed a cab, and Joe and I followed somewhat unsteadily behind.

'Where we goin'?' Clay asked.

'We?' I whispered, drunkenly. 'Well, you and I are goin' to try and lose G.I. Joe there somewhere down the next block, and then we're goin' to get laid.'

'I'm right here, Marty,' Joe seethed. 'I can fuckin' hear you.'

I waved a dismissive hand as if making a funny, and Joe just about bought it. It was just then, however, as we were set to climb into our cab, that we all nearly bought it, for the sickening snap of pistol fire, plus the accompanying splintering of hardwood and plaster above the bar's façade, indicated that someone either wanted our cab real bad or we were once again knee-deep in doo-doo.

I dived to the sidewalk as another three or four shots raked the cab, pulling Clay down alongside me, only to notice Joe already down there, snipering off for cover. As I hit the ground, I noticed the shooter was driving a Daimler, which was now careering up the street towards us.

As yet another volley of shots ripped into the façade of the Moose and we were showered in a rain of plaster, I became aware of the shrieks of passers-by as the Daimler bypassed the bar at speed. In the midst of it all, Joe sidled up alongside me. He was clutching at his shoulder again – the one he'd caught a bullet in outside Chez Shale – and it looked as if another gunshot had just grazed him a little further down his arm. Still, he didn't seem too worried. He just kept his eyes on the shooter's car as it sped off into centre city, even as he fumbled about in his flak-jacket, took out his elephant gun and loaded it.

'So, what you plannin' to do about that, Marty?' he said coldly.

I raised my palms-heels hurriedly, memories of an unusually irate Gus Diamond and his little pseudo-handgun fresh in my mind. 'Nothin',' I told him. 'We're just goin' to let it slide. It's probably some guy lettin' off steam. And that's why we all have guns, right? To shoot at things and stuff...'

Joe lowered his voice, raised his eyebrows and said levelly, 'Yeah, I hear what you're sayin' – you've suddenly gone from sperm-whale to white-whale. Except we're forgettin' nothin'!' He levelled his gun at me and I'm nearly sure I saw the Grim Reaper standing at his shoulder urging him to pull the trigger. 'Now, you and the blue-boy there, get your big lard-asses into that cab, and do it now!'

SEVENTEEN

Night: The sky was congressman grey with the appropriately weak promise of rain, and a stiff breeze, ripe as a dancer's thong, wafted in across the city from the Siegel River. As usual, the gloom was threaded by garish neon, the slick pulse of traffic-lights high above the intersections, blurring silver trails of car headlights, and firefly pinpoints of feverishly smoked cigarettes. Here, too, as in every asphalt jungle, Hell's foremost agent, Chaos, flitted intermittently amidst the seething fleshpots in his vibrant, nocturnal dance, at times adding gentle excitement and mild drama to the otherwise repetitive lives of many, or on rarer occasions – should he chance upon a witless, if ever-willing soul-mate to advance him in his cause – darkly enacting some of his less tasteful fancies.

Tonight, needless to say, Chaos had struck rare gold: He'd found himself a servile wing-man in the form of Joe Sinto, and a less than willing booty-call in the form of Yours Flinchingly.

Still, as the Danger Ranger bundled Clay and I unceremoniously into that cab, I wasn't too surprised my recent bout of bad luck had taken a turn for the worse. After all, life forever seems to come at me fast and from angles, and I've never been too good at either self-defence or geometry. With Joe now at the wheel, however, I had the kind of itch under my skin even calamine couldn't ease, so it was time for some damage limitation.

'Uhm, Joe, you forget to take your meds again?' I feigned a toothy and finger-probed the latest wound in his arm, hoping to quicken his blood loss. 'How's about we get this vet to a doctor and you, uhm, *stand-the-fuck-down*, hmmm?

Joe, however, was much too busy psycho-ing himself up to obey me. He pulled away from me, and, with his eyes trained firmly on the shooter's car – which was now fleeing across the thoroughfare in the middle-distance towards centre city – keyed the cab to life. As the engine thrummed satanically under the hood, he then turned and stared four aeons of eternity at me in as many seconds. 'I've taken my meds, Whale,' he said sourly. 'And this is no flashback. I'm just heart-sick of gettin' holes pumped in me every time I step out the door, so it's payback time!'

'Aw c'mon, Joe, jumpin' to conclusions earns you contusions, you know that.' I feigned a cheesy, but the Ham was suddenly lactose-intolerant. Fittingly, my next words were geek-meek: 'But you said I could be the boss of you, remember? So couldn't I at least drive?'

'From the back? I don't fuckin' think so!' Joe secured the doors with the central locking. 'We're goin' after that guy, and you're layin' down coverin' fire. Short bursts, in concentric sweeps. Same as we did – well, *some* of us did – back in-country.'

'Sure, I can do that,' I muttered under my breath. 'Not!'

'You finished?'

I nodded uncertainly. 'Uh-huh!'

'Good, then flush!'

I quietened, crossed my parts and watched dismally as Joe released the handbrake, jammed the gear-stick into first and eased his mind into neutral. As the tires spat gravel beneath us, the Ham then bullied the cab through the traffic towards centre city, and it soon became clear his idea of recreation was wreck-creation. Every pavement was a bypass, and in that hellish ride we ploughed through several trash cans, downed a roadside payphone, freaked out a few oldsters exiting a jazz-club, and prompted one bleary-eyed drunk to throw his brown-bagged bottle at our wind-screen – and all this as the traffic-lights whizzed by in a psychedelic blur. In truth, Joe was a rebel without a pause, and he'd all the reasoning skills of a club-wielding cannibal who'd just asked you to lean over his cauldron to get a better whiff of his vegetable stew. I should perhaps also mention that, as we rode, Clay assumed a crash position more after than before, and I nearly laid a butt-cutlet in my shorts.

'Jeez, Joe, c'mon, this is fuckin' crazy!' By now, I was tumbling about heavily in the back, using Clay as an airbag as we took each corner. 'You do know, of course, that your drivin' licence is supposed to expire long before you do?'

'Got the bastard in sight, Whale! Look, up ahead there. Turnin' into Ness Avenue. See him?' He put his head closer to the windscreen, narrowed his eyes. 'Hey, and maybe I'm wrong, but it looks like another fuckin' Chuck from here!'

My stomach double-flipped at that statement, and my hand seemed to move of its own accord towards my gun. Just then, I knew this was no longer a life or death situation: It was way more serious than that, and I began to harbour more unhealthy ideas than a necrophiliac in a shed filled with dead sheep. Don't get me wrong, I'm all for living in the past at times – mainly because it's cheaper – but I was now heartsick of Joe forever frogmarching me down the war-torn ruins of Memory Lane whenever he saw fit. Besides, it was near impossible to see who was driving the Daimler in the gathering darkness, so our shooter was probably more schmuck than Chuck.

As I was considering my options, however, Clay tugged at my jacket and pointed between my gun and Joe. 'Take him out, Marty,' he whispered tersely. 'Short bursts. Concentric sweeps!'

I ignored Clay's plea and shook him a definite no-no, partly because there was a chance Joe would only bleed sap, but mostly because it's never a good idea to shoot the guy who's driving you across town at speed. As Clay reached for my gun in a bid to show his obvious disagreement, I backhanded him across the jaw, after which he quietened down. Truth be told, I'd rather have been whacking Joe like a piñata just then, but this was hardly the time to be picky.

'You having any trouble back there, Whale?' As I was about to reply, Clay – now lying foetally across the back seat – grabbed my gun and quickly drew back the hammer. As I tried to wrestle it off him, Joe's ears pricked up quicker than those of a rabbit that'd just accidentally crept into a pound of sleeping dogs. 'I'll take that as a maybe, eh partner!' he chortled.

Despite my best efforts to retrieve the weapon, it went off at the convergence of Hoover and Diamond, yet the bullet only shattered the front windscreen as we two-wheeled it around the corner, and not Joe's cranium as Clay planned.

Joe, however, didn't bat an eyelid, which near-instantly psyched me out of another ten pounds, and all of them fully digested! He sure had added an exciting new facet to nausea.

'Open the window first,' Joe called back with a grin. 'You'll blow someone's head off if you go at it like that! And is there any chance you could get Clay to simmer down, man? I'm tryin' to concentrate here.'

Joe stuck the pedal to the metal, and the needle struggled to 95mph. By this stage, my mind's eye had developed a nervous tic, Clay was trying to kick out the side window in a bid to escape, and Joe was again shouting something macho which involved icing, but didn't involve cakes. It was then I knew I'd no choice: Joe's hatred for all things oriental ran deeper than the crack in a bricklayer's butt, and no amount of reasoning was going to coax him from his belfry.

But what were my options? If I shot him with his foot on the accelerator I'd have to simultaneously clamber into the front seat before he croaked, toss his lifeless form from the car and bring it to a halt before we crashed, all of which was slightly impossible for a man of my limited dexterity.

Or, I could go with a hastily formed Plan B.

Plan B was spontaneous and involved strangling Joe into submission using a choke which probably shouldn't have been used by anyone other than a Shaolin monk under a doctor's supervision. Still, I went for it!

But as I did, Joe began making funny, satisfied noises, and I released him instantly. Strangling him to death I could live with, but helping him get his rocks off was morally unacceptable. Still, all that became irrelevant in the ensuing nanoseconds, for by then we were of one voice – or, one scream, rather – as the cab rounded a blind-curve in the road and jack-knifed over a low-loader, leaving us airborne and spinning through the night, with Joe still wearing the grin of someone who'd struck it lucky in the Mile-High Club. And, as the road slowly unfurled above our heads and the night sky trailed below, I stuck my hands over my eyes in denial.

Then gravity reared its ugly head, and the cab struck and rolled over a grass verge, only to come to a shaky halt in a waterlogged gully. It seemed – without getting too philosophical here – that we'd all been momentarily circling the drain just then in more ways than one.

I was shaken and stirred, but alive. Quickly, I checked my parts, ensuring I still had one of everything down the centre, two of everything down the sides. I was fine except for a few cuts and bruises. Beside me, Clay groaned dimly, yet seemed otherwise alright. In the front of the cab, Joe was slightly dazed, yet he quickly shook that off and crawled out the front door. As he did, I kicked one of the mangled rear doors open and struggled through the opening. Outside, I rested shakily against the dilapidated hulk, watching as the Ham attempted to stand.

'You hurt?' I asked him. Joe shrugged, pursed his lips, then ran his hands tentatively over his body. 'Yet?' I added menacingly.

Joe grinned a good-old-boy grin. 'Shit, Whale, I'm made of wounds! Sometimes I think it's only my stitches hold me together.' As he spoke, he clutched at a few of his more tender ribs, then stared after the car we'd been chasing as it disappeared into the night. 'Besides, it's good to unwind every now and then, don't you think?'

I tottered unsteadily towards him, raising my hands into fists. 'Yeah? Well, I'm sick of you windin' me up, Joe. Now I'm goin' to show you how *I* like to unwind!'

Joe gazed at me momentarily, realising I was serious, after which he quickly adopted a boxing stance. 'So, now it's blubber whale to killer whale, eh? Well, bring it, Shamu, while we're both still young!'

He was semi-upright – and perhaps vaguely reminiscent of something that'd been swinging from the topmost branches of his own family-tree in the not-so-distant past – when I sucker-punched him hard in the ribs. He fell to the ground with a moan, and I kicked him a few times in the legs, before stomping his wounded arm for good measure. I stepped back as he was choking on his grin. 'You want to fight the King, Joe?' I balled my fists, then threw a few air-punches that near put me under. 'Then, let's go! I'm sick of you clangin' my bell!'

I was shaking by then, and my mind was a whirlwind of emotion – pain, fear, elation and depression. In fact, I was on the verge of insanity and about to leap, whereas Joe wasn't suffering from insanity, he was enjoying it! Still, I'm not entirely stupid, so I didn't let him get all the way up from the ground for his shot at the King. I kicked him again like a pigskin football, twice, and as hard as I could without dislocating my foot.

But he just kept grinning, and even emitted another almost sexual groan as he rose to his feet with the eagerness of a cub-scout at a crossing of little old ladies. I realised then that I'd forgotten one of my own golden rules: Never kick a man when he's down unless you're absolutely certain he'll never get up again.

'Fuckin' A, Marty!' Joe said, posturing up for another round. 'Fuckin' A!'

At that stage, I was exhausted and I'd nothing left but psychology. So I went at the Ali Shuffle, criss-crossing my legs and dancing around him in confusing semi-circles. Thing about the Ali Shuffle is, I only know the first half: I'd neither figured how to throw punches while moving, nor how to set up a decent defence. Still, Joe seemed impressed, and I think that's why he put his first punch on half-stun mode. It cleaned me off my feet and threw me against a broken fence. Then he came in fast, bouncing punches off my stomach with the speed of a professional. I was in Rope-A Dope mode now – not by choice, but because my trousers were snagging on the fence – and, after a few moments, Joe stopped, stepped back and admired my technique.

'Wow, you can fairly soak it up, Marty!'

I took that erstwhile opportunity to hit him a kick in the eggs. He clutched at his clutch, then fell to the grass, unconscious. Within seconds, I freed myself from the fence and kicked him again a couple of times more for good measure. I think I was getting to the stage where I couldn't stop when Clay came stumbling towards me.

'Marty, you're goin' to kill him!' he warned, pushing me aside. 'Do it like this!' He kicked Joe square in the back of the legs, twice. 'That'll just keep him sore!'

I heard the approaching siren of a police cruiser. 'Cool it,' I warned Clay. 'The police won't appreciate our efforts, even if they are for the good of the community.'

The city's finest were led from the front by a beefy cop who looked as if he'd just stalked across four continents to get there. As I tried to explain that Joe and I hadn't been fighting, we'd merely been separating each other, he hit me twice with his baton across the skull and hauled me bodily into the back seat of his car. Before I passed into unconsciousness, however, I remember smiling as a thought slipped through my mind at the speed of liquid mercury: At least, it informed me happily, I didn't have to wash out the stains in my own slacks when I got home.

***

I came awake some time later, yet it was hard to determine exactly when, due mainly to the fact that time had seemingly ceased to exist in the bowels of Police Administration. Within moments, I became aware that I was lying upon a thin metal cot in my favourite cell. Clay was lying upon the lowermost bunk across the way, and he was singing the prison blues. In the bunk above, Joe was accompanying him on the mouth organ. They both stared at me as I came awake – malevolently.

I heard a voice on the periphery of those darkly hypnotic glares. Tork Malone was standing just outside the cell door. He smiled sourly, and I slipped back into unconsciousness – voluntarily.

EIGHTEEN

We were in Tork's office. The senior detective stood with his back to me, gazing out of the window across the sun-sparked and slowly awakening city. I sat close to his desk, sipping at lukewarm coffee and dragging on a cigarette. Behind me, Mo leaned against a bookcase, his arms folded, his eyes mining the back of my head.

'Y'know, Shale' Tork sighed. 'Einstein once defined madness as doin' the exact same thing each day and expectin' different results. And that's what I think of each time I see you.'

'Einstein?'

'No, *madness*, you oversized fuckin' dog-rocket!' He took a deep breath, glanced momentarily down at me, then stared back out over the city. 'What I mean is, you wake each mornin', gorge on lard, then somehow stumble onto an unsuspectin' client. Several hours later, that same client's ready for the Happy Farm, you've become a professional target, and the city's crime rate has climbed 500%. So, at times, I reckon it'd be better for everyone if you just disappeared.'

'Hey, this isn't downtown Bolivia,' I feebled. As he turned and stared me a stormy, I added, 'And people saw me comin' in here. People with eyes...'

'Oh, don't worry, I'm talkin' legal here.' Tork suddenly produced a rap-sheet from his pocket and turned on me faster than a disgruntled postal worker. 'If I wanted, I could charge you with hijackin', reckless drivin', dischargin' a weapon in public, and countless traffic violations. Instead, I think we can perhaps exchange a few truths.' He leaned across the desk, wafted the sheet in my face. 'You remember what the truth is, don't you? It's where you don't have to keep recallin' what you said last. And if you agree to fall in with me now, *this* might even disappear.'

I grinned a sugar-coated toothy so sweet it should've died instantly of decay, yet I'd a feeling my own and Tork's idea of the truth were poles apart. To me, the truth wasn't a stranger, we'd just never been properly introduced, whereas to him and most 'law-abiding citizens' the truth was the latest delusion our present-day Uncle Sam had convinced them all to share. Still, even though I knew just then that sharing any leads I had with Tork would free me from my temporary bind, that new information might then allow him to solve the case before me, leaving me fee-less, knee-less and, inevitably, me-less soonafter.

The secret, therefore, lay in not lying to Tork, merely telling him the truth in a different way; and I'd no qualms about doing so. After all, can you actually deceive someone who doesn't really trust you? So, with that rationalisation predominant in my mind, I told Tork Malone the truth – or, at least, my version of it.

I told him how I suspected the real killer had been trying to frame both Abel and Frank; and, though I hadn't determined a motive, I figured it'd had something to do with their primary business venture. I also told him how the transmitter and earpiece was used to monitor the movements of the two men from the moment they entered room 18a; how the tracks of a table directly under the vent signified the perp was small, possibly a woman; and how the plan involved Rick being a very necessary witness. I lamely admitted, of course, that the actual time-line of the shooting was wrong, though assured them I'd work that out soon. And, as I spoke, Tork and Mo actually listened, sneered less than I expected, and even offered me more coffee. Finally, to cement the deal, I handed Tork the Shirinski letters.

'Maria said she got similar mail,' I said as Mo sidled alongside his boss to examine the letters. 'But Frank destroyed them.' I raised a hand as both men regarded me wryly. 'Yeah, she may be tryin' to enhance her alibi, but I believe her. As for those particular letters, I spent hours examinin' them under strict lab conditions...'

Tork held one to his nose. 'This one smells of wine,' he mused, raising a quizzical eyebrow. 'And this other one's got seaweed and sand on it. It smells like fish...'

I nearly choked on my coffee. 'Uhm, well, they're neatly written, correctly spaced, and have no spelling errors and proper margins, so they were obviously typed by someone with secretarial experience. And the way they're worded suggests our perp planned to reveal more than details of a supposed love-triangle.'

As Tork and Mo further scrutinised the letters, I poured myself some more coffee and mulled over what I hadn't told them. I hadn't mentioned that Gus Diamond and his merry men were on my case and may possibly have shot up both my house and the exterior of the Moose just to ensure I kept working this one. I hadn't mentioned that Marcie was equally volatile and perhaps equally responsible for those attempted assassinations. Nor had I included details of the luminous trail in room 18a, though frankly that was because I felt it was no longer relevant. And, finally, I'd omitted to add that I now suspected Patricia Shirinski had more to lose financially with Abel dead, as that simple detail merely eliminated one more female suspect and left Maria Ellis deeper in the frame.

After a few moments, Tork handed Mo the letters. 'Have Forensics check these. Oh, and get a few guys over to Skytowers to check out both that closet and room 18c.'

As Mo left, Tork relaxed into his chair, steepled his fingers under his chin. 'Right, Marty, I'll tell you what *we* know. Just to humour you, we decided to go with your theory. We interviewed the doorman who worked in Skytowers on the night of the murder, and he recalled seein' a woman leavin' shortly after the shootin'. So, we examined the security cameras and found he was right. She's seen exitin' a room on the 18th floor – we can't be sure if it's 18c or 18d, due to the camera-angle – and then in the lobby minutes afterwards. An outside camera also shows her drivin' off in a Daimler, but we didn't get the plate number. Still, it's hardly vital evidence because business-types enter and leave that place all the time.'

'But the entire 18th floor was closed for paintin', right? So she'd no cause to be up there. And whoever shot up the Moose was drivin' a Daimler...'

Tork shook his head. 'That's still not enough, Marty.'

'Hey, it fits with my hunch that the killer's female. And it's probably revenge, maybe somethin' to do with Frank and Abel's old business partner, Jim Harrison.'

'We followed the Harrison lead,' Tork said sourly. 'He bought a farm several years back in Honolulu, worked it for a while, then bought-the-farm again for good a few years later. So, that lead's as dead as he is. As for those letters, it *does* look as if the typist had secretarial experience. Of course, Maria Ellis was once a secretary...'

'As was Patricia Shirinski,' I cut in. 'And as *is* Anna Delaney.'

Tork nodded thoughtfully. 'Well, of the three, Patricia Shirinski seems to have more reasons for killin' her husband, primarily because she's named in his will...'

'There's a will?' I frowned a deepy. 'How much are we talkin'?'

'A cool two, maybe even three million.'

I shook my head, wondering if Anna Delaney had told me the truth about Patricia being in financial difficulty. 'Wow! And Anna, you, uhm, dig anythin' up on her?'

'She's from Iowa, and has absolutely no connection to anyone in this case.' He stared at me blankly. 'So, Marty, is there anythin' else?'

I shrugged and pouted easily. 'That's me, I'm all hunched out for now.'

'Well, hunches don't buy lunches,' Tork growled, waving me casually towards the office door. 'Now go. And, in case you didn't hear first time round, you've got two days to come up with new evidence, after which the D.A. has ordered that Frank Ellis stand trial for the murder of Abel Shirinski, and Maria Ellis stand trial for the attempted murder of Frank. So you're goin' to have to do a bit of work. And, if you want a definition of *that* word, it's sweatin' when you don't necessarily want to!'

I smiled an appreciative which depreciated as soon as I got into the corridor. But Mo was there, sporting a grim, and he set a firm hand between me and the wall to stop me moving on. 'A word to the wide, Marty,' he began. 'I've been told that a few members of a certain *family* are lookin' to leave you messier than usual over a debt you more-recently incurred. Is that right?'

I shook him an almost puritan no-no. 'Uh-uh, gamblin' isn't my Jones, Mo!'

'What the fuck does that even *mean*, Marty?'

'Look, Mo, I'd love to explain, really, but I'm hot on the heels of a suspect here, so, if you don't mind…' I gingerly removed his arm, then hurried towards the elevator. 'Oh,' I called back, 'you might want to get Malone some indigestion tablets. He's just finished eatin' shit, crow *and* his words. And, if all goes well in the next two days, he'll also be swallowin' large chunks of his pride and toppin' that off with a big slice of humble pie for desert!'

***

There'd been more than a little bravado in my exit from Police Administration, for the stark truth was that, in an investigation filled with swings and roundabouts, I was seemingly forever on the slide. I had to go see Patricia Shirinski again and ascertain her true financial status, then take things from there. I decided to drop in at the office first to see if Marcie had turned up anything new, but when I arrived the door was locked and the blinds drawn. I was set to leave again when Marcie dismounted from a cross-town Greyhound, her arms weighted down by files and bags, and her hair three sheets to the wind. She didn't seem in a good mood, but neither was I. All this eight-hour catnapping was eating away at my already uneven temperament. Marcie, therefore, was in the wrong place at the wrong time. She stared meekly at me from beneath her horn-rims.

'I slept in,' she squeaked apologetically.

'You sleep at home as well?' I barked. I allowed her to fumble the door open, pushed past her and made my way upstairs. Marcie stumbled into the office moments later. 'And what's with the windswept and interestin' hairdo, huh?'

Marcie mumbled something petty before moving off to fix herself in a mirror. I was thinking of something even pettier to say in reply when the door swept open and in walked Clay and Tommy Ellis. Thankfully, the Ham wasn't with them, though I kept my eyes on the empty doorway, my hand on my gun. 'Well, where is he?'

Clay regarded me sourly, then spoke in a tone you usually reserve for escaped lions or imminent pandemics. 'Out there. Somewhere.' He paused, before adding brightly, 'Oh, and young Tommy here has somethin' to tell you.'

Which wasn't the right thing to say to me to get me relaxed. Tommy Ellis was another doomsayer, and he wouldn't have had a cheery word to say about a carnival under the effects of laughing gas. I regarded him cynically.

'Well, spit it out, kid.'

'The Daimler...' he began hesitantly. 'The one outside the bar last night with the shooter inside?' I nodded tolerantly. 'Well, I saw it about an hour earlier outside your office. We were hangin' out down there, the guys and me, and it drove by real slow. I didn't see who was drivin' it, though, as the windows were blacked out.'

'Hangin' out as in *burglarisin' my office*, or just plain hangin' out?'

Tommy shrugged dumbly. 'How do you mean, Mr Shale?'

'Forget it. Anyhow, you get a look at the plates of the Daimler?'

Tommy's eyes lit up. 'Better than that,' he said. 'We hot-wired a car and tracked it as far as the Moose. Then we saw the shootin', so we hung back a little, before followin' it to the old warehouse district outside of town. Whoever was drivin' it hid it there, then took off on a motorbike. They were movin' too fast for us to follow after them. But they didn't see us, and I'm sure they'll return. I've got someone watchin' over the car as we speak.'

I clapped him on the shoulder. 'Great work, kid. Thing is, this guy of yours will have to stay there a while. I have to go extract a confession from a potential killer.'

Clay regarded me solemnly 'He didn't exactly tell you everythin', Marty.'

I was on my way to the door. 'What then? What else is there?'

'His man out there in the field,' Clay winced. 'It's Joe.'

I looked between the two of them, barely able to breathe. 'Tell me you didn't let him do that.' Clay nodded sourly and my heart dropped into my stomach. 'Jeez, do you know what you've done?'

Clay and Tommy shrugged and nodded almost guiltily. It was then I recalled Harry Truman once saying that you never set a fox to watch the chickens in the henhouse, no matter his experience. I shook my head and left the office in a daze. And I was still in something of a daze three hours later when I got out of my Buick outside Patricia Shirinski's house looking the best I'd looked for a long time.

***

Patricia Shirinski stepped back in surprise as she noticed the suave, well-coiffed and quite youngish-looking man on her doorstep. That man was me: A man more used to turning stomachs than heads, and a man who usually only ever wore a suit in the hope it would reduce the charges. It was wave a stick or dangle a carrot time. And I'd decided, for want of a better phrase, to dangle my proverbial carrot in Patricia's face in a bid to see exactly what sort of dame I was dealing with.

'Mr Shale, isn't it?' she asked, uncertainly. She was wearing an off-the-shoulder, nearly off-the-chest sort of frock that would normally have made me turn tripod immediately. Restraint set in, however, and I merely winked at her seductively. 'Mmm, yes,' she shuddered, 'I didn't recognise you. You're very – how can I put it? – *clean*. Yes, clean, that's the word.' She crossed her arms defensively. 'So, what can I do for you?'

'Well, this is a kind of social call.' She went to slam the door, but I blocked it with my foot. 'But not entirely,' I added quickly. 'It's, uhm, mainly business.'

She let me in rather reluctantly, and we moved into her grand sitting room and sat down – though not together, as I would've preferred. 'I suppose you'd like some coffee?' she said disinterestedly. I nodded. 'How do you take it?'

I wanted to say hot, black and wet, like my women, but I'd have to use that line another time as she was definitely none of those. 'White would be good,' I told her instead. 'White, lukewarm, and perhaps just a little too sweet to be wholesome.'

She poured the drink, passed it to me. Then I got into a little small-talk, mentioning casually that both Frank and Maria were going up the Swannee for double figures. That lightened the mood a little. Or, should I say, it lightened her mood at least.

'I'll be honest here,' I said when she'd stopped laughing ten minutes later. 'There are some people in Police Administration who think you're as guilty as sin on this thing. But I'm there for you. I know you're innocent. In fact, I've known it since I laid eyes on you, and, to be honest, I think you're a very impressive lady.'

'Why, thank you, Mr Shale,' she smiled. 'That's very nice of you. I'd like to say the same thing about you...' She shrugged, down-turned her mouth apologetically. 'But then obviously I'd only be lying, so I won't.'

I smiled wanly 'Mmm, well, anyhow,' I continued, 'I get this feelin' you and Abel had a few marriage difficulties. Am I right?'

'No more than any normal couple,' Patricia confided. She seemed ill at ease with that line of questioning – I could see that from the way her chest muscles tightened when she frowned. She rose from her seat and went to get herself a drink. 'I think I need a stiff one,' she told me.

You talk about tact: With that verbal opening, I could've gone for it there and then. But I held back, knowing I had to get the interview out of the way first.

'What I'm sayin', lady, is that there's an old joke which says marriage is an institution in which he loses his Bachelor's degree and she gains her Masters, and yet another which says a good wife laughs at her husband's jokes, not because they're clever, but because she is. Was that how it was with you and Abel?'

She regarded me haughtily. 'If you mean what I think you mean, no. We were equals. We were in love, and we were always honest with each other.'

'And he left you quite a bit of money in his will, isn't that right?'

'I don't know where you heard that, Mr Shale, but it isn't true.' She lowered her gaze. 'In fact, it will be common knowledge soon, so I'll tell you. Our company was set to go into liquidation, and we had to sell off most of our assets just to keep afloat the last three years. There's no money in Abel's will. In fact…'

'…that's why you're relyin' on the insurance,' I cut in. She nodded blankly, sipped heavily at her drink. 'But if Abel is now found to be complicit in the crime, you'll end up with zilch?' Patricia nodded again and she seemed set to go all watery and feminine, but I kept pushing. 'That aside, it's quite clear both you and Maria are hidin' somethin'. I still say it has somethin' to do with Frank and Abel's primary business. So why don't you let me in on this one? I can help you clear Abel's name. Then, the insurance is yours.'

She took a deep breath, lowered her head. 'I think you should go, Mr Shale. You've upset me enough for one day, and I really don't feel all that well.'

'Maybe I could help you,' I said with a wink, instinctively feeling she was maybe acting devitalised and distressed in the hope of being revitalised and undressed. 'We could maybe have a bath, lock lips, swap tongues and do some squishy stuff.'

'Mr. Shale,' she snorted, 'I'd appreciate it if you'd leave. Or…'

'…or even moreso if I stayed?' I grinned a 36 carat, feeling that line was a clincher.

'No, *or* I'll call the police.'

I raised a cocky eyebrow. 'Hey, what are they goin' to charge me with – assault with a friendly weapon?

Patricia rose quickly and rang a bell at her side. Her gardener was suddenly framed large in the doorway, bigger and nastier looking than I recalled.

'Only a suggestion,' I grimaced. 'I'll leave you my card.'

Her gardener took that rather opportune moment to trail me unceremoniously from my seat and out to the door, wiry seventy year old that he was, from which particular vantage he flung me unceremoniously onto the lawn.

I picked myself up and walked off down the drive. Well, she hadn't fallen for the old Shale charm, I mused, and that was so much temptation in itself, so maybe I was wrong about her after all. Maybe Patricia Shirinski had loved her husband, and maybe she wasn't a bed-hopping mattress-back like one or two others in this case. Still, I'd let that go for now, I decided as I began my long walk home, and I'd maybe think about her again later when I was getting into my hobby.

NINETEEN

They say true friends are never more than a phone-call away. And you've got to hand it to Clay: Despite knowing I'd swing on his nuts if short of a rope, it took one call to convince him to fetch Tommy and Muds over to my place shortly after 8-00pm. Now, I'm not big on apologising, and usually only do so if purposely laying down a mild I-told-you-so foundation for those who'll have just cause to judge me soon afterwards on ever-worsening offences. Still, I'd organised that little get-together on the pretext I was apologising for Joe's behaviour the previous night. Truth was, of course, I'd another ruse up my sleeve, yet I needed some help to pull it off safely.

Now, we sat around the kitchen table, upon which Greta had assembled heaped plates of nuts, chips and dips, all of which we planned to wash down with several cases of cheap lager. I nudged Clay over on the bench, passed him another beer. 'Say, buddy,' I grinned, 'you, uhm, mind if I sit alongside you?

'Only if you promise not to talk or gaze in my direction,' Clay soured. Still, he took the beer from me and gulped at it as if it was some vastly improved sort of oxygen. 'Oh, and if you could maybe die on the spot, too, that'd be nice!'

Now, I know they say we see in others what we know in ourselves, but, as a superior detective, I'm often required to think outside the box. And just then, as I slugged my beer and stared hard at Clay, it struck me the events of the last few days had either taken a hard toll on my friend or he was developing an alcohol problem. It may've had something to do with the way his favourite drink always seemed to be the next one, or the way he toasted other people's health so much he was ruining his own. However, in truth, it probably had more to do with the fact he was drinking more of my beer than I was. Despite this troublesome breach in our friendship, I still had high hopes of getting him back on my side. All I had to do was give him a thwarted 'If we don't hang together, we'll hang alone' speech, albeit minus the levity and with a side-order of gravity. And I intended doing so, but only after I'd filled him, Muds and Tommy in on the latest breaks in the case.

'So,' I chuckled, 'I'm on Patricia's sofa, notebook out, and all set to probe her in-depth, when she says she's off to get into somethin' more comfortable. Two minutes later, she's back wearin' a one-ounce negligee, squirmin' in my lap and tryin' to catch me in a lip-lock. Now, I'm a professional, as y'know, so I push her off and start askin' a few direct questions, but she's soon back cooin' in my ear, "What are you like in bed, Marty?"

'Wow!' Clay drawled, not a bit impressed.

'Yeah', I said, eager to maintain the facade. 'Well, as you guys know, I'm a very funny guy, so I say, "Six-foot-four and sleepy, lady, but I'm here to work!"' I chuckled softly. 'Now, don't get me wrong: Ordinarily, I'd turn tripod in a heartbeat with a broad like that, yet I know she's just tryin' to distract me because I'm onto her. Christ, and Abel just a cinder-ball, can you believe it? I'll tell you, they say bigamy is one wife too many, but you can't help thinkin' monogamy is often the same!

I adopted a bewildered, lit a cigarette and stared around the table, only to be met by several more incredulous stares. Momentarily guilt-ridden, I downturned my gaze, aware it perhaps wasn't right to tarnish the reputation of the recently bereaved. And hadn't yesterday's fiasco been my own fault in a way? Hadn't experience taught me I should never interview female suspects when carrying around a Cornucopian Horn of Plenty as I've a tendency to end every sentence with a proposition? Saying that, what harm was I actually doing? I wasn't lying, merely telling the truth in a way nobody recognised, although it probably wouldn't hurt any if I toned it down a bit.

I raised my head. 'Now, imagine the scene here. She's lap-dancin' me, swirlin' her plastic titties in my face, and I'm calmly interviewin' her. But then she loses it when I don't take her on, rings a bell at her side, and, seconds later, in walks this hulk of a man.' I extended my arms in a vertical fisherman pose. 'He's as big as a small horse, looks like the Bulgarian shot-puttin' champion, and he circles me for a time before pullin' out a switchblade. But I jump up and I'm on him like a tramp on fries. And, after about ten minutes of all-in, he's all-out. I swear, I laid him flat as a tortilla, and didn't even wrinkle my jacket in the process!'

Muddy and Tommy managed a smile. Even Greta managed a lopsided Aryan grin. Clay, however, didn't exercise his chuckle-muscles even slightly. 'So, apart from comin' on to her,' he said coldly, 'and failin' dismally in your attempts to woo her, did you uncover any new evidence which might eventually put her away?'

Everyone there, especially Tommy, stopped smiling, and regarded me expectantly.

'Wow!' I snorted indignantly. 'So, now you think I actually want to bed that refugee from a recyclin' plant? Jeez, I wouldn't take her out if it was foggy, and I'd rather French-kiss a skunk! Besides, she's all about the money, but even then it's probably never made her happy, merely allowed her to grumble in style. As for sex, my guess is she just uses that as a chance to have another good fuckin' moan…'

'Thou doth protest too much,' Clay retorted, raising a stalling hand. 'All I'm askin' is if you got any new evidence which might prove she killed her husband.'

I shook my head dolefully, now all too aware that sometimes a problem shared is a problem quadrupled. 'No,'

I admitted flatly. 'I didn't. But that doesn't mean she's innocent, does it?' As everyone there regarded me blankly, I turned to Tommy, who was now slumped dejectedly in his seat. 'Look, kid, don't worry,' I told him. 'I've still a few interviews to conduct. It's not over until the fat, uhm, whatever...'

'You look very pensive, uncle Whale,' Muddy said.

'Nah, kid, I'm just thinkin'.' As Muddy raised an inquiring eyebrow, I added, 'Y'know, about the car used in the drive-by. And about Joe.'

'I'm tryin' to enjoy my beer,' Clay shuddered. 'Why'd you mention *him*?'

'Yeah,' I pouted, lowering my gaze. 'We have ourselves a problem there.'

'We?' Clay belched. 'What's with this *we* shit, paleface?' He spat a bunch of half-chewed pretzels over my table. 'Is that what this little party is – a bribe?'

'Jeez, Clay, you're so fuckin' cynical! This is all, uhm, for free...'

'You only ever get free cheese in mousetraps!' Clay rasped. 'What do you want?'

I paused a second, thinking it only mannerly. Then I said, 'Your pick-up truck. And maybe one or two of you to help me on a stake-out. Any, uhm, volunteers?'

'Joe's there,' Clay replied coldly. 'So, why do you need our help?'

'Because Joe's there.'

'I'm with you, uncle Whale,' Muddy beamed.

'Me too, Mr Shale, sir,' Tommy added. 'This is for my family anyhow.'

I thanked them sincerely, though I can't be sure I meant it as I'm always sincere whether I mean it or not. Still, the Good Ship Shale had nearly press-ganged itself a full crew, so all we needed now was a skipper before setting off for our personal Bermuda Triangle. Of course, a couple of beers later, that problem was also solved, because by then Clay was putty-like in my hands.

***

If you've ever seen a stake-out movie, it may've struck you that sitting in a car the night through is exciting. Thing is, no one ever mentions the cramped conditions, the stale air, the sweaty feet and the hours of boredom and anxiety as you try to stay alert in case you miss anything. Fact is, it's about as much fun as your weekly crap.

It was approaching midnight and Clay had parked the jeep upon a secreted hillside verge overlooking the only road in and out of the abandoned warehouse district on the city outskirts. Tommy sat in the front passenger seat, and I sat in the back seat alongside Muddy. The car used in the drive-by, Tommy informed us, was stashed in the warehouse immediately behind the high wire fence to our front. I'd already told the others this might be a fruitless operation, but they didn't seem too worried. I noticed, however, that I was the only one who'd come prepared.

'What's with the pyjamas, Marty?' Clay asked. As I ignored him and took out a bag of cookies, a few sleeping tablets and a flask of warm milk, he said, 'Hey, Whale, you hear me back there?'

'Sure I can hear you, but I'm prepared to swap places with someone who can't!' As he glared an icy at me, I nibbled on a cookie. 'You'll see. I've done this before.' I looked over at Muds. 'Hey, kid, could you stop pickin' your nose? You're examinin' that thing like it was the lost treasure of Tutankhamen.'

Tommy stared back at me. 'Is it you that keeps blowin' off, Mr Shale?'

'Uh-uh,' I replied, offended by his tone. 'These are special anti-flatulence cookies, purpose-baked for stakeouts.

I'm even smokin' less so none of you will have to hook up to an iron lung when you get back.' I glowered at each of them in turn from an overhang of forehead. 'So how about stickin' your *grrr* on the end of your *attitude*, and showin' me the *grrr-attitude* I so rightly deserve!'

Obviously unaware that a fine pun is its own reword, Tommy ignored me and stared wide-eyed beyond the mesh of shadows now clinging to the surrounding bushes. 'Do you think Joe's out there somewhere?' he asked quietly.

I burped loudly, stared off at the full moon and nodded sourly. 'Oh, he's out there, kid, he sure is. But don't worry, I always expect the unexpected...'

It was then, at that moment, that *It* chose to appear at my window: Swamp Thing! He'd smeared his face in black and grey stripes, was garbed in green and brown camouflage, and his helmet sported enough foliage to thatch a small cottage. The whites of his eyes, however, were luminous as flying saucers and just as eerie.

'Joseph H Crucifix!' I spluttered. I fumbled about for my gun, which was now somewhere under my seat. As I was doing so, Clay released a lungful of scream, Tommy ducked under the dash for cover, and Muddy tucked in neatly behind me.

'Can it, guys!' Joe rasped. 'It's only me.'

I took a deep breath, suppressing an urge to plug him. 'Jeez, Joe, you scared the doo out of us! And why the get-up? You're like a walkin' Army and Navy store!'

'Chucks out there,' Joe whispered, taking on a big-eye. He looked at me hard, with that deadpan-makes-you-want-to-reach-for-the-bedpan look he's always able to pull off with ease in his attempt to make others uneasy. 'I'm just waitin' to see the reflection of the moon in his little yellow eyes. Then I'm gonna fuckin' pop him!'

Joe had some type of Gattling gun strapped across his back, with a magazine of armour-piercing, wall-removing and city-levelling ammunition feeding into it. If that was his pop-gun, I didn't envy Chuck in the slightest.

'You like the weapon?' he grinned. 'Marty, meet Bertha.'

I nodded an awkward how-do. Then, calmly, I said, 'So, uhm, what's up, Joe?'

'I came over to see if you've forgiven me for the drivin' thing.'

I frowned, unable to believe he'd reduced last night's Demolition Derby to 'the drivin' thing'. 'Hey, what's to forgive? You forgive me for the, uhm, kickin' thing?'

'Shit, Marty,' Joe cheesed, 'you couldn't punch your way out of a wet paper bag!'

'Uh-huh,' I nodded, grinding vice-like at another cookie. 'And what's with, uhm, *Bertha*? They say you should walk softly and carry a big stick through life, Joe. You're not exactly adherin' to that little snippet of wisdom, are you?'

Joe pouted a De Niro. 'Hey, they also say tact is fur on a gauntlet, Whale, know what I'm sayin'?'

I didn't know what he was saying, and I so wanted to explain that tact was actually the art of making a point without making an enemy, yet this was a man who'd forged a career tactlessly making enemies, so what was the point? Instead, I smiled wanly and said, 'Mmm, snappy retort, Joe! Anyhow, do you think you could just go back and keep watch, and maybe *not* shoot at our perp, even if you see him?'

Joe sighed and nodded dimly, then vanished into the blackness of the night.

'Is he for real?' Tommy asked in horror.

'Oh, he's the real deal, kid,' I nodded. 'His sole purpose in life is to serve as a warnin' to others. Like, back when we were neighbours, I went over to his place one time to complain about the mines he was layin' in my yard.' They all stared at me, horrified. 'Yeah,' I nodded. 'Seriously. Anyhow, there were posters all over his wall: Visit Russia before she visits you; Stalin's grave is just another Communist plot, stuff like that.' I turned to Tommy. 'Does that sound real enough to you?'

As Tommy nodded thoughtfully, I shook my head and cursed under my breath. Yeah, Joe was too real for my liking. His family crest was probably made up of a Dodo, a Cuckoo, and a Bat, all sitting around eating bananas.

'He's a pain in the neck,' Tommy cut in.

'I've a much lower opinion of him,' I seethed. I handed Clay my gun. 'Listen,' I told him. 'I'm goin' to grab a half-hour's shuteye. If Joe comes back, just shoot him and we'll talk consequences later.'

Clay nodded uncertainly and I went to sleep, hoping against hope that, just for once, someone would follow my instructions to the letter.

***

Wishes don't do dishes, I'll say it again. I awoke shortly after 10-00am to hear from my bleary-eyed colleagues that Joe hadn't died in a hail of gunfire, and that our perp hadn't returned to pick up the Daimler. So, after convincing Joe that I'd drop by to relieve him in a few hours time, I had Clay drive me home. There, I showered – even though I didn't really feel the need, as I'd showered two days back – before sprawling on my settee and catnapping a few hours away.

At 2-00pm, shortly after I'd drunk breakfast, I climbed into the Buick and drove over to the Shirinski Gadget shop. Anna Delaney was there, looking far too beautiful to be guilty of even Original Sin. Still, I had to follow every lead, no matter how insane. It was either that or acknowledge the fact that, once Maria and Frank Ellis began their stretch, I'd once again be circling the proverbial drain.

Little Plum was wearing a raspberry red dress and strawberry blouse, and cherry-red lipstick made her bee-stung lips a focal point of her peach complexion. She also had the nicest set of melons I'd ever seen, just sitting there in a fruit basket inside the door. As she shook my hand in greeting and led me inside, her little plane-on-a-chain dipped low into the valley of her breasts, and never in my life had I so wanted to be a Kamikaze pilot than just then. Inside the main office, I sat down, lit up and a cigarette and got straight to the point.

'Miss Delaney,' I began. 'A certain officer by the name of Tork Malone has been tossin' your name around in this murder case like a Frisbee at a beach party.'

Little Plum turned olive green. 'Me?' she gasped, incredulously. 'He thinks I killed Abel?'

I raised a palm. 'You're no more surprised than I am, Miss Delaney. In fact, when I heard he was blamin' you, I went down to Police Administration and mounted a steamin' protest all over their station floor. Seriously. Now, I *know* you're innocent. It's just that I need a bit more evidence to convince me to, uhm, convince him.'

'But what can I tell you that you don't already know?'

'Well, was Abel givin' you..?' I had to be tactful here, because she looked shocked enough as it was, so Italian hand-signals were definitely out. 'Well, was he givin' you anythin' in the way of, uhm, *extra*, if you know what I mean.'

She cocked her head like a curious spaniel and shrugged. 'I don't understand...'

I cursed inwardly. How did you ask such a beautiful young girl such an awkward question? Was he giving you the Gorilla's Finger, a Prime Rib, the Beef Dagger or the Mutton Message? Did you and he ever play Bury the Bratwurst? Or did he ever offer to take the temperature of your Bearded Clam with his Love Thermometer?

'What I'm tryin' to say is, was he givin' you, y'know, a *bonus*?' As I spoke, a hand-signal slipped out, and just when I thought I had it all under control. A big Italian one, complete with clenched fist and slapped bicep. Shit!

Anna blushed and lowered her head. 'Were we lovers, you mean?'

'Yeah, that's what I mean. Sorry, I haven't spoken to any real ladies in a while.'

Anna nodded, then shook her head sadly. 'No, Mister Shale. Abel was a sweet man, and we were friends, but nothing more. I couldn't imagine...' She shivered a little as if the thought repulsed her, and I smiled, because women tend to do that when talking about me. It was sort of nice to see I wasn't out there on my own.

'Alright. Well, is there anythin' you may've forgotten to tell the police?' I hedged. 'Like maybe what you were, uhm, doin' the night Abel was killed?'

She shrugged easily. 'On the night of his death, I was at a dance class downtown. I left about 7-15 and went straight home. I saw no one for the rest of the evening.'

'Surely you must realise you then had a few minutes in which you could've reached Skytowers. Time enough to get in, polish Abel off, escape in a Daimler and...' I threw up my hands. 'Clean as a whistle, worlds your lobster, know what I mean?'

Anna dropped her head, and I saw tears forming in her eyes. I offered her a congealed handkerchief and, for one brief moment, as her little aeroplane came flying out from the valley, I caught a glimpse of her initials upon it.

'You ever get hitched?' I asked. 'Ever married?' I glanced at her left hand, though she wasn't wearing a wedding ring.

She tried to open my handkerchief, then handed it back to me as the thing refused to separate. 'They say that marriage is an institution, Mr Shale,' she said simply. 'And who wants to live in an institution for the rest of their life?'

I smiled sadly. 'Yeah,' I agreed. 'My thoughts exactly. Though they also say it isn't the way they say it is, y'know?' She shook her head and I shrugged, not really wanting to clarify that statement. I got up instead and shook her hand. 'Well, I better be goin'. Thanks for your help.'

She smiled again, and nodded, before getting up and escorting me to the door.

I walked out into the fresh air, my mind a jumble of half-thoughts. And something stirred in the inky cauldron of my mind just then, an idea that I didn't really want to contend with. Of course, most times I don't usually let ideas get in the way of my thinking, and yet, at that particular moment, I felt I might actually have to.

TWENTY

Wednesday night is Greta's night on the town. She usually starts out at a bingo hall with a concealed hip-flask and a box of cigars to tide her over, then heads into centre city to the sort of bars where they have plasma on drip. During the small hours of such evenings, no mother's son is safe, even though Greta could personally stroll naked and unmolested through a roomful of sailors on shore-leave, such are her redoubtable charms. To be candid, she's got a face like a blind carpenter's thumb, stay-out-of-bed eyes, and a nose that should've come with training wheels. On the upside, however, she has everything else a man could wish for – sideburns, biceps, and a punch that could stun a lowland gorilla into a seizure. Unsurprisingly, therefore, she usually returns home most Wednesday nights alone.

At the start of our tempestuous relationship, this had always been a problem – for me. Being the only available male at so late an hour upon whom she might yet sate her primeval lust, Greta tried everything from bribery, blackmail, chloroform, drugs and heavy coshes in her attempt to bed me. Now, I'm no saint, and, even though I've never gone to bed with an ugly woman, I've woken up with plenty. Still, there's a line even I won't cross: Pug-ugly and Bug-ugly I can take, but Fugly is way off-limits! So now, each Wednesday night, I deadlock my bedroom door, wreath the door with garlic and have at least one silver bullet in my Magnum, just in case.

On this particular Wednesday evening, the pungent whiff of one of Greta's perfumes in the hallway – it was either Eau de Colon or Eau Dear – told me that pensionable-unmentionable had already left Chez Shale to engage in her weekly manhunt. So, after de-tabbing a beer, I decided to make my own supper. Of course, as I too have a natural disposition for making the already unpalatable indigestible, I tend to stick with much easier recipes. As I slipped the bread in the toaster, however, the phone rang. In truth, I wasn't feeling too sociable, but I decided to answer it anyhow: After all, there was always the chance that Patricia Shirinski could no longer suppress her urges and had decided to invite Yours Seductively over for a post-ash-bash.

Still, in much the same way as the inevitable always happens, the improbable rarely does. The caller – even though he hadn't the manners to state his name – was my old bottom-feeding non-friend, Chester Hardcastle. And, like me, he obviously believed that good news should be delivered face to face in the hope of reward, and bad news briefly by phone in a strange accent. But I was onto him instantly. He couldn't ditch the slime in his voice, and I swore I heard his scales crackling as he spoke.

'This is a friend,' he slithered. 'I've got a lead on the Ellis case. Word has it that the Mayor is going to come down hard on Maria and Frank Ellis. He's up for re-election soon, and he's been told he needs to get tougher on crime in the city.'

Chester shouldn't have gone all inside-info on me, but then he didn't really know that, unused as he was to slithering about in the cess-fest of anonymous phone-calls. Besides, anyone calling me a friend usually wanted something for free; and, as a not-so-wise mouse once squeaked, you only ever got free cheese in mousetraps.

'Go ahead, *friend*,' I said shortly. 'I need the help.'

'So, if you want to save them, you should be looking into the girl called Anna Delaney. She knows far more than she's told you.'

As Chester spoke, my toast suddenly sprung from the toaster and fell to the dusty floor. 'Is that it?' I seethed. 'I'm in the middle of whippin' up dinner here.'

'I'm doing you a favour. But you obviously don't deserve my help.'

'No, and I don't deserve haemorrhoids either, but I've fuckin' got them!'

'Look into what I'm saying,' he rasped. 'You won't be disappointed.'

'Uh huh! Well, I might do that. And hey, Chesty...'

'Yes? Uhm, I mean, sorry, vere you talking to me?'

I ignored his sudden switch to a German accent. 'No, I'm talkin' to my sofa, Chesty the Chesterfield. Anyhow, don't you want paid for this? I mean, I'm guessin' you're just a poor, trainee ambulance-chaser who's simply lookin' to scam some moolah for his law degree fees, right?'

'Giff it to the Underappreciated Private Investigator's Fund!'

As Chester hung up, I ignored the five-minute rule about dropped food, picked up my toast and began buttering it. Christ, I mused, if that guy ever went in for brain surgery, they'd charge him a search fee! Still, I could see his line of thinking: He needed a scapegoat to keep Maria out of the Big House until he got paid. And, as he couldn't fob his imaginary lead off on Tork Malone, he figured I'd work it for him. As to why he'd chosen Anna Delaney, it may've been because the field of suspects was narrowing, or because, like me, he actually suspected her of telling a few lies. The second initial on her little aeroplane had been scraped away. She also wore an engagement ring embossed in diamonds which had been fashioned into two letter A's, though what that meant I didn't know. Anna and Abel? That was one possibility, because porking secretaries had been one of Abel's hobbies after all.

I was thinking it over and eating my toast when the phone rang again. Mo was on the line, so I hung up. I did that six times, but he kept ringing, same as I do with him.

'What is it now, Mo?'

'I need some info on that guy, Joe Sinto,' Mo said wearily.

'Joe, eh?' I spat out some of the hairier toast, continued munching. 'Well, his last reality check bounced, he's a shiver forever in search of a spine, and he's slower than a herd of wild snails stampedin' through treacle. More importantly though, Mo, he's *not* actually my responsibility, so why are you askin' me about him?'

'I just got word he was seen drivin' down the warehouse district in a T62 tank,' Mo sighed. The incredulity in his voice told me that even he doubted the validity of that report. 'It was taken from outside the Karpis Stadium. The Army and the Navy are holdin' their annual game there. Is someone windin' my clock here?'

I rose hurriedly, pulled on my sneakers. 'Yeah, sure, he's your solid, everyday Joe is Joe, but he couldn't tell left from right with two guesses, never mind drive a tank! You just ignore that one, Mo, and I'll go check it out.'

'Yeah, well, I get the feelin' you know *exactly* what he's doin', Whale, so it better not be true, for both your sakes!' The line went dead, and I cursed under my breath, then got straight on the phone to Clay and explained the situation.

After laughing like a loon for several moments, Clay said, 'Beats me why everyone is forever tryin' to stick you on a shame-spiral where Joe is concerned, Whale. Don't they realise it's not your fault you never learned how to accept responsibility?'

I ignored the sarcasm. 'Look, Clay, I don't need Joe throwin' his frag grenades into my bunker. If you help me find him, I'll help you out with that plane-bill thing.'

'Yeah? How much are we talkin'?'

As Clay brightened, it suddenly struck me that personal calamities can be sorted into two types; there's the kind which brings misfortune to us, and the other sort which brings good fortune to others. Clay had obviously decided he could profit from this sudden downturn in my ever downturning misfortunes. 'Mmm, a few hundred.'

'A couple of hundred or a few hundred? The difference could be several hundred.'

'Five...'

'Eight,' he said sharply.

'Four and a half.'

'Five it is,' Clay agreed swiftly. He knows I'm the first to put my hand in my pocket, though I'm also the last to take it out. Still, he hadn't gotten his money yet and there he was, gloating. Jeez, would he ever learn?

Thirty-minutes later, Clay, Muddy and Tommy were at my door; and, at about 8-45pm, we reached the warehouse district. Clay dimmed the jeep's headlights, and, under a bruised sky, we took the dirt track off the main road into the scrub that grew up thick beyond the warehouse we'd surveilled the previous night. As we drew to a halt and scanned the overgrown hedgerows that grew up around the rusting fences, I whispered, 'Right, Sergeant Daffy of Looney Corp, where the hell are you?'

Clay took on a big eye. 'He'll find us,' he mused bleakly. 'He'll find us.'

Clay was right. Swamp Thing suddenly rose up without warning beside my window like something from way down the food-chain, Bertha strapped across his back. Still, on the upside, as we were expecting him this time, it saved us from having to bunch up and hire a stable-hand to clean out Clay's jeep when we got back to town.

'What's happenin', Joe?' I asked, casually surveying his armour for chinks. 'You, uhm, commandeerin' tanks now, is that it?'

'I just figure anythin' worth fightin' for is worth fightin' dirty for,' Joe grinned. He regarded me through such pain-wracked eyes that I wanted to go at him with a morphine-filled syringe. 'And the guys down the stadium said I could borrow it, so it seemed like a great idea to me.'

'Yeah, well, you get an idea, Joe, you should treat it gently.' I regarded him sagely. 'Remember, it's a long way from home, and probably very scared, what with it bein' all alone and stuff.'

'Hey, man, sorry for fuckin' tryin' to help!' Joe shook his head despondently. 'Y'know, man, it's just that I've spent my whole life fightin' for peace, and now I'd just like a little piece of what I've been fightin' for…'

I sighed deeply. Clay had been right earlier: I had to start taking responsibility for my own actions. At the beginning of this case, I could've ignored Joe's pleas to let him help me out, but somewhere at the back of my mind – in a stroke of Einsteinian genius comprising 1% inspiration, 9% perspiration and 90% desperation – I'd decided he'd come in handy when the going got rough, even though I'd known exactly what he was like. Now it was time to man-up and bring him back into line.

'Look, Joe, you're a good guy, and I appreciate you helpin' me out. Still, while it's great to be an individual just the same as everyone else, you should never stray too far from the herd, know what I'm sayin'?' He nodded dimly. 'Good, now, I'd like you to go back over there and fire off a single warnin' shot – into the air – *if* our suspect comes back to collect his car. Do you think you could do that?'

Joe pouted a solemn, then beamed a freaky. 'Good pep talk, Whale. I'm on it.'

I gnawed at my lower lip. 'Great! Well, off you go. And make sure you keep your helmet on.' Joe saluted, then shimmered like a chameleon into the brush and vanished. Quietly, I added, 'In case there are any fuckin' woodpeckers about!'

'I reckon that guys all talk,' Muddy said when the Ham had vanished out of earshot. 'He probably wouldn't know a

Communist if he saw one. And the other night in the bar, he told me he was in 'Nam when the first shot was fired. Told me he'd actually fired it. But I reckon he was stateside when they fired the second.'

'Yeah,' I sighed. 'You could be right. But he's the man with the tank, y'know. And you never argue with the man with the tank, that's my motto.'

Joe suddenly appeared back at the car window. 'Words fly on the wind, Muds,' he said eerily. 'And I know all about Commies, kid', he rasped. 'They're the guys who have nothin' and want you to share it with them. You remember that when they get a foothold on our shores.' Muddy nodded in horror. 'And never try talkin' pygmy to a dwarf, y'hear?'

Muddy nodded again, and Joe vanished as if he'd never been.

I shrugged. 'He's the man with the tank. And you never argue...'

'...with the man with the tank,' Muddy whispered. 'Yeah, I see that.'

Seldom, as a bunch, do we ever agree on anything, yet we agreed on that one. The conversation changed after that philosophical rejoinder, and we spoke of many lesser things, most of little consequence. Soon the blue-black evening sky succumbed to a night as pitch as a bucket of tar, and the temperature dropped into the 50s. We grew apathetic, tired and generally disgruntled, and one of us might soon have lost his temper and started taking his life out on the others had it not been for Joe.

Or, should I say, Bertha.

I was half asleep when the gun-battle started. I'm saying gun-battle here, because few people would argue with the fact that anything over a hundred shots qualifies for that title. The sky lit up like July 4th, and my comrades, noisy little tykes that they are, decided to go at the flailing and the wailing, the sighing and the crying, the shouting and the pouting, and the hitting and the shadow boxing.

But not me. Long since used to not only having nightmares when I was asleep, I was calm, unshaken and unstirred, with my Magnum poised to fire at my enemy… who was coming towards me in a fucking tank!

'Clay!' I stormed as the glare of massive headlights near blinded me. 'Get us the hell out of here!' I shook him bodily and he responded rather well, so I kept doing it, even as he thrust the gear-stick into reverse and revved the engine until the pick-up was skidding back into the brush. A motor-bike flashed by the side window and I heard the sound of automatic fire dashing off the road, the trees and everything else within a fifty yard radius. Seconds later, the T62 rumbled past us after the bike, ploughing up the surrounding brush as it moved. I wound my window quickly down as Joe made to reload Bertha.

'Jeez, Joe!' I screamed after him. 'What the hell are you doin', man?'

Joe cupped his ear above the roar of the engine. 'Can't hear you, Marty!'

'Go MIA!' I said frostily. 'Go *dee-dee-mau*, or whatever the fuck it is!' He looked a little hurt. 'And stay there,' I added sourly. 'We'll take it from here.'

Joe saluted sadly and the T62 ground to a halt, but not before flattening 200 yards of wire-fencing and several signposts. Bertha fell to half-mast in Joe's arms like a deflated dragon, belching reams of smoke and puff-balls of flame. Clay pulled the pick-up around and we drove off in the direction the motorbike had taken.

The driver of the motorbike was suited up in black in the time honoured fashion of all baddies, and kept to the country roads that led into centre city. Clay pushed the needle on the clock to 85mph, then 90, and further. He had us hurtling along the roads and taking hairpin bends with the aggrieved attitude of a Formula One driver who'd found he'd only a day to live. The biker remained several hundred yards ahead of us, but glanced back on occasion to gauge his distance. He was heading in the direction of Masseria Park, though when he reached it, he raced on. In the distance I saw the shining beacon of trellised lights that made up the tall, rectangular phallus known as Skytowers.

The motorcyclist made towards it, and we stayed hot on his tracks. I didn't know what we'd do when we caught him, as someone would firstly have to prise my fingers out of the dashboard and my head out of my ass if Clay kept on driving the way he was. I'd stopped shaking him a while back and now he was on automatic.

The biker skidded to a halt outside the massive complex, fired two shots into the air, then cast the bike to the ground and ran into the building's lobby. Clay parked the pick-up in the lot at an angle as yet undecided upon by geometrists. I disengaged my fingers from the dash, picked my Magnum up from the floor and got out. Clay, Muddy and Tommy followed after me like lost sheep.

Gingerly, I strode up the steps into the lobby. The security guard lay unconscious on the floor, so we bypassed him and fanned out, moving towards the elevators. When we reached them, I summoned one down. As I did so, I asked Tommy to go reconnoitre the stairwell, and to let me know by way of either a shout or a stifled scream if he found anyone. The lift had been sitting on the 18th floor and down it came. As the door opened, I stepped back in surprise and my gun dropped down to my side.

Anna Delaney stepped out of the lift. She was dressed in black leather and had a sad, almost committed smile upon her face. She made no rush to escape past me.

Instead she held out her hands. 'Take me, Marty,' she said softly. 'I'm all yours.'

As my jaw dropped, I stared at her hard. In other circumstances, I would've had a pole on me that Paul Bunion couldn't have chopped down, and you would've had to hold me back with a crane, pulleys and forty-pounds of chain. But in this instance, my heart dropped into my stomach and the only thing I could raise was a frown.

TWENTY ONE

'Why?' I asked, shaking my head in disbelief. 'Jeez, I never figured you for a Marty Miller, lady.'

Anna seemed puzzled, and once again she cocked her head like a Spaniel.

'It's English rhymin' slang,' I told her uncertainly. 'A Marty-Miller is a killer. A Marty-Urderer, on the other hand, well, I can't, uhm, remember what that is...'

'Oh.' She dropped her head and shrugged as if I'd simply accused her of stealing candy from the corner shop. 'I see.'

'I see – is that all you can say?' I grabbed her shoulders and shook her bodily. As I did so, she wobbled in all the right places and I cursed inwardly, knowing that in a few days she'd belong to some butch curtain-muncher in the state-pen, and that it'd probably take years to get her back on solids! I shook my head and whistled softly. 'Wow, I took you for an All-American, and you turn out to be an Attila the Honey! You weren't even in one the Grand Draw in my books. '

'It was me. I did it. That's all you need to know, Mister Shale.'

We went over and sat upon a bench in the lobby. After a time, Clay trotted off to rouse the unconscious security guard, and Tommy sidled off to phone the precinct. I could've pulled out my gun and trained it on Anna, but there was still this belief lurking deep within me that she was about as violent as Ghandi on sedatives. She raised her head and looked me calmly in the eyes.

'I have my reasons,' she said easily. 'They don't really matter. All that matters now is that I surrender peacefully and do my time.'

I nodded sadly, my eyes searching out her eyes, her breasts, her eyes. And then her breasts again. A short time later, my hypnotic gaze was broken by the sound of Tork's booming voice leading him up the lobby. He can be a man of few words at times, though seldom are they few enough. This was one of those times.

'Ah, Shale,' he intoned as I turned. 'It's about time you did somethin' right. At one stage you were makin' this case harder than the Twelve Labours of Hercules. And what is it with you and this midnight shit? Is there some kind of an annoyin', nocturnal animal in you that has to constantly deprive everyone else of sleep?'

Tork is a master of the boomerang compliment: The spiked and poison-tipped, razor-edged boomerang. He throws it at you at speed, and then, when it strikes, he drags it back instantly, pulling little pieces of you away with it as it leaves.

'I'm just brilliant, and I'll be the first to admit it.'

Often, despite opinions to the contrary, self-praise is the only recommendation.

He looked at me, through me, then sort of around me. Then he dragged his dead-eyed glare away and stared at Anna for a moment, though she didn't return his gaze. She sat silently, knitting her fingers into complicated little knots.

'We've a lot to talk about Miss Delaney,' he said evenly. 'Startin' with the murder of Abel Shirinski, and the attempted murder of Frank Ellis.' He turned back to me. 'You can go now, Shale. I'll have Maria Ellis on the street tomorrow mornin', and Frank as soon as he's able. Go hang from a rafter, or whatever it is you vampires do best.' As an afterthought he added, 'Make sure it's a strong one. We don't want to spend the rest of the night pullin' you out of yet another hole.'

'I'm goin' to have a shower and wash away the memories of these last few days,' I told him sourly. 'I feel dirty, violated and abused.'

'Yeah? Well, there's a car-wash down the block, if that's any help,' Tork said snidely. He watched sourly as our bedraggled group made towards the door, then returned to his business.

Outside, Tommy shook my hand excitedly. 'Thanks, Mr Shale, sir,' he beamed. 'If it hadn't been for you...for all of you...' His Cheshire cat grin stuck a period to the end of his sentence.

I put one of those friendly little rabbit punches on is chin, though I made it a little harder than was perhaps necessary, knowing it was probably the last chance I'd get to have a good dig at him. Come Monday morning, it'd probably be business as usual between us.

As we made our way over to the pick-up, Mo Breasley passed us by. 'I hear congratulations are in order, Whale,' he grinned. 'So why've you got a face on you like a warthog lickin' a nine-volt battery?'

'Eat me, Mo!' I replied, giving him the finger before climbing into the jeep.

'Huh!' he snorted, flicking a cigarette stub in my general direction. 'Huh!' And with that, he entered Skytowers as if he'd done *me* the favour.

Clay had just keyed the ignition, when I heard a rumble of thunder somewhere in the middle distance. After a few moments, however, it became clear the noise was far too consistent for that. My gaze was drawn towards nearby Masseria Park, and I noticed a very large piece of machinery coming our way. I urged Clay to hurry up and get us out of there, then down-turned my head as the Danger Ranger drove obliviously past us and turned his T62 onto the highway.

'What's eatin' you, Whale?' Clay asked when the tank had rumbled by. 'You just found the murderer, and you're not happy. What gives?'

'Let me get back to you on that one,' I shrugged. 'I say we go eat. Anyone got some money on them – all my available funds are tied up in cash.' I turned and smiled a feeble at them. 'Just makin' a funny. C'mon, I'll buy.'

'I was supposed to meet Martha earlier,' Muddy cut in. 'We could go down to her work. They do good food there, and we'll be entertained while we eat.'

We nodded our agreement, though I think we all despaired for Muddy just then. This was his wife-to-be he was talking about: This girl with the Community Chest; this harlot who, if you tripped in front of her, would've been under you before you hit the ground. Poor Muds, I'd have to give him some sound paternal advice, and soon. So, we drove over to the strip-joint known as Lickin' Lips. Martha worked there as a dancer, though I'd seen her before and she was about as erotic as an on-stage enema. More lapdog than lap-dancer, she wasn't exactly pretty, not was she exactly ugly; in fact, she was somewhere in between – pretty ugly!

Still, it's all about personal taste, and Muddy obviously had none. Anyhow, as it turned out, it wasn't Martha's turn to juggle her jugs when we got in, which wasn't so bad as we were planning to eat.

The place was dimly-lit and half-full of the sort who frequent such places – the sort who are frequently half-full. Shady, devious, badly-shaven people who may indeed have resembled us physically, yet who weren't possessed of our moral standing. The pianist in the corner wasn't much better: He couldn't have carried a tune in a bucket, his songs were more decomposed than composed, and I reckon I could've eaten a tin of alphabet spaghetti and shit better lyrics. Still, I'd been here too often to run the place down, so I called a young hostess over and asked for a food menu.

The drinks we didn't need a menu for – anything fluid, with the ability to preserve everything except secrets was fine with us all. We began by ordering soup-in-a-basket and legs of salmon just to get our hostess to smile a little, but she wasn't up for that. So then Tommy and Muddy ordered pasta and meatball sauce. Clay and I ordered the soup and a dinner for four between us. After all, that car-chase had left me slightly peckish, and these days you never knew where your next meal was either coming from or going to.

'Beats me why you eat out so much,' Clay said as he ogled a set of swivelling hips and mammaries on stage. 'You havin' a maid an all.'

'The grass always looks greener on the other side of the kitchen fence,' I told him thickly. 'Greta can't cook for shit! I came home one night and found a load of charred sausage skins on my plate, y'know. I asked her what the deal was. Know what she said? "I gutted them, Herr Shale. I gutted them!"'

We all laughed loudly, though Tommy laughed louder than everyone. It was the first time I'd seen him smiling in a week that had been as funny as a fire in an orphanage. Soonafter, our bountiful hostess arrived with some soup, four pitchers of beer and some bread.

'I didn't order this,' Clay said sharply. 'I want somethin' you can crunch.'

'You haven't tasted the soup yet,' she snapped defensively. She moved around us and laid the table as if she hated it. Then she growled, 'The meat sauce and pasta is on its way.'

Clay, uncouth character that he is, started slurping at his soup so loudly that four people got out of their seats to do the Tango. Our main course arrived shortly afterwards, and I picked at mine, unable to get Anna Delaney out of my mind.

Something inside didn't feel right, and it wasn't just the soup. Anna had owned up to Abel's murder, yet I couldn't believe she was guilty. I know my theory on equating breast size, good looks and innocence has inherent flaws, yet it had always worked until now. Questions coursed through my mind. Why had Anna raced into town and rushed into Skytowers? And even if Abel had been giving her the bell-end before ditching her for another woman, why had she attempted to wipe out Frank Ellis as well? And last night, why hadn't she tried to run off or hide? In a building the size of Skytowers you would, more often than not, have needed tracker dogs, a heat-scanner and the help of a medium to find her. So what had she not been telling me when she was telling me her reasons for not telling me what she should have told me?

And finally, why was Clay dribbling soup all over my slacks?

'What are you doin', Clay?' I snapped nastily. 'Your mouth not big enough, because it sure fuckin' looks it from here!'

He didn't reply. His eyes were fixed on the stage. His future daughter-in-law was up there wearing nothing but a Boa Constrictor and a smile. I shook him out of his trance and he pointed at Muds, who was smiling the way you do when you're on an over-measure of Quaaludes and someone threatens to cut your head off.

I glanced up at Martha for a while, trying to figure out what the kid saw in her that was extraneous to what everyone else saw of her. As I did so, Clay clutched at my shoulder despairingly. 'What can I do to bring him to his senses, Whale?' he whispered. 'That little hussy will be the death of us. She's so domineerin' she writes her diary a month in advance, for Chrissakes! And he just sits and wastes his time there at home, doin' nothin' for hours, waiting for her to phone or call.'

'How do you know?'

'Because I sit and watch him.'

'Ah!'

Quickly he added. 'You tell him, Marty. He'll listen to you. You owe it to me.'

I snorted loudly. 'How'd you figure? I owe you nothin' but money.'

'True,' he returned quickly. 'So, maybe we could let that slide if you can convince him she's the original good time had by all.'

Now he was talking my language. Clay wasn't getting his money anyhow, but this way I wouldn't have to pretend to feel guilty about it. 'All or nothin',' I said hopefully. 'You have to remember, he's a stubborn little tyke. Talkin' to him is like drawin' pictures in water, know what I'm sayin'?'

'All or nothin',' he agreed with a nod.

I patted Muddy affectionately on the shoulder, and, when he turned and grinned at me, I offered him a beer. 'Listen, kid,' I said. 'I think you and me should talk.'

'Can't it wait, uncle Marty. I want to watch this part where the snake hides...'

I spun him around by his lapels. 'C'mere, you dirty little bastard!' I realised instantly that I was being a little harsh when he started choking for breath, so I let him go. 'Sorry, kid, the drinks a demon when it gets a hold of me.'

'It's alright,' Muddy said, sporting a wide-eyed. 'What is it you wanted to say?'

Ah, he was an innocent! And here I was, hypocritical as a tiger wearing rosary beads, all set to ask him not to follow a lifestyle I followed to the letter. Don't get me wrong, I like giving advice as it passes the time, yet I'll tell you that you should never put a leper in a wind-tunnel, never ask an elephant to pass the peanuts, and never bury a corpse in a drift of snow. It's all rather negative and obscure, even though I give it in all sincerity, and about as deep and meaningful as my sex life. Still, I had to give this thing a go, so I put a hand on Muddy's shoulder to accentuate the bond between us. That, and to stop him turning back to watch his fiancée doing the Rumba with her Mamba.

'What I have to say may seem a little vague,' I told him. 'And maybe it is, Muds, I don't know. But, well, bats are birds in birdless lands...'

Muddy looked at me as if I had a touch of the crazies going on. 'You want to tell me about bats when my girl's dancin'?' he said with a frown. 'What are you tellin' me about bats for?'

I took his other shoulder solidly in my hand. This advice shit was hard enough to give freely without begging the attention of the receiver. 'No, Muds. Look, what I'm sayin' is this: Marriage is a process of findin' out what kind of man your wife would really have preferred. It's a period of rest between romances, and not every married woman is a wife. Though, and I'll say this now...' I raised a hand as if under oath. '...a woman's tongue is the sword that never rusts!'

He gazed at me blankly. 'I don't get it, uncle Marty. Could you let me go now?'

'Sure, kid. Sure. But listen up, Muds. When I talk of bats here, what I'm really talkin' about is birds, if y'see what I mean. I mean, you can go lookin' for a bird and they're not all bats, if you get me. It's like, y'know, there are birds in this birdless land, and not every one of them is a bat... Jeez, Muddy!'

Muddy shrugged. 'Honestly, uncle Marty, I don't get it.'

'Well, I can't put it much plainer without tellin' you the truth, kid.' I took a deep breath, then drew on my beer for courage. As I did so, I noticed Clay throwing a hand over his mouth and vehemently shaking his head.

'What is the truth, uncle Marty?'

'She's a tramp, kid!' I blurted out. 'A regular fuckin' knockin' shop. A mattress with legs!' I threw an arm around his shoulder. 'Jeez, kid, don't cry! C'mon, it was a joke for Chrissakes! Get up from there, you're snottin' my slacks!'

Clay pushed me aside and pulled Muddy up towards him. 'Great stuff, Whale. Tactful as a fox in a coop. Is that the best you can do?'

'Yeah, it is actually!' I snapped. 'You can't always go around slappin' lipstick on the face of honesty. But, no, you want it all ways, Clay. If you went out and shot a penguin you'd expect it to be roasted and covered in pepper sauce when it fell out of the fuckin' sky.' I shook my head, slurped back the remainder of my beer and got up. 'I'm outta here. I'm sick of people always usin' me to their own ends, 'cause I always come out of things the worst!'

The piano player stopped thrashing his piano as I passed him by. 'Any requests?' he asked pleasantly.

'Yeah,' I growled. 'Hand out some fuckin' ear-plugs, then go train your voice never to come back when you throw it!'

Outside, I took in the air for a while, then walked a few blocks to clear my head. It was after 3-00am as I turned off Brady and made my way north, and I was in a foul mood with the wrong people for the wrong reasons. Gulls wheeled overhead and a light, warm rain blew in across the river. As I walked, Anna Delaney and her mammaries were heavy on my mind. Why did I still think she was innocent? Were her breasts real or surgically enhanced? Could she have actually killed her boss in cold blood? And how come her bra straps didn't strap under such strain?

My mind was in turmoil, so much so that I should perhaps have realised that I'd strayed into Bundyville, one of the city's more dangerous districts.

'Hey, bud!' a voice said on the periphery of my vision. 'You got a light?'

I turned around and broke wind immediately. There were six of them.

And they hadn't got a single cigarette between them.

TWENTY TWO

Bundyville is one of the city's less sociable districts, the kind of place where you can recognise a stranger by the fact he has two ears, and where any dog with a tail is a tourist. And there I was on that muggy night, dicing with the Reaper over whether or not I should play the mug-ee. I took a brief inventory of my situation. A few of my adversaries looked as if they'd been foddered on raw meat and steroids, the rest as if they took turns working shifts in a Notre Dame belfry. As I upturned my gaze, I also saw several curtains twitching in the tenements across the way, though, sadly for me, I knew the words 'intervention' and 'mediation' in this particular area of town would never hold anything more than legal connotations.

Yeah, I was alone, and it didn't look good. Well, I was carrying a *friend*, of course, but six corpses would be difficult to hide, and there wasn't a snowdrift in sight.

'You got a light?' the voice asked again. The tone oozed malice, and I farted again, this one a real canary-killer.

'Well, I've definitely got a light head if that's any good to you,' I wheedled, hoping for a tension-breaking laugh that never came. 'Look, my money's in my, uhm, hotel. If you escort me there safely, I'll give you ten dollars each. What do you say?'

It was then they chose to laugh. But somehow, as they did so, the tension intensified and cold reality kicked in, the way it does at times when one of my more astute clients threatens to pay me precisely what I'm worth.

'Well, actually, I *have* got a light.' I stuck a hand into my jacket, knowing then that they weren't going to see the light, but they were definitely going to feel the heat.

'Not so fast, wide-load!' a more unpleasant voice cut in from directly behind me.

I turned to see another goon behind me, bat in hand. I sighed a dismal, aware he'd go baseball on my softballs if I played hardball, so I raised my arms in surrender, a voluntary spinectomy kicking in. Time slowed as I did so, yet another cocoa-motive chugged through my colon towards my now heavily-puckered exit-wound, and I found myself pondering the intricacies of life and death. They say you have to wake up to make your dreams come true, so had I lived my dreams or wasted my life dreaming? Had I done everything and everyone I'd wanted to do? And was I now going to accept my fate like a man, or was I going to be a mouse and run?

I turned, squeaked, and hot-footed it out of there. And my six friends sloped after me. They must have all been dying for a cigarette real bad!

It's quite amazing how fast a guy can run when he has cause. And if you're farting lumps, of course, it's like you're on turbo-power. I was a cheetah in an elephant's body by the time I reached the Lickin' Lips, my hands fumbling beneath my jacket for my Magnum – which was unfortunately now tangled in its holster – and my heart pounding like a pneumatic drill in a phone booth.

Until I heard the voice.

'Fuckin' A!' it chuckled. 'Fuckin' A!'

I never thought I'd think or say it, yet I wanted Him to be there so badly I'd have sold my soul. Or re-mortgaged it, whatever. And never in my life had I wanted to see Joe Sinto with something less than capable of First Strike capacity in his arms.

Well, he didn't have Bertha with him as it turned out, but he wasn't alone. Behind him stood Muddy, Clay and Tommy, and they were all as welcome as a stray pig at a low-budget barbecue. I wheezed to a stop and stood semi-upright before my friends, I their General, they my troops. My aggressors halted just yards behind, reassessing what might well have now turned into their predicament.

'Well, come…and …get it,' I wheezed. 'If…you've…the gonads!'

They obviously had the gonads, and, had I taken a proper look at my team swaying about like pendulums behind me, I might've understood why. Still, in they came, swinging and cursing like demons at an exorcism. I got into the Shuffle straight off: Hook, cross, counterpunch, puff, pant, wheeze, stuff like that. And, even though my friends were rat-assed, they were triers, and at one stage we were actually winning. Though it wasn't during the latter stage, which would've been nice.

Still, even though the fight was a regular Chinese Fire-drill, we held our own. In fact, I held my own most of the time, even as one guy tried kicking them off me with a pair of steel toe-caps. In-between throwing the odd hook or kick, I also threw the odd tantrum, or I faked serious wounds before coming at my startled foe like a Cobra out of a can.

Muddy and Tommy threw punches in bunches, connected ever now and then, and generally confused the situation. Clay fought like a Girl Guide at a wet sponge stall while getting seven shades of brown kicked out of him. And Joe, well, he screamed the oaths of regiments and the rants of the insane at full moon without adding anything of real value – until, that was, he drew a handgun and fired a shot into the air. It was the final bell in a fight definitely going the wrong way. But the resultant bang had the desired effect, in that it allowed us to keep our lives, our dignity and, more importantly, our money. Moments later, Tommy and Muds chased our assailants into a side-street with gusto. My battalion seemed alright in the main, though Clay was lying dazed in the gutter.

Clay had been in the gutter on several occasions in his life, of course, but this time was markedly different in that somebody else had put him there.

'You alright?' I asked, trying to put feeling into my voice. Which is difficult when you've none in your lips.

Clay blew a few puddle-bubbles, then lifted out his head. 'Sure, Marty,' he sneered. 'I just found a parkin' space, send Muddy back for the pick-up!'

It was an attempt at humour that went over my head. Still, I laughed, perhaps because it was genuinely funny, or perhaps because I'm like most people in that I can occasionally find humour in even my best friend's faults and troubles.

'What about the rest of you guys?' I asked. The smiles on all of their faces told me they were fine. 'Y'know,' I added sternly, 'you should've stayed out of that. I was just bringin' those guys back onto my own turf to polish them off.' I pointed to a few sticks and bin-lids, before faking a few air-punches. 'Yeah, they're lucky men.'

Joe chuckled darkly. 'Get real, Marty,' he chided. 'You were nearly toast!'

The Chinese say that even the most welcome stranger becomes bothersome after three days. Joe had condensed that to somewhere within the space of three minutes. Still, I held my tongue and merely smiled at him dagger-like.

'Man, I'm fired up!' Tommy grinned. 'That was cool, Mr. Shale, sir. Any chance you could take me in and teach me a few things? As an apprentice, maybe.'

'I'll get back to you on it,' I told him, knowing I never would. I looked at Muds. 'You alright, kid?' I asked.

He nodded, but held his head low. I knew then I owed him an apology. We strode past the club and turned into a side-street off the expressway. There was a night-club there, the sort that didn't open until decent people were home in their own, or other people's beds. It was the kind of place where the Hole in the Wall gang might've run to if all other bolt-holes had turned bad. But still, it was somewhere, and anywhere is somewhere when there's nowhere else to go.

I paid us all into the place with the remainder of Clay's money, then bought the guys drinks with some of mine. Then I drew Muddy aside for a chat as Joe and Clay went walkabout. It was your average meat market, with wall to wall floors, floor to floor walls, and ceiling to floor walls. The dames were wet and wild, the beer wild and wet, the floorboards warped and twisted, and the patrons twisted and warped. I'd seen it all a thousand times, and forgotten it as many.

'Look, Muds,' I began. 'I wasn't tryin' to rattle your cage earlier, I was just tryin' to be your pal. Y'see, good advice is like a kidney machine – you may think it's only takin' the piss out of you, but it's actually there for your own good! And sure, I said a few harsh things about your girl, but I was brought up to believe the only men who should fall to a woman's feet are chiropodists. And men, well, whereas we want all we can get, women want all they can't get, so we start off wantin' to smother them with rubies and diamonds, then end up wantin' to smother them with either a duvet or a pillow. Know what I'm sayin'?'

He nodded uncertainly. I hugged him in close and he smiled.

'But you, Muds,' I continued. 'You're all over that girl like a bad case of the pox. Remember, she's only a woman. They're the same as us, but without our skills and talents. For example, they talk of the sufferin' of childbirth, but I've got piles and I don't boast about them.' I adopted a corrugated. 'Yeah, I too have suffered, and I've got to shit once a week whether I want to or not.' I shook my head contemptuously. 'Childbirth!' I snorted. 'Jeez, I've laid tougher eggs!'

Muddy smiled, raised his head up a little. 'I get what you're sayin' now, uncle Marty. But they aren't all bad. I mean, some of them are alright, aren't they?'

'Sure they are. But I was talkin' to you about bats earlier, remember?'

Muddy grinned at me and hung his head sheepishly. 'Yeah.'

'Well, what I was tryin' to say is you have yourself a bat in a land full of birds. And it's time you gave that bat the bird, y'know? I mean, look around you...'

Muddy glared through the strobe and neon at the crowded dance floor. He smiled and nodded eagerly. 'Sure,' he agreed. 'There's more out there, I just have to go for it.' He moved off to dance, and he was soon strutting rooster-like amongst the available fowl. As he did so, Clay approached me, a thin smile on his lips.

'How do you do that, Marty?' he asked. 'How do you drive people to the edge, then stop them jumpin' and have them love you for it?'

'I've got a way with kids, Clay,' I told him sagely. 'Y'see, most guys don't realise it takes you eighteen months to teach them to stand up and talk, then eighteen years to get them to sit down and listen. I do, because I'm gifted. It's as easy as that.'

Clay nodded, raised a doubting eyebrow. 'Uh, huh! You just jam it, Marty, if you ask me. I wouldn't normally ask a monkey to sort out a row about bananas, but I'm glad I did this time out. Look at him. He's a heart-breaker. Got them all over him!'

We watched The Muds strutting his stuff all over the floor with a budding Wendy Whoppers. I shook my head. Thing was, she could well have been mine if young Muddy hadn't been there. Ah, well, I thought, let her dream!

For whatever reason, Clay chose to leave me as Joe chose to join me. The Ham handed me a few bottles of beer. I took them, then bit hard at my lip. 'Listen, Joe, thanks for showin' up when you did. Seriously, I might've killed the six of them.'

'No problem, Marty,' Joe smiled magnanimously. 'Anyhow, I might need you there for me when the Whitehouse falls. In a few months time, maybe.'

'Maybe sooner,' I told him as seriously. 'I hear Nixon's runnin' again.'

While he was pondering the implications of a return to some of our foggiest days, I said casually, 'Say, did you, uhm, return that tank yet?'

'Sure did. Malone wanted to charge me with stealin' it, but since I borrowed it there's nothin' he can do about it. He's a hard-case, Marty. I told him I'd heard him on the police radio puttin' it around town that I'm a loony. He admitted straight off it was him, and said he didn't know I wanted it kept a secret.' Joe clenched his jaw hard. 'He and I are goin' to have words some time soon, I can feel it'

Joe kept talking. Then he began sub-plotting, and talking inanely of lesser things. As he did so, I gulped back my beers, hoping my beer-muffs would kick in. When they did, I fixed my eyes upon the podium dancers high above the disco floor, feeling my libido rise. Watching is fine, but all that stuff is like handing a hungry man a picture of cakes. So, within moments, I began looking around for something female that might've been starting to look around for something male like me.

She stood beneath the staircase at the furthest end of the room, hugging the shadows like a cockroach with migraine. Unfortunately, as I approached her, I noticed the resemblance didn't end there. By this stage, however, the anaesthetic was kicking in, and Yours Altruistically was all set and willing to become a boner-donor.

Joe followed close behind. 'I know her,' he told me with a shake of his head. 'You got your self a pig in a poke there,

Marty.' He snorted derisively as I shoo-ed him away. 'Yeah, well, I'll just go siphon my python,' he added sourly. 'Oh, and they'll be doin' the same with yours in the mornin' if you do what I think you're goin' to do.'

Joe had used the right words, but in the wrong context, because right then I had a pig *and* a poke in mind. Nor did his dark reference bother me, as I prefer women with a past because there's a chance history will repeat itself. As it was, she recoiled as I neared, yet I stopped midway as I espied something on the dance-floor; something which sparkled ever so briefly beneath the strobes, before disappearing as quickly. Whatever it was, it sparked an idea in me, yet that same idea was as quickly doused by the sour waters of my passion bubbling to the surface. I moved hurriedly on, my eyes fixed firmly upon the eyes of my intended. In return, one of her eyes remained fixed on mine, even as the other stared off some 90° to her right.

Some five feet away from her, I turned once or twice to let her see what I had on offer. From her lopsided and semi-demented grin, it was difficult to tell whether she wanted to have me there and then or skewer me with meat-hooks. But I held the Good Ship Shale on course, my gonads my rudder and my pecker my mainmast. Moments later, I stood before her, allowing her to both see what she was getting and getting herself into. Then, I went at a fifty-watt cheesy.

'How do you like your eggs in the mornin'?' I asked her coyly.

'Unfertilised,' she replied wittily. 'You got any love-gloves on you?'

'Never use them, baby. It's like tryin' to swim in a sack. When I burn rubber it has nothin' to do with prophylactics.'

'Coitus interruptus?' she grinned.

I shook my head forcefully. 'Uh-uh! That's like dinin' in the Waldorf, then goin' outside to throw up all over the veranda.'

She licked her lips, then one of her eyebrows. 'I can eat a tomato through a tennis racket,' she told me invitingly. 'That sound good to you?'

I nodded. Our haggling was over, sealed by that one promise. She stalked out into the light and it struck me that the last time this girl had gone to the beauty parlour she must've used the emergency exit. Still, just so long as she was lukewarm, it was definitely enough for me.

I took her outside, using the shadows for cover until I found the cab rank. Finding a cab with a broken light in the back was easy enough, because that's the type of thing you do for yourself. Cab drivers expect it. It's like stealing towels from hotel rooms. Anyhow, as it turned out, my cab driver took one look at my partner and broke every one of the vehicle's internal lights himself.

I won't go into details about my animal exploits. It's suffice to say that beauty is in the eye of the beer-holder, and that by bedding my latest conquest I kept well within the boundaries of bad taste. She left shortly after we made the beast-with-two-backs – which saved me the trouble of gnawing off an arm – and sloped north as the sun cringed behind the tower-blocks until she'd gone to ground. It's funny, because rumours abounded in my neighbourhood for months afterwards about the Yeti-like creature that'd been seen in my street. House prices also dropped dramatically in Vesperville shortly thereafter, stories were told to naughty children at Christmas and Easter, and a guy on the corner made figurines of the creature he'd only sell to people over eighteen.

None of which was my immediate concern. When I awoke late Thursday evening there was something buzzing in my head and begging for release. Yet it wasn't a fly or some such other insect that had found a vacant space and decided to move in for the weekend. It was another idea.

But this was one I didn't want to disappear.

TWENTY THREE

Greta's date left about 7-00am. I heard him and his guide-dog competing to get over the back fence shortly after my own conquest had sloped away. Me, I slept a little longer, actually until about 7-00pm, when I rose gluey-eyed and hungrier than a lab-rat on a drip. When I got downstairs, Greta was in the kitchen, chirping a tuneless and flaying the previous day's greasy pans under the cold tap with a sponge. I shook my head wearily, lit a cigarette and poured myself a coffee.

'My dinner warm?' I grunted. I knew she'd been cooking from the fresh ashes on the hot-plate and the acrid pall of smoke that hung, fog-like, over the table.

'Should be – it on back of fire two hours.' She grinned a chummy-gummy, and I winced at the sight of it. 'Is only joke. Here dinner.'

Greta handed me a plate of something that been on the back of the fire for three hours. It looked as if it had started off as a chicken, one that had maybe run itself to death in the Boston marathon. I was psyching myself to eat it when the door-bell sounded and saved me the trauma. Maria Ellis stood on the step, her thin smile just about pinned in place by common courtesy. From the way she moved through Chez Shale as if it were shark-infested waters, however, I guessed it was the commonness of me and mine which was heavy on her mind. This woman was obviously class-conscious to the extreme; unlike me – I'd no class and was very conscious of it. Saying that, I do know which fingers to stick in my mouth when whistling for restaurant service, and rarely do I slurp the dregs of my coffee from the saucer anymore, so some of it must be kicking in.

As Maria stood at the kitchen door, I noticed she was wearing a figure-hugging blouse which kept her pendants extremely pendent, and an even tighter-fitting skirt which firmly swaddled her waddle. If that'd been any other dame just then, I'd have complimented her instantly on her rack, maybe even patted her ass, yet I'd long figured her as the type of broad who'd view such positive charm as negative smarm. So, instead, I merely allowed my gaze to wander unfettered all over her voluptuous body until she coughed abruptly to regain my attention.

'I hope I'm not disturbing you, Mr Shale,' she frowned. 'I just came to give you your money.' She waved a beefy envelope to her front. 'And to thank you,' she added unenthusiastically. 'I suppose...'

'Grab a stool,' I told her. 'You can stay for coffee, can't you?' She deserved some of Greta's coffee with that fucking attitude!

'No, really,' she replied. 'I have to go back and see Frank and Tommy. I'm busy, uhm, all week actually.' She lobbed the envelope at me as if she was pitching for the Yankees, no doubt thinking that a suitable conclusion to our business.

Some people can run a wad of notes past their lug-holes and count it easily. I can do it through an envelope. 'It's all there,' I told her. 'So, how's Frank doin'?'

'He's fine,' she winced. 'Though he'll never play the piano again, as they say...'

She smiled sourly and I nodded, realising she was making a funny. I could've replied that it didn't really matter so long as he could play the organ, but again I held off; after all, I had my money now, so the need for witty shit-chat was over. I feigned a smile. 'Mmm, well, I'll drop by and see you all sometime...'

'No, you can't,' Maria replied hastily. 'We're moving. Yes, that's it, we're moving. Out of town. So, we'll see you in a few years time. Maybe...'

'Sure, lady, whatever. Well, you give my best to Tommy and Frank. And if you ever need me again, I'm in the book.'

She left in a flash, her aerodynamic snoot so high in the air it looked like a flag-less mast. Still, to be honest, I didn't mind her rushing off, as I'm not too sociable first thing in the evening. Don't get me wrong – the fact I'd now enough moolah to stop Happy Valentine from sending me south to my maker was nearly enough to give me a boner, but I was dog-tired, planned to have a few beers and watch a game, then sleep like a hibernating bear. So, I freshened my coffee and sidled into the sitting-room. There, Greta was now using a feather-duster to redistribute dust from the blinds to other parts of the room, caterwauling in falsetto, and generally getting in the way. I was about to point that out to her in rather brusque sign-language when the phone rang. Clay was on the other end of the line.

'So, how'd you get on with your, uhm, *date*?' Clay asked brightly. 'She get back into her coffin before the sun came up?'

I laughed shortly. 'Yeah, I suppose I should've asked her what she looked like when I was sober. What about you? You manage to ditch Joe?'

'He hooked up with somethin' too,' Clay replied easily. 'Somethin' that may've had a hook in it at one stage, actually. A female MP, with hands like spades and more scar-tissue than a battlefield commander.'

I laughed shortly, urged Greta from the room with a flip-off finger, then flicked on the television. 'And Tommy and the Muds, they do alright?'

Clay went at the descriptive, telling me how their night had only been beginning when it was ending, filling me in on an episode that had more sun than an Aussie soap, and generally running off at the mouth. I half-listened and supplied a few grunts when called for, but, to be honest, none of it was really sinking in.

Y'see, like anyone, even if I'm deep in conversation, I turn soundproof if something more interesting grabs my attention. Just then, it was a picture on my TV. It was nothing of shock-value, simply an image of a flashing light in a discotheque someplace. Yet that image jolted a hazed memory of the previous night, which in turn harnessed several seemingly unrelated facts, and within moments they were all tumbling around in my mind like pieces of a jigsaw, until at last they clicked into place. As they did so, I leapt excitedly off the sofa, phone in hand.

'I've got it, Clay!' I roared. 'I've fuckin' got it!'

'Yeah, Joe said that would happen…'

As I jumped off the sofa, Greta rushed back into the sitting-room and stared at me the way I often stare at her before she goes out kerb-crawling down the docks late of an evening. I pressed my hand against the phone. 'Greta, iron me some fresh slacks.' I paused, wondering if I'd be better off wearing soup-strainers the way my month was going. 'Make that my brown slacks, just in case.' I removed my hand from the phone. 'Listen, Clay, I need you over here – I've just solved the Shirinski murder and I need to go arrest the perp. Oh, but I'd like you to go and get Joe first, bring him over here too.'

'Let me get this right,' Clay gasped. 'You're tellin' me you've just *re-solved* a murder you just solved? Not only that, after puttin' my life on the line several times this week, you now want *me* to help catch your perp along with that one-man freak-show, Joe Sinto? Why'd you even think I would do that?'

Shit, I hated the way he could see through me! After all these years, he'd finally figured our friendship was akin to a motorbike and detachable sidecar, which – unless he was driving – was necessarily unencumbered when nearing hilly terrain. As for Joe, of course, I made no secret of the fact I only ever allowed him to hitch his war-wagon to my caboose when we were on board the Runaway Train and rapidly approaching Dead Man's Curve, and only then because I'd have the satisfaction of taking him with me when I died. But now I needed them both again: Joe, not because he was a knight in shining armour, but a retard in body-armour, who'd proven he'd take one for the team; and Clay because, if it came down to it, I'd rather his jeep got messed up than my Buick.

Still, despite Clay's negative reply, there was no point in me getting all pessimistic, because that attitude would never work for me, ever. All I had to do here was remember two things: Firstly, Clay was the sort of friend who could see right through me, yet on some level he must've enjoyed the view; and secondly, he had a nose which began between his eyes, but which couldn't help ending up in other people's business.

'Look, Clay, there's an old sayin' which states that today's mighty oak is just yesterday's little nut that held it's ground. And when I think of that nut I think of Clay Rivers...'

'Wow, thanks, Whale!'

'No, I mean, you've been with me all the way in this until now, and now's your chance to finally blossom into that mighty oak. Don't you want to be one of the first to find out who the murderer is? I mean, you'll know before even Tork Malone. And don't you want to take some of the credit for their capture?'

Clay sighed a heartfelt and thought it over for a minute. 'Mmm, well, if you put it like that. Give me a while to get Joe, and we'll be right over.'

On that note, he hung up. Knowing I'd a long night ahead, I had Greta fix me some beans and eggs, then I called Mal Brennan at his home address. And, even though he didn't agree with everything I said, Mal and I are basically on the same page where investigative theory is concerned: In short, we both believe in getting our facts clear first, then distorting them later. After that, I phoned Rick in Skytowers. As usual, talking to him was a bit like paddling through glue, but he eventually agreed to help me out. I came off the line then, knowing that, before the night was over, my credibility was going to be at an all-time high.

***

It didn't take Clay long to find Joe's house, ringed as it is by a high barbed-wire fence. What took him longer was finally plucking up enough courage to work his way through the minefield and press on the correct doorbell – the one that didn't trip the system. Joe came out to greet him happily, explaining that these days few people ever bothered to call around anymore, except for maybe placard-bearing locals, the riot squad, or an occasional U.N. emissary under a flag of truce.

That done, they arrived at the door my brownstone shortly after 3-30am: Three of them, if you included Bertha.

'We won't need her where we're goin',' I told Joe with a grimace. I could just picture him chasing flies around his house with an axe. 'Here's somethin' a little quieter.' I handed him a Colt Automatic, fully loaded with the safety-catch on.

'You sure about that, Marty?' he asked. 'We won't need Bertha in City Hall?'

'I'm afraid it doesn't go that far up, Joe,' I told him sadly. 'So Greta will look after, uhm, Bertha for you.' I studied Greta's animated face for a second. 'But take the ammunition out before we go. Oh, and maybe the firin' pin as well, if you would.'

'Don't I get a gun?' Clay asked, as if it were a reasonable proposition. Behind Joe's back, he softly mouthed, 'Self defence. Just in case.'

I shrugged, realising he had a point. I handed him my Derringer. It's a ladies gun, a one-shot pop pistol, just about right for Clay.

'Right, Clay, we'll take your jeep,' I said, checking my own gun was loaded.

'Where?' Clay asked.

'Skytowers,' I said. 'That's where we'll find the second-last piece in this jigsaw.'

***

We reached Skytowers shortly after 4-00am, in fact so late it was nearly early. As arranged, Rick met up with us on the 18th floor, torch in his hand. He was understandably wary about meeting Joe again, and kept his distance as I introduced him to Clay.

'Is this the one you're lookin' for?' he asked, handing me the torch.

'Yeah, that's it,' I told him. It was the torch with the special blue filter – the same one he'd given me the first time I'd been there, but not the second. It was the sort used for finding hairline cracks in pottery, and it had come into Rick's possession the way tools do with every handyman – he'd stolen it. He led us to room 18a, now devoid of its yellow banner-tape, where he keyed open the door and flicked on the light. I immediately moved towards the central closet and peered around inside, my gaze finally drawn to a small, barely noticeable hole in the left-hand side of the ceiling. I smiled happily and returned to the main room.

'Now, could you turn that light off a moment,' I told Rick.

'Is it safe?' He eyed Joe warily. 'You know the way he gets.'

'Flick the switch,' Joe cut in. 'Or have your switch flicked. Your choice.'

I waved a nonchalant hand at Rick. 'He's just jokin',' I grinned. 'He never really bears a grudge against anyone he's wronged. That right, Joe?' Joe smiled wryly and I turned back to Rick 'Just switch the light off, you'll be fine.'

Sighing heavily, Rick knocked the switch off as I turned the flashlight on.

'Well, look at that!' Clay exclaimed.

As I pointed the torch-beam at the carpet, a thin, sparkling trail was revealed, the same one I'd seen the first night. It was dimmer now, though still plainly visible. I smiled smugly, awaiting a barrage of queries that never came. Yep, no one said a fucking word! And, believe me, there's nothing more annoying than having all the answers when no one is asking you any questions.

So I just stood there in silence, said nothing, and waited. And waited. And waited.

'Well, go ahead,' Clay rasped. 'Tell us what it is.'

'Thought you'd never ask.' I smiled sagely, then asked Rick to flick the light back on. As he did so, the trail disappeared instantly. 'It's a substance that emits phosphorescent light,' I grinned. 'And, as you may or may not know, phosphorescent light dissipates more slowly than fluorescent light when the energy source is removed, depending on the temperature. The heat in this room kept this stuff glowin' for about a week, which is about right accordin' to Mal.'

'But what is it exactly?' Clay asked.

'Eggshells,' I replied, matter-of-factly.

'I don't get it,' Joe frowned. 'You're sayin' someone was walkin' on eggshells?'

'In more ways than one, Joe.' I turned to Rick. 'So, how long have you been coverin' for Vic Fellows?'

'Me?' he gasped. 'I haven't been covering for anyone.'

'I mean coverin' his shifts, like you did on the night of the murder.' I regarded him levelly. 'He was supposed to be workin' here that night, wasn't he?'

'He was,' Rick shrugged. 'But I cover for him all the time, so it's no big deal. When I told him about the murder the next day, he asked me to keep the swap under wraps as our boss frowns on us doing that sort of thing. So, I did. After all, the murderer was caught, and it had nothing to do with us.'

'Well, normally that swap wouldn't have been relevant, but this time it was. Y'see, Vic Fellows murdered Abel Shirinski. So, uhm, where is he now?'

'Are you sure?' Rick seemed seriously surprised. 'Wow! Well, he doesn't start until midnight, so he's probably at home.'

Joe stepped in towards him. 'Don't you go phonin' him when we're gone, y'hear! You fess up, you mess up, and I'll put so many holes in you, you won't know which to bleed from first.'

Rick faded Caucasian and I gave him another wan, understanding smile, before allowing Joe to lead us out into the darkened parking lot towards the pick-up.

**

As night's warm, foul breath quelled the city, I sat quietly in the back of the jeep as Clay drove us down to Vic's apartment block, my head aswirl with thoughts. The Ham sat upfront beside Clay. He'd removed a single bullet from the Colt, tied a napkin around his head, and was now playing a game of Russian Roulette, yet he kept on winning despite the odds. Clay seemed somewhat happy with that, though it may simply have been because he was in the proposed flight path of Joe's brain cell and any other debris that would certainly come flying his way.

About ten minutes later, we reached Cahn Street, where the tenement in which Vic Fellows lived lounged against the night sky as if it had just gotten home from an all-nighter. The street was bleakly lit by the pulsating neon of a mini-mall and a burlesque club on the corner. In this part of town, the rising damp had short-circuited the street lamps, and, while most local apartments had roaches, there were reportedly as many with shrimp. Due to the prevailing darkness, therefore, Clay had a bit of trouble parking the jeep, and he used some guy's rust-bucket to the front of us as a brake. Unbeknown to us, the owner of the car was still in it at the time. And yet, all too aware he lived in a very dangerous district and was outnumbered three to one, he was polite enough when he exited his vehicle and stepped casually around to survey the damage.

'So, hey, how do you guys stop when I'm not here?'

Clay simply shrugged and offered him fifty bucks. The guy hmm-ed and haa-ed for a while, after which Joe produced his gun and showed him how he stopped other people permanently. Unsurprisingly, the guy got quietly back into his car and drove off into the night without so much as a backward glance. Moments later, we entered the run-down tenement, with the Ham once again on point.

TWENTY FIVE

They say a clear conscience never fears a knock on the door after midnight. Vic Fellows put two bullets through his front door before even asking who was there.

We'd reached the 3rd floor via the urine-sodden stairwell, labouring up past a rag-tag assembly of slumbering or semi-conscious druggies, dipsos and bag-ladies, all of whom had taken advantage of a broken lobby door and were now irregularly sprawled upon a sickly grey stair-carpet that looked as if was shampooed daily in toxic waste. This was your typical south-side city block in every respect, the kind of place where every absurdity had a champion, and where collective reality was little more than a basic hunch. Due to the broken air-conditioning, the building's interior was also hotter than the lowermost cavern of Hell. As we neared the top of the stairwell, I was sweat-drenched, my mouth was drier than a nun's crotch, and I'd this ominous feeling that if any of my internal organs had escaped being pickled over the years, they were soon about to be poached.

Upon regaining my breath, I'd pointed Vic's apartment out to Joe. He'd then edged forward to knock on the door, even as Clay and I squatted low at the first bend in the hallway, our hands over our ears. In truth, it was fun to watch Hambo Tibetan-Two-Stepping it back to join us as the bullets pinged harmlessly off the walls around him, but nowhere near as funny when he regrouped and seemed set to return fire. So, before he'd time to commit, I bundled the disgruntled vet behind me and warned him to silence. Then I shouted: 'Alright, Vic, are you comin' out peacefully? Or, should I say, are you comin' out, *Jim Harrison*?'

As I spoke, Clay gasped in confusion. 'Wow, I'm lost!'

Clay was saying nothing new there. But, to be fair, it was a genuine Scooby Doo moment, much like the one in which the intrepid ghost-busting team finally unmask Old Man Winters, the doddering, if kindly owner of the Hillside Lodge, who's actually been chasing them around the mansion for the last half hour with the vigour of a Tasmanian Devil on PCP. Before I could fill Clay in on what I knew, however, Jim Harrison – aka, Vic Fellows – eased his front door slightly open and fired a further four shots up the corridor. 'You're obviously very smart, copper!' he then called out in Cagney-ish. 'But you aint takin' me alive, y'hear?'

'I'm no copper,' I flustered, staying low to the carpet as the bullets struck the wall high above us. 'I'm just a brilliant Private Investigator with some great contacts downtown. So, hand yourself in now and I'll fix it so you get only a year in the can at most, with maybe time off for good behaviour. What d'ya say?'

I was lying, of course. Jim Harrison was going downriver to do a stretch that'd turn Mr Bendy green with envy, and we all knew it. But honey catches more flies than vinegar, and honey-coated clichés are nearly as good. I know, because I've watched as much Cagney and Lacey as any woman.

Jim laughed snidely, and when he replied his tone was thickly defiant. 'Do you really think I'm goin' to leave my fate in the hands of twelve people who aren't even smart enough to dodge jury duty? Uh-uh! And the state pen isn't for me: By the time I got out and reached pastures anew, I'd be too old to climb the fence. No, sir! I'm goin' out of here feet first, cold as a penguin's pecker!'

'Well, I'd rather not kill you,' I pouted. Which was half-true. After all, everyone leaves life a little better, though I admittedly still had to work out if Jim Harrison would make his contribution to the world simply by leaving it. 'Just remember, any day above ground is a good one, and old age is always preferable to the alternative.'

'Who said anythin' about *you* killin' me, copper? I've rigged this place to blow and kill everyone around here for miles just as soon as I make my confession.'

It was suddenly very much hotter in that No Man's Land of a corridor. Not hot enough to kill a camel, true, but hot enough to grant me a marked insight into my next port of call if Jim Harrison was telling the truth.

I loosened my tie, and, as I did so, I could've sworn a rat passed me by wearing a flak-jacket and Kevlar helmet. Jeez, this heat was making me delusional, I was bloated with gas from my last meal of beans and eggs, and, to stick the tin hat on it, I'd a real tough call to make: Should I take a chance and hear Jim Harrison out, thereby leaving myself open to either spontaneous or involuntary combustion, or should I get the hell out of there and ultimately let the police take credit for solving a case that'd definitely brighten up my currently all-too shabby résumé?

'Look, uhm, Jim,' I feebled. 'Anna will only get off the hook if one of us lives to verify your confession. But if we all die here, she'll end up in the clink drinkin' from the hairy cup, and all those attempted murders and the actual murder of Abel Shirinski will have been a complete waste of time.' I pouted uneasily. 'That last part bein', uhm, from your perspective, obviously.'

As I'd spoken to Jim, I'd kept my gaze firmly fixed upon his front door. Now, it creaked slowly open to reveal his blacked-out apartment. Seconds later, when the pulsating neon strobe in the backdrop briefly lit the place up, the crazed janitor was starkly silhouetted in the midst of the opening looking like something you'd sketch left-handed. As I scrutinised him further, I realised he'd a gun in one hand and a remote-control in the other. He laughed dryly and I nearly wet myself.

'Right, copper, you listen to what I have to say and we'll take it from there. But if any of you moves an inch when I'm talkin', I'll blow us all to kingdom come!'

I managed a paper-cut grin, gingerly placed my gun down on the carpet, then urged Joe and Clay to do the same. As my uncertain companions followed suit, I said. 'There. Our weapons are down, let's talk.'

Seeing this, Jim Harrison nodded stoically and slumped into a sitting position just inside his doorway. He frowned sadly, as if he was lost in thought and it was darkly unfamiliar territory, then he began to speak:

'I was thirty-years-old when my papa died,' he sighed. 'So, I sold our chicken farm in Honolulu and moved to the city, where I planned to invest in computers. That's how I met Frank and Abel, who'd just gotten into that line of business. At first, I considered those guys world-wise go-getters, but I soon found out they were otherwise from the get-go. They figured straight-off I'd an inferiority complex – if not a very good one – and they used it to con me out of all I owned. I mean, back then I was a frugal guy – you'd tell me what you needed, and I'd tell you how to get along without it – but when I joined forces with them, they told me I had to keep pourin' money into research and the ongoin' modernisation of all our gadgets and components. Needless to say, my inheritance soon dwindled, we got deep into debt, and the business downturned. So the guys agreed to buy me out for a pittance after a year. But it was a scam: The business was actually doin' fine. And, after I'd gone, they sold out to a conglomerate for a small fortune.'

Jim sighed sadly. 'Still, I was a realist. My papa always said, "Son, expectin' life to treat you right is like walkin' into a tiger's den and expectin' it not to eat you because you're a vegetarian!" and he was right. So I returned to Honolulu and bought back our old farm. I'd such dreams for that place, too. I planned to breed chickens with parrots so that when they laid an egg they'd come tell me. Then I began feedin' them sawdust so they'd lay planks. Then I got them drunk on whiskey so they'd lay scotch eggs. If it had worked, it would've been poultry in motion!' Jim raised a stalling hand and sighed darkly. 'But it didn't work – obviously – because how could it? Y'see, my thinkin' hadn't been clear since Frank and Abel left me with egg on my face, so I'd lost heart and begun relyin' on my liver. Inevitably, my proverbial, if not my actual chickens, came home to roost; and, as I'd no money left, I had to reduce my stock until I was simmerin'. But one glimmer of hope remained in my life. Around that time, I'd accidentally knocked up an old sweetheart, who, though she didn't want the kid, agreed to leave her with me. So, I had a baby daughter. For a while…'

'You're obviously a fuckin' maniac!' Joe growled. 'If the relatives of those chickens knew what you'd planned for them, they'd turn in their gravy!'

Filled with a sudden, if understandable rage, Jim began firing once again in our direction. As he did, Clay and I went pancake, but Joe lifted his Colt and returned fire. Obviously a firm believer that no un-aimed bullet ever misses, Joe emptied his weapon in seconds and basically hit everything he wasn't aiming at. But as both men paused to reload, I dragged the Ham to the ground, pushed his head deep into the fungal carpet to sedate him, then sat on him. As I did so, I shouted: 'Right Jim, now we're getting' somewhere with this whole communication thing – that, for example, is the exact *opposite* of what we're lookin' for!'

'Just tell him to stop talkin'! I don't even know him, but I've taken laxatives that didn't irritate the shit out of me as much!'

'To be fair, he has that affect on everyone,' I reasoned. 'Look, just keep talkin', it's gettin', uhm, real interestin'.

As Jim was set to continue, however, several more shots rang out. Briefly, I was confused, yet I suddenly realised these were coming from the floor below. Now, to me, dawn is Nature's way of telling you to go to bed, yet it struck me that, around here, this was your regular dawn-chorus, maybe even a sincere form of non-verbal communication between neighbours. It was another sad proof, should it be needed, that this city was merely a large community where everyone was alone together. Still, as I pondered that philosophical enigma, Joe began struggling beneath me like Fido at bathtime, so I let him up, but only on condition he once again move behind me and remain quiet. Jim Harrison, however, didn't seem at all fazed by that latest interruption.

'I was sayin' things weren't goin' well,' Jim rasped. 'The bank reclaimed the farm, I was drinkin' heavily, and, as I was now homeless, Welfare Services took Anna into custody, then fostered her out to new parents in Iowa. But before I'd come to the city I'd taken out life-insurance, so I faked my death in that plane crash just so Anna would have money when she was older. I couldn't tell her, of course, and I couldn't go see her, so I returned to the city, got a job in Skytowers and kept my head down. Yet sometimes, just when you think you've hit rock-bottom, life throws you a shovel and tells you to keep diggin'! What I didn't count on was Anna returnin' here to retrace her roots. Nor did I think Abel would offer her a job as his secretary. Around the same time, Frank also returned from Canada, and everythin' seemed to be goin' well for him too. That was difficult to watch, those two guys doin' as well as they were, and me with less than nothin'. And I soon realised I had to do somethin' I should've done years before...'

'So you sent them both a series of letters containin' details of their sordid pasts,' I trumped. 'And in the final ones, you had the two of them meet up in Skytowers in a bid to find out who'd sent them. 'Of course, you were in the closet listenin' in on the receiver as they argued, after which you stepped out wearin' a mask, warned them both to be quiet, knocked Frank out and shot Abel. Thing was, you'd put a silencer on the murder weapon, which you removed just before you placed it in the unconscious Frank's hand. You then put another gun in Abel's hand, ran back to the closet, fired the shot that struck the wall close to the door of 18a, and then pulled the closet door after you. *That* was the shot which roused Frank and alerted the janitor, who came into the room seconds later to find a very confused Frank Ellis standin' over the body of his old business associate with the murder weapon in his hand.'

'You're good, copper.'

'I'm a Private Eye, but, yeah, they say I'm the best. Now, tell me about Anna.'

Jim laughed shortly. 'Like I said, she didn't even know I was alive. But then, a few months back, she found a photo in the local paper, one in which I'd stupidly posed in the background of an official picture. So she tracked me down and we talked. I asked her to get away from Abel, but she told me they were havin' an affair and he'd planned to leave his wife for her. I told her I'd seen him promise other girls the earth, then treat them like dirt, but she wouldn't listen. So I just pretended to accept it. Secretly, though, I was plannin' my revenge, and I knew she'd get over him. After all, love isn't blind, it just makes you blind, and it's way better to lose a lover than love a loser...'

So Abel had been giving Anna the message after all. It's not often I envy the dead, I'll tell you now. Nevertheless, I still had to find out if Anna was totally innocent or if her father was merely covering for her.

'So who typed those letters?' I asked thickly. 'And how come you had access to that spyin' equipment?'

'Before Maria came on board, I did the typin',' Jim replied coldly. 'So I had a lot of experience. As for the spyin' gear, when Anna told me where she worked, I went down there one night, broke in and stole a heap of stuff. I figured it'd be ironic if I planned Abel's murder usin' his own equipment.' He laughed shortly. 'How'd you figure it was me anyhow?' he asked. 'Copper!' he added irately.

'There were several clues,' I replied loftily. 'Firstly, you have an apartment like a barnyard, and when you answered the door to me last time, I noticed the same phosphorescent glow I'd seen in Skytowers on your floor each time the Cola sign flashed in the window, though I thought nothin' of it back then. But Anna was the real clue. There was a photo of her on her desk in Honolulu. She wears a little plane around her neck – a Cessna if I'm not mistaken – which is the sort you supposedly died in, and upon it were the initials A. and what looked like the letter H., which I presume stand for Anna Harrison. Then there were the initials on her ring – the two letter A's – which I now believe stand for Anna and Abel. One thing confuses me, though: The footprints in 18c were made by ladies shoes. How was that?'

'That was how I exited Skytowers on the night of the murder. I figured people would be less likely to be lookin' for a woman.'

'And you dressed as a nurse to enter the hospital?'

'Yeah,' Jim chuckled. 'That was me too. Thought I'd have a stab at Frank. Literally. I didn't think he was sufferin' quick enough.'

'Right, so one last thing: How did Anna come to be in Skytowers last night?'

'She came by here shortly after the murder and said she knew I killed Abel,' Jim sighed. 'She said she'd never forgive me, but that she wouldn't rat me out if I went away and never saw her again. By that stage, of course, the police had let the investigation drop, but you were still on my trail. I rifled through your office, tryin' to see what you'd dug up, but it looked like a herd of wildebeests beat me to it and I found nothin'. I decided to kill you anyhow, just in case, but you've got more lives than Frankenstein's cat, so I let that one go too. I still had to get rid of the car though, and I planned to do that, then skip town straight after. I told Anna this and she agreed to wait for me in Skytowers to see me off, but you chased me back and the jig was up. When I reached my office, though, Anna didn't want me to get caught. She knocked me out with a wrench, dressed in my leathers and went downstairs to take the fall. She's a gutsy girl.' He shook his head. 'Yeah, you're obviously the best, and I probably shouldn't have kept a few chickens here in my apartment, but what can I say – old habits die hard! Same as me, I suppose: I lived hard, and now I'll have to die the same way!'

'And what about the midgets?' Joe growled. 'How'd they get the laundry baskets out of Skytowers?' As I attempted to clamp a hand around Joe's mouth, he drew away from me sharply. 'Hey, calm the fuck down, Marty! I'm tryin' to conduct an investigation here!'

Almost instantly, Jim Harrison fired another shot down the corridor in our direction. 'Didn't I warn you to keep that imbecile quiet?'

'I'm tryin', really I am.'

As I'd spoken, I'd shoved Joe around the corridor bend, yet that dynamic quickly changed as he pressed his Colt tight to my nose and stared at me through eyes deep and dark as snow-ringed piss-holes. As Clay – forever possessed of the balls of a eunuch – took a whitey and scrambled out of our way, I stepped back, my gut churning. I needed this bull-crap now like a moose needed a hat-rack, but how did I tell Joe that those who tell us to calm down are often the same ones who rile us up in the first place, or that he should never speak unless improving the silence? After all, according to the Ham, he didn't have an attitude problem, everyone else had a perception problem.

'Look, Joe, I don't mind you gettin' things off your chest, but keep your shirt on, okay?' He nodded evenly. 'Good! Now, this guy's no chicken. In fact, he's hard-boiled enough to roast us all rather than leg it or ultimately fry, and I get the feelin' that tryin' to talk him out of here is goin' to be like pickin' chicken bones out of an egg. But I have to try, or, at worst, incapacitate him with a kick in the giblets, caprice?' Joe nodded blankly again. 'Alright. Because if this goes down wrong, *you'll* end up gettin' the blame, know what I'm sayin'?'

Joe eyes darkened to an indecently blacker shade of jet. He cocked his gun and pressed it deeper into my nose. 'Are you sayin' this is all my fault, Whale?'

'Uh-uh, I said I'll be blamin' you – there's a big, *big* difference!'

Joe pouted solemnly. 'Fine! You've got a minute. Then I'm goin' in!'

I frowned darkly, realising I should've known it would come to this. After all, to the man whose only tool is a hammer, all problems soon begin to look like nails. But then I had to take some of the blame, because, when all was said and done, a lot had been said and nothing done. I turned to stare wryly at Jim Harrison. He was huddled behind his bullet-ridden apartment door, swigging heavily at a gin bottle. I shook my head sadly. Like all those bent on revenge, he'd let yesterday take up too much of today, and, all wrapped up in himself, he'd become a very small package.

I had to find common ground with him – I had to say something to tug at his heart-strings, to make him see life was worth living. I took a deep breath, nodded solemnly, then said: 'So, Jim, are you, uhm, comin' out or what?'

Jim spat an oyster of phlegm into the corridor and raised both his gun and the remote control defiantly. 'No way, copper!'

I looked at Joe, he looked through me, and I was happy enough just then that I'd thought of wearing my brown slacks. Still, it was crunch time: Should I allow Joe to storm the apartment and take my chances, or should I run off and let Joe storm the apartment?

It was definitely a time for firm decisions.

Or was it?

As it was, that decision was taken from me. Joe, who'd long figured that nothing exceeds like excess, and that you can do far more with a gun and a kind word than merely a kind word, raised himself to his full height, raised his gun higher, then stared me down. So I stepped back, stooped low at the corridor bend and prepared for the worst, more uncertain then than I'd ever been in my life. Jim Harrison, an immoveable object, had lost his will to live, and Joe Sinto, an irresistible force, hadn't lost his will to die, so if my limited knowledge of physics was in any way correct, things were about to get real physical.

As happens in such life-changing moments, however, everything occurred in slow-motion. And, from the way Joe went running up that corridor, cat-quick, without firing a shot, it was obvious that, in his mind at least, true heroes only ever got winged in gun battles, and all potential wounds were only flesh-wounds.

Yet nothing much happened. Joe charged the door and shouldered Jim to the floor. The crazed janitor then pressed the remote-control, and, for one heart-stopping second, the world stopped. But then his TV set flickered to life. It was an anti-climatic moment to say the least, yet there wasn't one amongst us who wasn't relieved. Except maybe Jim. Still, minutes later, the Ham regrouped and led his captive down through the building and into the jeep, all the while looking happier than a clown in a roomful of hyenas. And I didn't even try to stop him, because, well, he still had one or two bullets left in his gun.

TWENTY FIVE

Tork Malone was at his desk, deep in conversation with Chester Hardcastle when our weary troop of three paraded Jim Harrison into the lobby of Police Administration. Still, as the detective and I weren't currently at loggerheads, he simply stared rather warily between us, before allowing his cold gaze to finally fall upon me.

'Well, well, the ego has landed! So, Marty, to what do we *now* owe the displeasure?'

I stood aside as Joe pushed a dishevelled Jim Harrison in Tork's direction. Before the detective could utter a word, I then loudly explained the crazed janitor's emotive motive for both the murder of Abel Shirinski and the frame-up of both Frank and Maria Ellis. Now, there are times when I rely heavily upon exaggeration to see me through a weary plot, and, in truth, there's little I can't blow out of proportion. Yet this time it was unnecessary, for this tale contained all the colours of the rectum and more besides. When I'd finished relating it, Tork pouted in subdued admiration, though Chester Hardcastle was the first to speak.

'I'm none the wiser,' the Attorney to the Damned pouted.

'No,' I sniped. 'But you are better informed. And in your case, Chesty, that's maybe the best we can hope for.'

Chester smiled wanly, and, in the way of all those who should have an inferiority complex yet never do, managed to stare up at me whilst looking down upon me.

'I have to say I wasn't expectin' this,' Tork grinned finally. 'But I'm actually more surprised at you, Marty. Usually, when you stumble upon the truth, you pick yourself up and walk right on by as if nothin' has happened. But this time you got it right. I'll tell you, it's a great day for idiots – you've done your tribe proud!'

By now, of course, I so wanted to out-smarty Tork Malone, yet this was one guy I'd forever have to disagree with without being too disagreeable as he'd manpower enough at his disposal to subject me to a perpetual pest-in-a-blue-vest-fest. So, even though I'd nothing to say, I had to say something – to Chester.

'Yeah, well, they can take the gallows down now and let yet another of his clients back on the streets. My *friend* Chester here won't be happy about that, naturally, seein' as how this is the third client he's tried to fry this week, but that's showbiz!' I got in close enough to Chester to hear his scales crackling. 'Y'know, *friend*,' I seethed. 'No matter how much you practice law, you'll never have enough practice. So do everyone a favour. There's a bus leavin' town in an hour – be under it!'

'You finished with the Wyatt Earp scenario?' Tork asked me coldly. 'If you are, you can get on your horse and go. And take Doc and Calamity with you.' He looked Joe squarely in the eyes. 'Because if I see either of them around here in the future, I'm gonna come lookin' for you. And that might not be fair, Marty, but I don't give a monkey's cahooey, you dig me?'

Joe saluted him stiffly. 'I hope we're fightin' on the same side in the next war,' he returned evenly. 'Sayin' that, it'll hardly matter if it's confusin' enough!'

Tork leaned in close to Joe. 'You shouldn't growl if you can't bite,' he seethed. 'And as for you gettin' close enough to give me your best shot, you'd have more luck tryin' to tie knots in smoke!' He raised a quick hand to stall any more incoming. 'Now, gentlemen, I've really had a wonderful evenin', but this wasn't it. So why don't you all go somewhere where I can be alone?'

Because Joe can only shut his mouth after he's put his foot in it, the conversation came to an abrupt end, and Tork's recalcitrant glare informed me that I wasn't getting another word in, not even if I cut off the crusts and folded it in two. So, Clay, Joe and I moved out through the revolving precinct doors into the night. As luck would have it, Chester's car was parked directly over the road in a badly-lit lot. Shortly afterwards, it didn't look anything like the Chester's car that we all knew and he loved. Satisfied I'd done my bit for society, however, I pocketed my paint-flaked keys, walked nonchalantly back down the road and got into the front of the pick-up alongside Clay. Joe got into the back.

'Drop you off anywhere, Joe?' I asked. The asylum maybe, I thought.

'Bus stop's fine with me, Whale,' Joe beamed a freaky. 'That girl I met the other night, she lives just a few blocks from here. Me and her have plans to move to Waco, Texas. Hear some guy's set up a mighty fine commune down there, so might drop in for a spell. You don't fancy comin' down that way, do you?'

I feigned an undecided. 'Nah, I have to go pay off a small debt, so I'm sort of busy.'

He nodded and we left him off at the corner. 'Yeah, well, next time you've got a case you're havin' trouble with, get me on the horn. I'll be there in minutes.'

'I'll do that, Joe.' I shook his hand, then watched as he walked off towards the depot. 'Not!' As Joe disappeared from view, Clay wheeled the pick-up around and drove back in the direction of Vesperville proper. Some three or four streets away I turned to him and said, 'Y'know, I've actually got a soft spot for that little guy.'

'Yeah?' Clay was surprised.

'Yeah, the Florida Everglades!'

We laughed loudly.

'That's the way I feel about you,' Clay chided.

'I'm touched,' I said mockingly.

'You sure are,' he agreed.

I had Clay drive me to the brownstone, and we were laughing hard when we got inside. The Muds and his latest bit of fluff were there, sipping at beers and chowing down on something that looked as if it needed carbon-dating. Clay – one of several people who I'd like to believe I'd taught over the previous week that you can grow out of childhood but never adulthood – seemed content enough with his son's latest date, and I told him to make himself at home, that I had to go out, though I'd be back in a while. Greta left me to the door, and, after warning her not to host any rallies on my lawn, I got into the Buick and drove off into centre city.

***

Gus Diamond's place is a seedy, gambling den hidden beneath an Italian deli on Capone Avenue. Much like a prohibition-era speak-easy, it was accessed by a reinforced metal door that prohibited access to those who reinforced the law and spoke in less than subtle tones. As I strode confidently towards it, I noticed Happy Valentine chatting to two of his cronies outside. At the doorway, I passed him two envelopes – one for him, a thicker one for his boss – and he smiled warmly, clasped me firmly by the shoulder and shook my hand.

'Marty, great to see you! Hey, guys, it's our old pal, Marty.' The two henchmen – who each looked as if they'd gargled briefly at the Fountain of Knowledge – grinned thinly and shook my hand solidly in turn. With the formalities over, Happy then led me inside. On our way into the main room, Happy chuckled lightly and said, 'Hey, Marty, I hope you didn't take our last encounter too seriously. It's just that, years ago, I was told happiness is like peanut butter – you have to crush a few nuts first before you spread it around. And that's my philosophy, basically, to make everyone happy, thus my name. So, we were just tryin' to scare you a bit, and I'd never hurt anyone's feelin's unintentionally.'

'Hey, you were just doin' your job. And it was a great incentive to find work.'

As we spoke, I peered into the main room, soaking up the atmosphere. Some of the pros and cons of this place were that it was full of pros and cons, yet there were six card tables, a couple of waiters plying the players with free drinks, and a little snack bar at the end of the room with a stock of fresh food forever on the go.

'You want to stick around a while, Whale?' Happy smiled. 'We're havin' an easy game, no big stakes, a few girls dancin' later on, and quite a bit of free food. My mom cooked up a mean chilli for the guys, and it's goin' down a treat.'

I stood there a moment, considering his offer. Many might have considered me crazy for doing so, yet what were my options? I could go home, listen to Clay, the Muds and Greta droning on, maybe have a few beers, then go to bed and engage in a ménage-a-moi.

But, let's face it, I'd had a bad few days, I needed to unwind, and for once I didn't have too much month left over at the end of my money. And these guys weren't the worst in the world when it came down to it. Alright, we'd fallen out a bit the last time, but then maybe I shouldn't have started doing card tricks in front of the guys I was playing poker with, and maybe every time I'd lost the winning hand I shouldn't have lost my head.

'Well, Happy,' I said, as he placed a fraternal hand around my shoulder, handed me a cigar and led me towards a table. 'I said I wouldn't, but what the hell - old habits die hard!'